D   UE

Secret Smile

Secret Smile

Nicci French

THORNDIKE
WINDSOR
PARAGON

This Large Print edition is published by Thorndike Press®, Waterville, Maine USA and by BBC Audiobooks, Ltd, Bath, England.

Published in 2004 in the U.S. by arrangement with Warner Books, Inc.

Published in 2005 in the U.K. by arrangement with Penguin Books Ltd.

U.S. Hardcover 0-7862-6585-X (Basic)
U.K. Hardcover 0-7540-7972-4 (Windsor Large Print)
U.K. Softcover 0-7540-6886-2 (Paragon Large Print)

The text of this Large Print edition is unabridged.
Other aspects of the book may vary from the original edition.

Set in 16 pt. Plantin by Christina S. Huff.

Printed in the United States on permanent paper.

British Library Cataloguing-in-Publication Data available

Library of Congress Cataloging-in-Publication Data

French, Nicci.
    Secret smile / Nicci French.
        p.   cm.
    ISBN 0-7862-6585-X (lg. print : hc : alk. paper)
    1. Sisters — Fiction.   2. Man-woman relationships —
Fiction.   3. Triangles (Interpersonal relations) — Fiction.
4. Large type books.   I. Title.
PR6056.R456S43 2004
823′.914—dc22   2004051606

Secret Smile

Chapter 1

I've had a dream recently, the same dream, over and over again, and each time I think it's real. I'm back at the ice rink on the afternoon I first met Brendan. The cold stings my face, I can hear the scrape of the blades on the ice and then I see him. He's glancing over at me with that funny look of his, as if he's noticed me and he's got something else on his mind. I see all over again that he's good looking in a way that not everybody would notice. His hair is glossy black like a raven's wing. His face is oval and his cheekbones and chin are prominent. He has an amused expression on his face as if he has seen the joke before anybody else and I like that about him. He looks at me and then gives me a second look and he's coming over to say hello. And in my dream I think: Good. I've been given another chance. It doesn't have to happen. This time I can stop it now, here, before it's even begun.

But I don't. I smile at what he says to me and I say things back to him. I can't hear the words and I don't know what they are, but they must be funny because Brendan laughs and says something and then I laugh, and so it goes, back and forth. We're like actors in a long-running show. We can say our lines without thinking and I know what's going to happen to this boy and this girl. They have never met before but he is a friend of a friend of hers and so they are surprised that this is the first time they have come across each other. I'm trying to stop myself, in this dream that I both know and don't know is a dream. An ice rink is a good place for a boy and a girl to meet, especially when neither of them can skate. Because they have to lean against each other for support and it's almost compulsory for the boy to put his steadying arm around the girl and they help each other up and laugh at their joint predicament. Her laces are frozen together and he helps her to untie them, her foot in his lap for convenience. When the group starts to break up, it's only natural that the boy asks the girl for her phone number.

The girl is surprised by a moment of reluctance. It's been fun but does she need something like this at the moment? She looks at the boy. His eyes are shining from the cold. He is smiling at her expectantly. It seems easier just to give him the number and so she does, even though I am shouting for her not to. But the shouting is silent and in any case she is me and she doesn't know what is going to happen but I do.

I'm wondering: How is it that I know what is going to happen? I know they are going to meet twice — a drink, a movie — and then, on her sofa, she'll think, *Well, why not?* And so I'm thinking if I know what's going to happen, it must mean that I can't change it. Not a single detail. I know they'll sleep together twice more, or is it three times? Always in the girl's flat. After the second time she sees a strange toothbrush in the mug next to hers. A moment of confusion. She will have to think about that. She will barely have time. Because the next afternoon, her mind will be made up for her. It's at about that moment — the girl coming home from work, opening the door of her flat — that I wake up.

After weeks of grayness and drizzle, it was a beautiful autumn afternoon. A blue sky just beginning to lose its electric glare, a sharp wind that was shaking bright leaves from the trees. It had been a long day, and I'd spent most of it up a ladder painting a ceiling, so my neck and right arm ached and my whole body felt grimy and sore, and there were splashes of white emulsion over my knuckles and in my hair. I was thinking about an evening alone: a hot bath, supper in front of the TV in my dressing gown. Cheese on toast, I thought. Cold beer.

So I opened the door to my flat and walked in, letting my bag drop to the floor. And then I saw him. Brendan was sitting on the sofa, or rather, lying back with his feet up. There was a cup of tea on the floor beside him and he was reading something that he closed as I came in.

"Miranda." He swung his legs off the cushion and stood up. "I thought you'd be back later than this." And he took me by the shoulders and kissed me on the lips. "Shall I pour you some tea? There's some in the pot. You look all in."

I could hardly think which question to ask first. He hardly knew what job I did. What was he doing, thinking about when I finished work? But most of all, what was he doing in my flat? He looked as if he had moved in.

"What do you think you're doing?"

"I let myself in," he said. "I used the keys under the flowerpot. That's all right, isn't it? You've got paint in your hair, you know."

I bent down and picked up the book from the sofa. A worn hard-backed exercise book, faded red, the spine split. I stared at it. It was one of my old diaries.

"That's private," I said. "Private!"

"I couldn't resist," he said with his roguish smile. He saw my expression and held up his hands. "Point taken, I'm sorry, it was wrong. But I want to know all about you. I just wanted to see what you were like before I met you." He reached a hand out and gently touched my hair where the paint was, as if to scratch it away. I pulled away.

"You shouldn't have."

Another smile.

"I won't do it again then," he said in a playfully apologetic tone. "All right?"

I took a deep breath. No. I didn't think it was all right.

"It's from when you were seventeen," he said. "I like to think of you at seventeen.

I looked at Brendan and already he seemed to be receding into the distance. He was on the platform and I was on the train that was pulling away and leaving him behind forever. I was thinking how to say it, as cleanly and finally as possible. You can say, *I don't think this is working anymore,* as if the relationship was a machine that has stopped functioning, some vital bit having gone missing. Or, *I don't think we should continue,* as if you were both on a road together and

130691

you've looked ahead and seen that the road forks, or peters out in rocks and brambles. You can say, *I don't want to keep on seeing you.* Only of course you don't mean *see*, but touch, hold, feel, want. And if they ask why — *why is it over? what have I done wrong?* — then you don't tell them: *You get on my nerves, your laugh suddenly irritates me, I fancy someone else.* No, of course you say, *You haven't done anything. It's not you, it's me.* These are the things we all learn.

Almost before I knew what I was about to do, I said the words. "I don't think we should go on with this."

For a moment, his expression didn't alter. Then he stepped forward and laid his hand on my shoulder. "Miranda," he said.

"I'm sorry, Brendan." I thought of saying something else, but I stopped myself.

His hand was still on my shoulder. "You're probably exhausted," he said. "Why don't you have a bath and put on some clean clothes."

I stepped away from his hand. "I mean it."

"I don't think so."

"What?"

"Are you about to get your period?"

"Brendan . . ."

"You're due about now, aren't you?"

"I'm not playing games."

"Miranda." He had a coaxing tone to his voice, as if I were a frightened horse and he was approaching me with sugar on his outstretched palm. "We've been too happy for you to just end it like this. All those wonderful days and nights."

"Eight," I said.

"What?"

"Times we met. Is it even that many?"

"Each time special."

I didn't say, *Not for me,* although it was the truth. You can't say, *It really didn't mean much after all. It was just one of those things that happened.* I shrugged. I didn't want to make a point. I didn't want to discuss things. I wanted him to leave.

"I've arranged for us to meet some mates of mine for a drink this evening. I told them you were coming."

"What?" I said.

"In half an hour."

I stared at him.

"Just a quick drink."

"You really want us to go out and pretend we're still together?"

"We need to give this time," he said.

It sounded so ridiculous, so like a marriage guidance counselor giving glib advice to a couple who had been together for years and years and had children and a mortgage that I couldn't help myself. I started to laugh and then stopped and felt cruel. He managed a smile that wasn't really a smile at all, but lips stretched tight over teeth, a grimace or a snarl.

"You can laugh," he said at last. "You can do this and still laugh."

"Sorry," I said. My voice was still shaky. "It's a nervous kind of laugh."

"Is that how you behaved with your sister?"

"My sister?" The air seemed to cool around me.

"Yes. Kerry." He said the name softly, musing over it. "I read about it in your diary. I know. Mmm?"

I walked over to the door and yanked it open. The sky was still blue and the breeze cooled my burning face. "Get out," I said.

"Miranda."

"Just go."

So he left. I pushed the door shut gently, so he wouldn't think I was slamming it behind him, and then I suddenly felt nauseous. I didn't have the meal in front of the TV I'd been looking forward to so much. I just had a glass of water and went to bed and didn't sleep.

My relationship with Brendan had been so brief that my closest friend, Laura, had

14

been on holiday while it was going on and missed it completely. And it was so entirely over and in the past that when she got back and rang me and told me about what a great time she and Tony had had — well, after all that, I didn't bother to tell her about Brendan. I just listened as she talked about the holiday and the weather and the food. Then she asked me if I was seeing someone and I said no. She said that was funny because she'd heard something and I said, well, nothing much and anyway it was over. And she giggled and said she wanted to hear all about it and I said there was nothing to tell. Nothing at all.

Chapter 2

Two weeks after Brendan had walked out of my door, I was up a ladder and just reaching with the brush to get into the corner when my mobile went off and I realized it was in my jacket pocket and that I didn't have my jacket on. We were working on a newly constructed house in Blackheath, all straight lines and plate glass and pine. I was painting the wood in a special almost transparent oil-based white paint that had been imported at great expense from Sweden. I scrambled down and put the brush on the lid of the tin.

"Hello?"

"Miranda, it's Kerry."

That was unusual enough. We met fairly regularly, every month or so, usually at my parents'. Maybe once a week we would talk on the phone; I was always the one who rang her. She asked if I was free that evening. I'd half arranged something but she said it was really important. She wouldn't ask if it wasn't. So of course I had to say yes. I started to discuss where we should meet, but Kerry had it all worked out. A very straightforward French restaurant had just opened in Camden, fairly near where I lived, and Kerry would book a table for eight. If I didn't hear back from her, I should assume it was set.

I was completely baffled. She'd never arranged anything like that before. As I slapped the paint over the huge pine wall, I tried to think of what she could possibly have to tell me and I couldn't even come up with a plausible answer to the basic question: Was it likely to be something good or something bad?

Within families, you're stuck with the character they think you are, whatever you do. You become a war hero and all that your parents ever talk about is something supposedly funny you used to do when you were in nursery school. You can end up moving to Australia just to get away from the person your family thinks you are or who you think they think you are. It's like a room made out of mirrors, with reflections and reflections of reflections going on into infinity. They make your head ache.

I hadn't fled to Australia. I lived less than a mile from the house I grew up in and I worked for my uncle, Bill. Sometimes it's hard to think of him as my uncle because he is so unlike my father. He has long hair that he sometimes wears in a ponytail, and he hardly ever shaves and what's more, rich and trendy people queue up to employ him. My father still calls him a painter and decorator and when I was a child I remember him working with a raggle-taggle collection of no-hopers, usually driving a dodgy van he'd borrowed from someone. But nowadays Uncle Bill — which I never call him — has a big office, a company, a lucrative agreement with a team of architects, a waiting list that you can hardly even get onto.

I arrived at La Table at about one minute past eight and Kerry was already there. She was sitting at the table with a glass of white wine and the bottle in a bucket by the side and I knew immediately that this was good news of some kind. She looked illuminated from the inside and it showed through her eyes. She'd changed her appearance since the previous time I'd seen her. I have my hair cut quite short. I liked the look anyway and it made particular sense when I was working so that my hair wouldn't get dipped into resin or caught around a drill. Kerry wasn't someone who had ever had much of a particular look, just medium length hair, practical clothes. Now she had had her hair cut short as well and it suited her. Almost everything about her was different. She was wearing more makeup than usual, which emphasized her large eyes. She had new clothes as well: dark, flared trousers, a white linen shirt and a waistcoat, of all things. She had an elfin, eager look about her. She waved me over to the table and poured me a glass of wine.

"Cheers," she said. "You've got paint in your hair, by the way."

I wanted to say what I always want to say to this, which is: *Of course I have paint in my hair because I spend half my life painting.* But I never do and I especially wasn't going to this evening when Kerry looked so happy and expectant. Expectant. It couldn't be, could it?

"Occupational hazard," I said.

It was around the back where I couldn't see. She scratched at my hair, so that we must have looked like two grooming chimpanzees in the middle of the restaurant and I even let her do it. She said it wouldn't come off, which was comforting. I took a sip of the wine.

"This place seems nice," I said.

"I was here last week," she said. "It's great."

"So how's things?"

"You're probably wondering why I called you," she said.

"There doesn't have to be a special reason," I said, lying.

"I've got some news for you," she said. "Some pretty startling news."

She *was* pregnant. That was it. That was all it could be. I looked at her more closely. A bit surprising to see her drinking, though.

"I've got a new boyfriend," she said.

"That's wonderful, Kerry. That's great news."

I felt more puzzled than before. I felt happy for her, I really did, because I knew that she hadn't had a boyfriend for some time. It was something that worried her. My parents were always a bit concerned about it, which didn't help. But for her to announce it in this formal way was bizarre.

"It's a bit awkward," she said. "That's why I wanted to tell you before anybody else."

"How could it be awkward?"

"That's right," she said eagerly. "That's right. That's what I've been saying. It really shouldn't be a problem at all, if we don't let it become one."

I took a sip of wine and forced myself to be patient. That was another characteristic of Kerry. She veered between being so in-communicative that she wouldn't say a word to a sort of babbling incoherence.

"What problem?"

"He's someone you know."

"Really?"

"Actually, it's more than that. It's some-one you went out with. It's an ex-boyfriend of yours."

I didn't respond to this because I started thinking frantically. Who could this be? Lucas and I had had a massive bust-up and he was with Cleo anyway. I'd been with Paul for a year and he'd certainly met Kerry once or twice. But wasn't he still in Edinburgh? Then it was back to ancient history. There were a few odds and sods from college but that was at a time when I was hardly in touch with Kerry at all. I tried to imagine the massive coincidence that could have brought Kerry together with some figure like Rob from my distant past. But they hadn't even met, had they? Or perhaps it was way back even beyond that into my pri-meval past at school, with someone like Tom. That must be it. Maybe there was a school reunion . . .

"It's Brendan," she said. "Brendan Block."

"What? What do you mean?"

"Isn't it amazing? He's just about to arrive. He said he thought it would be good if we all got together."

"That's not possible," I said.

"I know it might seem a bit odd . . ."

"Where did you meet?"

"I'll tell you," she said. "I'll tell you everything. But I wanted to tell you something quickly before Bren arrives."

"Bren?"

"I just wanted to say straight away, my lovely Miranda, that Bren has told me all about it and I want you to know that I hope it won't be embarrassing."

"What?"

Kerry leaned across the table and put both her hands on mine. She looked at me with big sympathetic eyes.

"Miranda, I know that it was painful for you when you parted." She took a deep breath and gave my hand a squeeze. "I know that Bren broke up with you. He's told me how upset you were, how angry and bitter. But he has told me that he hopes you're over it. He says he's fine about it."

"He says he's fine about it?"

And at that moment Brendan Block came into the restaurant.

Chapter 3

Kerry met him in the middle of the room and he bent down to kiss her lingeringly on the lips. She closed her eyes for a moment, looking tiny beside his tall, bulky figure. She stood on tiptoe and whispered something in his ear and he nodded and looked across at me with his head slightly to one side and a very small smile on his lips. He gave a nod and walked toward me with both arms outstretched. I didn't know quite what to do. I half-raised myself from my seat, so by the time he arrived at the table I was crouched awkwardly with the chair jammed behind my knees.

"Miranda," he said. He put his hands firmly on my shoulders, making me sink a bit lower toward my chair, and stared me in the eyes. "Oh, Miranda."

He bent down to kiss me on the cheek, too near my mouth. By this time Kerry had managed to wrap her arm around Brendan's waist so she bobbed toward me too and for one awful second we were all a few inches from each other's faces and I could see the sweat in the divot above his upper lip and the small scar in Kerry's eyebrow where I'd hit her with a plastic spade when I was four and she was six, and smell his soap and her perfume and something sour in the air between us. I pulled myself free and sank gratefully back onto my chair.

"So Kerry's told you?" By now he was sitting, too, positioned between me and Kerry so that we were crammed around a small segment of the table, our knees touching. He put a hand over Kerry's as he spoke and she looked up at him with her shining eyes.

"Yes. But I . . ."

"And it's really all right?"

"Why shouldn't I be?" I said and realized I'd answered a question that hadn't been asked. It made me sound tense, rattled, which I was, a bit. Anyone in the world would have been. I saw them exchange a glance. "I mean, it's fine."

"I know this must be hard for you."

"It's not hard for me at all," I said.

"That's very generous of you," he said. "Typically generous. I told Derek and Marcia you would be like this. I told them not to worry too much."

"Mum and Dad?"

"Yes," said Kerry. "They met Bren a

couple of days ago. They really liked him. Well, of course they did. Troy did, too, and you know how hard he is to please."

Brendan gave a modest smile. "Sweet kid," he said.

"And you told them . . ." I didn't know how to finish the sentence. I suddenly remembered a phone call the night before last, when both my parents had talked to me, one after the other, and asked me how I was feeling at the moment. A small tic started up under my left eye.

"That you would understand, because you were a big-hearted woman," said Brendan.

I felt myself getting angry now at the thought of these people talking behind my back about the way they thought I would react.

"The way that I remember it is . . ."

Brendan held up a hand large and white, with hairy wrists. Hairy wrists, big earlobes, thick neck. Memories bobbed to the surface and I pushed them back down again. "Let's not go any further right now. Give it time."

"Miranda," said Kerry pleadingly. "Bren just told them what we thought they needed to know." I looked across at her and saw on her face the luminous happiness that I wasn't used to. I swallowed hard and stared at the menu.

"Shall we order then?"

"Good idea. I think I'll have the *daurade*," said Brendan, rolling his "r"s at the back of his throat.

I didn't feel like eating anything.

"I'll just have the steak and chips," I said. "Without the chips."

"Still worried about your weight?"

"What?"

"You don't need to," Brendan said. "You look fine. Doesn't she, Kerry?"

"Yes. Miranda always looks lovely." For a moment she looked sour, as if she'd said *Miranda always looks lovely* too many times. "I think I'd like the salmon and a green salad."

"We'll have a bottle of the Chablis, I think," said Brendan. "Do you want a glass of red with your steak, Mirrie?"

That was another thing. I'd always liked the name Miranda because it couldn't be shortened. Until I met Brendan. Mirrie. It sounded like a misprint.

"White's fine," I said.

"Sure?"

"Yes." I gripped the table. "Thanks."

Kerry got up to go to the ladies' and he watched her weave her way through the tables with that small smile on his face. He ordered our meal before turning back to me.

"So . . ."

"Miranda."

He just smiled, then laid a hand over mine. "You two are very different," he said.

"I know that."

"No, I mean, you're different in ways you couldn't possibly know."

"What?"

"Only I can make comparisons," he said, still smiling at me fondly.

It took me a few seconds to understand. I pulled my hand away. "Brendan, listen . . ."

"Hello, honey," he said over my head, then stood up to pull back Kerry's chair for her, placing a hand on her head as she sat down again. The food arrived. My steak was fat and bloody and slid around the plate when I tried to cut it. Brendan watched me hack at it, then lifted a finger to a waitress as she passed. He said something to her in French, which I didn't understand, and she brought me a different sort of knife.

"Brendan spent time in Paris," said Kerry.

"Oh."

"But you probably knew that?" She glanced up at me, then looked away. I couldn't read her expression. Was it suspicious, resentful, triumphant or simply curious?

"No, I didn't." I knew very little about Brendan. He said he was between jobs. He'd mentioned something about a psychology course and about traveling around Europe for several months, but beyond that I could hardly think of a single detail of his life. I'd never been to his flat, never met his friends. He hadn't talked about his past and he had been vague about his plans. But then of course, there had been so little time. We had been approaching the stage when you start telling each other about your lives when I'd caught him finding out about my life in his own way.

I finally managed to insert a mouthful of steak into my mouth and chewed it vigorously. Brendan inserted a finger and thumb delicately into his own mouth and extracted a thin bone, laying it carefully on the side of his plate, then swilling back the rest of his mouthful with white wine. I looked away.

"So," I said to Kerry. "How did you two meet?"

"Oh," she said, and glanced up at Brendan sideways. "By accident, really."

"Don't call it accident. Fate," said Brendan.

"I was in the park after work one evening and it started to rain and this man . . ."

"That would be me."

Kerry giggled happily. "Yes. Bren. He said he knew my face. 'Aren't you Kerry Cotton?' he said."

"I recognized her from your photograph, of course. Then there she was in front of me in the rain."

"He told me he knew you — I mean, he didn't tell me about, you know — he just said he knew you. Then he offered to share his umbrella . . ."

"Like the gentleman I am," said Brendan. "You know me, Mirrie."

"We carried on walking together, even though it was belting down with rain. We got wetter and wetter, and our shoes were squelching with water."

"But we kept on walking through the rain," said Brendan, and he put his hand on her hair and stroked it. "Didn't we?"

"We were soaked through, so I invited him to come and get dry at mine . . ."

"I toweled her hair for her," said Brendan.

"That's enough," I said, lifting up my hand, pretending to laugh. "We'll stop with the getting dry, shall we?"

"I can't tell you how relieved I am that you know," said Kerry. "When I discovered about you two, well, for a bit I thought it would ruin everything. I would never do anything to hurt you. You know that, don't you?" She looked remarkably pretty: soft and slim and luminous. There was a small pain in my chest.

"You deserve to be happy," I said, turning my back on Brendan and speaking only to her.

"I *am* happy," she said. "We've only known each other for a few days, ten to be precise, and it's not been long since the two of you — well, you know . . . So perhaps I shouldn't say this, but I can't remember being so happy."

"That's good," I said. Ten days, I thought.

We ate our meal, drank our wine. Glasses chinked. I smiled and nodded and said yes and no in the right places, and all the time I was trying not to think. Not to remember the way his tummy bulged slightly over his boxer shorts, the black hair on his shoulders . . .

Finally I looked down at my watch and gave a fake start of surprise at the time it was, though it was only just gone nine-thirty, and told them I had to get back, early start tomorrow, long drive, no time for coffee, so sorry. . . . We had to go through the whole rigmarole of saying good-bye, with Kerry hugging me hard and Brendan kissing me too close to my mouth and I resisting the urge to wipe the dampness away with the back of my hand, and everyone saying how we must meet again very soon, oh yes, how lovely I'd been, how kind, how *good*.

He walked me to the door of the restaurant.

"It's been raining," he said.

I ignored him.

"It's an incredible coincidence," I said.

"What?"

"I break off with you and a few days later you meet my sister in the street and you start going out. It's hard to believe."

"There's no such thing as coincidence," said Brendan. "Maybe it's not surprising that I'd fall in love with someone who looked like you."

I looked over Brendan's shoulder at Kerry, still sitting at the table. She caught my eye and gave me a nervous smile and looked away. When I spoke to Brendan I smiled, so that our conversation would look friendly to Kerry.

"Brendan," I said. "Is this some kind of weird joke?"

He looked puzzled and a bit hurt.

"Joke?"

31

"If you're playing with my sister as some way of getting at me . . ."

"That sounds pretty self-centered," said Brendan. "If you don't mind my saying so."

"Just don't hurt her," I said. "She deserves to be happy."

"Trust me. I know how to make her happy."

I couldn't bear to be with him another second. I walked home through the damp streets, breathing in deeply, letting the air cool my face. Had he really fallen in love with Kerry? Did it really matter how they had met? I walked faster, till my legs ached with the effort.

I often think of positions in families, the difference it makes to you. Would I have been someone else if I'd been the oldest? What about Kerry, if she'd been in the middle, instead of me? Would she have been more confident and extroverted, more like me — or at least, more like the me the family assumed I was? And Troy — the baby of the family, who came along nine years after me? If he hadn't been all on his own, the obvious mistake, what would that have meant for him? Or if he'd had brothers who could teach him how to kick the football and use his fists and play violent computer games, instead of sisters who petted and ignored him?

But we were stuck with what we'd been given. Kerry had come first and had to lead the way, although she hated being a leader. And I was second, impatient to grow up and chafing to be first, always trying to overtake her, push her out of my way. And Troy was third and the only — very much the last but almost the first as well, thin-shouldered, wide-eyed, dreamy, strange.

I let myself into the flat. It was true that I had an early start tomorrow but for a while I couldn't get to sleep. I lay in bed, shifting to different positions, turning the pillow to find a cooler spot. There was no photograph of Kerry in my flat, of course there wasn't. But then I hadn't believed Brendan's story anyway, so what did it matter? He tracked down Kerry because she was my sister. Considered from a certain angle, it might seem romantic.

Chapter 4

As I drove home from work the following day, the buildings wavered in the drizzle, the skyline was soft and blurred. If it were this time in the summer, then it would be light for hours more, but now people were drawing their curtains, turning lights on. In my flat, I pulled off my overalls and stood under a tepid shower for thirty seconds before dressing in a baggy pair of jeans and a long-sleeved T-shirt. I stood in front of the mirror and pulled in my stomach. What had Brendan said about my weight? I turned sideways to the glass and gazed at myself, dissatisfied. Maybe I should start running. Every morning before going out to work, perhaps. What a horrible idea.

The phone rang as I was leaving to meet Laura.

"Miranda?"

"Hi Mum."

"I tried calling before but there was never any reply."

"My answering machine's screwed up."

"How are you? Are you all right?"

"Fine."

"Sure?"

I wasn't going to help her. "I'm fine, Mum. Just a bit tired. I've been busy at work, now Bill's away. How are you and Dad?"

"I spoke to Kerry. She said you'd had a lovely dinner together."

"It was nice to see her." I paused and then relented. "And Brendan."

"Miranda, you're being very good about this. Don't think we don't realize the effort. I just wish you'd told us when it all happened. I hate to think of you being miserable and not telling me."

"There wasn't anything to tell. Everyone's got the wrong idea."

"If it's any consolation, Kerry is transformed. You saw what she looked like yourself. She's like a different person. I'm happy. But I'm almost frightened as well."

"You mean, because Brendan might leave her?"

"Oh don't say that! Anyway, he seems to adore her, too." I was silent for a second too long and she said sharply, "Miranda? Don't you think so?"

"They both seem very happy," I said.

"So are you really all right?"

35

"Really. But I'm running a bit late."

"Yes, but before you dash off, will you come over at the weekend? How about Sunday lunch? Then we can all get together."

"You mean, with Brendan, too?"

"With Kerry and Brendan, yes."

My stomach clenched. "I'm not sure I'm free then."

"I know it's hard for you, Miranda, but I feel this is important. For Kerry I mean."

"It's not hard for me. At all. I just don't know if I'm free, that's all."

"We could make it Saturday lunch. Or even the evening if that suited you better. Or are you going away for the whole weekend?"

"All right, Sunday," I said, defeated.

"It'll be very casual. You'll be fine."

"I know I'll be fine. I'm not anxious. Not in the least. Everyone's got the wrong idea."

"Maybe you can bring someone with you."

"What?"

"Someone. You know. If there's anyone . . ."

"There isn't anyone at the moment, Mum."

"I suppose it's still in the early days."

"I've got to go now."

"Miranda?"

"Yes."

"Oh I don't know. It's just . . . well, you've always been the lucky one. Let Kerry have her turn. Don't stand in her way."

"This is stupid."

"Please."

I imagined her fist clenched tightly around the receiver, her frowning, intense face, the strand of hair that always hung loose over one eye.

"It'll all be fine," I said, just to stop her. "I promise I won't do anything to stand in Kerry's way. Now I really do have to go. I'll see you tomorrow when I pick up Troy though."

"Thank you, dear Miranda," she said emotionally. "Thank you."

"I never met him, did I?"

We were sitting cross-legged on the floor, backs against the sofa, eating jacket potatoes. Laura had dotted sour cream on hers, but I'd split mine open and mashed several large knobs of butter into it, then sprinkled grated cheese over the top. It was very comforting. Outside it was dark and wet.

"No, it was so brief. When you went to Barcelona it was before the beginning and when you came back it was after the end."

"*You* finished it with him?"

"That's right."

"So why do you mind?"

"I don't," I said before the words were out of her mouth.

"You do. I can tell you do."

I thought for a moment.

"Yes, I do. Because it's creepy. It feels incestuous. And the way my mum and presumably everybody else thinks I'm heartbroken. It makes me want to smash things."

"I can see it must be irritating, but it's quite funny, too."

"No," I said. "Not in any way at all. She calls him Bren."

"Well . . ."

"And he called me Mirrie."

"Families," said Laura vaguely. She wiped her chin.

"Mirrie," I repeated. Then: "Am I over-reacting?"

"Maybe."

"You're right, I'm overreacting."

I'd eaten all the potato and only the crisped skin was left. I put a bit more butter onto it and bit off a piece. Then I took a large swallow of wine. I didn't want to move; it was warm in here and I was full up and pleasantly tired, while outside the wind rustled in the trees and cars drove through puddles.

"How are things with Tony?" I asked after a while.

"Oh. All right. I suppose."

I looked at her. She'd pushed her glossy dark hair behind her ears, and her face looked very young.

"You suppose? What does that mean?"

"They're okay. You know. It's just sometimes . . ." She stopped.

" 'Sometimes'?"

"Sometimes I wonder what happens next." She frowned and poured the last of the wine into our two glasses. "I mean, we've been together for nearly three years. Do we just continue like this? I think that's what Tony would like, just to go on year after year, being comfortable together, as if we were already married except with separate houses. Or do we start living together properly, I mean. Buy a place together. A fridge. Plates. Put our books and CDs together. You know. And if we don't, then what are we doing together now? You have to keep moving forward, don't you?"

"I don't know. I've never been in a relationship that long."

"That's the thing. You have all these dramas and excitements in your life."

"Me?"

"Things beginning and things ending."

"And things not happening at all."

"Yes," she said doubtfully. "But I'm only twenty-six. Is that part of my life all over? Is this it?"

"Do you want to move in together?"

"Well, sometimes I think it'd be . . ."

But then there was the sound of a key in the lock and the door swung open.

"Hello," Tony called cheerfully, dropping his bag on the hall floor with a thump, kicking first one shoe then the other off his feet, so they skidded over the wooden boards. He came into the room, hair damp on his forehead, cheeks reddened from the air. "Oh hi, Miranda. How are you?"

He bent down and kissed Laura and she put one hand up to his cheek and smiled at him. It looked all right to me.

He was out of the door before I'd even parked the van, and running down the garden path. He couldn't wave because he had a bulging plastic bag in one hand and was holding his backpack in the other, but his pale face was shining and he was grinning and saying something to me that I couldn't hear. He tripped over something on the path and half stumbled. His backpack swung against his legs, but he kept on smiling and mouthing words. Sometimes it is more painful to see Troy happy than to see him low.

"Hi there," I said as he pulled open the door and clambered into the passenger seat, his bag getting tangled up with his angular body in the process. "How's it going?"

"Fine. Good. Really good." He wrapped the safety belt around himself and his baggage. "I've been teaching myself to play the guitar, you know. Do you remember your old guitar? I found it in the junk room. It's a bit clapped out but I don't suppose that matters much at the moment. Anyway, I thought I'd cook us supper tonight, all right? I brought the stuff with me. You haven't got any other plans have you?"

"No," I said. "No other plans. What are we having?"

"Savory profiteroles first of all," he said. "I saw them in this recipe book of Mum's and it says they're really simple. I haven't got any filling for them but you must have something I can put in. Cheese maybe? Or tuna fish. Even you must have a tin of tuna in a cupboard somewhere. Then kabobs. I have to marinate them first, though, so it might take a bit of time. I'll start when we get to your flat. I haven't thought about pudding. Do you actually want pudding? I thought we could just have the starter and the kabobs and that would be enough. I could make rice pudding. But hang on, we're having rice with kabobs so it's probably not a good idea."

"No pudding," I said. I could already picture the chaos that lay ahead.

Every Thursday I see Troy. It's been a pretty constant arrangement for the last two years, when he was fifteen and in trouble. I collect him from Mum and Dad's after work, and I bring him back later in the evening, or else put him up for the night on my sagging sofa bed. Sometimes we go to the movies, or to a concert. Occasionally he meets some of my friends. Last Thursday I took him to the pub with Laura and Tony and a couple of others but he was in one of his lethargic moods and he simply put his head on the table after his first sip of beer and went to sleep. Sometimes he seems paralyzingly shy, at other times he just doesn't bother. He'll pick up a book in the middle of a conversation or wander off when he feels like it.

Quite often we just go back to my flat and do stuff together. In the last few weeks he's become keen on cooking, with variable results. His enthusiasms flare up and then they die away again. He went through a phase of playing games of patience. He

42

would have to complete the game before he did anything else. If he managed to get out, it was a good omen, but he hardly ever managed it. In the summer he was fanatical about jigsaw puzzles: he brought one to my flat that was called "The World's Most Difficult Jigsaw." It had thousands of tiny pieces with pictures on both sides. And you didn't know what the final image was meant to look like. For weeks, I couldn't use my table because bits were scattered over it, straight sides at one end, and in the middle the gradually emerging picture of a street scene. Suddenly he got bored. "What actually is the point of doing jigsaw puzzles?" he said to me. "You work for hours and hours and then when you complete it, you break it up and put it back in the box." He worked for hours and hours, but he never completed it and it's now in a box under my bed.

Where did it go wrong? That's what my mother says sometimes, especially when Troy is silent and withdrawn, skulking in his bedroom, his face a sullen mask. He was always clever, sometimes bafflingly, dizzyingly clever, talking at one, reading at three, dazzling teachers with his aptitude. He was shown off to my parents' friends, paraded in assemblies, showered with school prizes, written about in the local paper, put into classes with children who were one, two years older than him and two feet taller than him as well, because he never seemed to grow. He was tiny, with bony knees and ears that stuck out.

He was bullied. I don't just mean pushed around in the playground or jeered at for being a swot. He was systematically tormented by a group of boys and excluded by everyone else. The bullies called him Troy Boy, locked him in the school toilets, tied him to a tree behind the bike shed, threw his books in the mud and stomped on them, passed notes around the classroom about him being a sissy and a gay. They punched him in the stomach, ran after him at the end of the day. He never told anyone and by this time Kerry and I were so much older than him that we occupied entirely different worlds. He didn't complain to the teachers or to my parents, who just knew he was quiet and "different" to the other boys in his class. He just worked harder than ever, and acquired a pedantic and slightly sarcastic manner that of course isolated him further.

Finally, when he was thirteen, my parents were summoned to the school because he'd been discovered throwing firecrackers at boys in the playground. He was wild with rage, weeping and swearing at anyone who came near him, as if eight years of abuse had surfaced all at once. He was suspended for a week, during which time he broke down and confessed to Mum who stormed around the school making a fuss. Boys were hauled in front of the head, given detentions. But how can you tell children they have to like someone and be their friend, particularly when that someone is like my little brother: shy, scared, socially dysfunctional, crippled by his own particular brand of intelligence? And how do you undo damage that's been built into the foundations? With houses, it's easier to pull the whole thing down and start again. You can't do that with people.

I had left college by this time. I didn't understand how serious it was until Troy did his GCSEs. Maybe I didn't want to understand. He was expected to do well. He said the exams had gone fine, but he was vague about them. It turned out he hadn't done a single one. He'd sat in the park near his school, throwing bread to the ducks, staring at the litter on the banks of the pond, looking at his watch. When my parents discovered this they were stunned. I remember being with them one afternoon when all Mum did was cry and ask him what she'd done wrong, was she such a bad mother, and Troy just sat there, not talking, but on his face he had an expression of triumph and shame that terrified me. The counselor said it was his cry for help. A few months later he said that Troy's cutting himself — dozens of shallow abrasions across his fore-arms — was a cry for help. And the way he sometimes didn't get out of bed in the mornings — that was a cry for help, too.

He didn't go back to school. There was a private tutor and more therapy. He goes three times a week to a woman with letters after her name to talk about his problems. Every so often I ask him what goes on in these forty-five-minute sessions but he grins and shrugs. "Often I just sleep," he says. "I lie down on the couch and close my eyes and then suddenly there's a voice telling me my session is over."

"How's it all going?" I asked as I made us a pot of tea and he cut red peppers into strips. Already the kitchen was a mess. Rice bubbled ferociously in a pan, making its lid bump and water splash over the sides. Egg-shells littered the table. Bowls and spoons stacked up in the sink. There was flour on the linoleum, as if there had been a light snowfall.

46

"Have you noticed," he asked, "that people always ask me how I am, in that careful, tactful kind of voice?"

"Sorry," I said.

"I'm bored to death of talking about me. How's it going with you?"

"Okay."

"No, you're supposed to really tell me. That's the deal. I tell you, you tell me."

"Actually, 'okay' is about the right word. There's nothing much to report."

He nodded. "Brendan's going to teach me to fish," he said.

"I didn't know you liked fishing."

"I don't. I've never done it. But he says one day we can go to the sea where a friend of his has this boat and fish for mackerel. He says you just haul them out of the water, one after the other, and then cook them at once over a fire."

"Sounds good."

"He says even if it's raining, it's nice to sit in a boat waiting for a tug on the line."

"Have you seen him much then?"

"A couple of times."

"And you like him?"

"Yes. Can't imagine you with him though."

"Why not?"

He shrugged. "He's not your style."

"What's my style?"

"You're more of a cat person than a dog person."

"I don't have a clue what you're on about."

"He's more like a dog than a cat, don't you reckon? Eager, wanting to be noticed. Cats are more independent and aloof."

"Am I independent and aloof then?"

"Not with me you're not. But with people who you don't know so well."

"What are you then?"

"An otter," he said immediately.

"You've really thought about this."

"And Mum's a kangaroo."

"Kangaroo!"

"And she can't quite get used to the fact we're no longer in her pouch. Except that I crawl in and out occasionally."

"What's Dad?"

"Brendan once had a kind of breakdown as well," said Troy. He started threading alternating chunks of lamb and pepper onto skewers.

"Did he? I didn't know that."

"He said he never tells anyone. But he told me because he wanted me to know that pain can be like a curse and like a gift, and that it's possible to turn it into a gift."

"He said that?"

"Yes. He's a bit of a hippie really."

48

"I'm going to have a beer, I think."

"Dad's a duck."

"I don't think he'd like that."

"Ducks are all right. They're optimists."

"And Kerry?"

"What about gazelle?"

"Has Brendan said anything to you about me?" I tried to keep my voice casual.

"He said he hurt you."

"Ah."

"Did he?"

"No."

"And he said you were too proud to admit it."

Chapter 5

"Are you all right?" said Mum, as she opened the door to me. I was all right. But the way she kept asking me, that sympathetic tone in her voice, it was like glass sandpaper being rubbed on my skin. And because she kept asking me, I had become more and more self-conscious about what to say in response. It was no longer enough just to say "fine," because that sounded defensive. I started to think of what a person who was fine would say, what I could say that would genuinely convince my mother that there was no awkwardness, because in actual fact there wasn't — on my side at least.

"I'm absolutely fine," I said. "There's no problem about any of this."

Too much. My mother was immediately sympathetic.

"You're looking lovely, Miranda," she said.

I was looking all right, but it had been a delicate balance. There's the old cliché that when you're dumped — and of course I hadn't actually been dumped, but that was neither here nor there — you should make yourself look dazzling to show the person who has dumped you, or who people think has dumped you, what they're missing. But because it's an old cliché that everybody knows, then making a huge effort in those circumstances can end up looking slightly pathetic. On the other hand, you can't go the other way and give the impression that you've been lying in bed all day crying and drinking cooking sherry. It should have been easy but it wasn't, and the only way I could decide what to wear was to think back to the last time I'd been out to meet someone socially (not counting Kerry and Brendan) and wear what I'd worn then. Unfortunately, that had been a hen night for an old friend and I'd worn a skimpy black dress that was completely unsuitable for a Sunday lunch at my parents. But the time before that had been a casual night out at a bar and I'd worn jeans and a white shirt and my new denim jacket with the suede collar, and that would do fine.

"You're looking very nice," said my mother, which made me think something must be wrong. "Everybody's here already. Kerry is looking gorgeous. I don't mean . . ." She glanced at me awkwardly. "Shall we go through?"

"Is Troy here?" I asked.

"Yes. He seems quite well. A bit less hyper than on Thursday, but on an even keel. Touch wood," she added and thumped the door for luck.

It seemed that all was well with the Cotton family. Kerry was happy. I was looking lovely. Troy seemed all right. I was tempted to make some sort of protest, but today was a day I was going to be on my best behavior. The sun was shining, as if in honor of the occasion, and although it was October everybody was out in the long, narrow back garden. Everybody except Troy, who was uncomfortable in groups. You'd see him there at first and then he would melt away, go upstairs somewhere and read a book or listen to music.

Even so, the small garden seemed crowded. Bill and Judy were there as well. My parents hadn't told me they were inviting my boss and his family. So they knew as well. "Knew." There should be a different word for knowing something that isn't actually true. The weather was so good that Dad had lit a barbecue. I could see him at the end of the garden, standing over it, poking at the coals with — yes, there was no doubt about it — with Brendan. The two of them were talking to each other with great animation but were too far away for me to hear what they were saying. Kerry was standing with Judy. She was wearing baggy black trousers and a tight-ribbed pink top and she looked the way she did at La Table — happy, confident.

I decided to put off any potential awkwardness for as long as possible and walked over to Bill, who seemed like the most neutral person in the garden. He gave me a friendly nod.

"Hi, Miranda," he said. "How are you doing?"

He handed me a bottle of beer from the table next to him.

"I don't see you here very often," I said to him.

"Marcia was most insistent."

I took a sip from the beer and looked up at the back of my parents' narrow terraced house, which was covered by scaffolding.

"What do you think?" I said.

"If it wasn't being redone it wouldn't be standing by next year."

"That bad?"

"Worse. You can almost see that crack growing."

"Miranda," said my father, appearing suddenly from the side. "How are you?"

I ignored the question, especially as

Brendan was hovering at his elbow dressed in new, ironed jeans and a light blue sweater with the sleeves pulled up to just below the elbow, and gave my father a little hug. He patted me on the back awkwardly. He's not a great hugger, my father.

"Hi, Dad," I said. "Lovely to see you."

"I've got to admit that Brendan is a master with the barbecue," he said.

"It's all about piling up the coal," Brendan said. "You make the briquettes into a pyramid and put several fire lighters underneath and then really get it all burning. You only spread them out when the flames have died down."

"Bill and I were talking about the house," I said.

"You should pay attention to Brendan," Dad said. "You might learn something."

"I don't make many barbecues in my flat," I said.

"You might need to one day," said Brendan.

"I've always thought it was something men liked doing," I said.

"We never had a barbecue, did we, Mirrie?"

I was tempted to say, *No, Brendan. We never had a barbecue because we only went out for about nine days, so we didn't have time for*

54

that for that or indeed almost anything at all. I didn't. I made myself take a deep breath. A silent, metaphorical deep breath.

"No, we didn't," I said.

"I'm afraid that I've been boring Brendan," Dad said. "He's been letting me talk shop."

"Boxes," said Brendan and rubbed his hands together. "So simple and yet imagine life without boxes."

Bill gaped. Even my father looked a bit startled by such enthusiasm.

"Yes, well," he said. "I don't know about that. I'm a practical man. I like making things. I've always been interested in problem solving. Finding solutions. You can do that with the packaging business."

"I know exactly what you mean," said Brendan. "On the face of it, packaging sounds obvious. But a few years ago, this man called Harry Vermont and me set up this dot com company."

"What company?" my father asked.

Brendan laughed ruefully. "One of those that was going to make us all millionaires," he said. "But it's gone now."

"What did it do?" said Bill.

"The point of it," said Brendan, "was that people could order different sorts of consumer goods from the Web site and we

55

would deliver them. We would be middle-men. Middle-persons, I should say. When it started, I thought it was all about technology. But once it started, I realized it was partly that but when it came down to it, it was also about packaging and delivery. You had to get the right packaging at the right place, you had to source it and do the actual packing, and then you had to deliver it on time. It was an amazing challenge for us."

"Who did you source it from?" asked Dad.

"Sorry?"

"Packaging in this country is quite a small world. I was wondering if you were dealing with someone I know."

"We were only in the planning stage," said Brendan. "Then the dot com collapse happened and we lost our funding. Poor old Harry never quite got over it."

"If you're interested, Brendan, I'll show you around sometime," said my father.

"I'd love that," said Brendan. "Meanwhile, I reckon it's time to get the food on the barbecue."

As it turned out, it wasn't time to put the food on the barbecue. While we had been talking, the barbecue had gone out. Brendan said that this sometimes happened when the briquettes had been left in the shed for a long time and had got damp. My father looked pleased and said that he wouldn't have been able to bear it if there was somebody better than him at lighting barbecues in the family. His position as lord and master would have been threatened.

I was disconcerted for a while by the notion of Brendan being "in the family" and I fell silent. I finished my beer and opened a second one, and then I started to feel more mellow about it all. I stood apart and looked at the family and looked at Brendan bustling around. I thought of this narrow strip of urban garden, one of dozens in the street, one of millions in London, and suddenly I was touched by the sight of Brendan going to so much effort, bustling between the barbecue — which had now been lit, quickly and efficiently by Bill — and my father and my mother. Every so often he would sidle up to Kerry and touch her or whisper something to her or give her a look and she would light up.

He helped my mother with sorting out the marinade for the chicken and salmon pieces. Somehow he went into the house and tracked Troy down to whichever hole he'd been hiding in. He chivied him out and got him to carry plates to the table, and the different salads that Troy and my mother had made that morning. It made me think about myself and I felt a little ashamed. I wondered if I had assumed that the Cotton family existed entirely for my benefit, like some sort of museum that I could drop into whenever I felt like it. And I could always rely on other people to maintain it. My parents were there to do things for me, and to blame when things went wrong. Had I thought enough about doing things for them?

By the time I was on to my third beer I was feeling thoroughly forgiving of almost everybody in the world, and certainly everybody in this garden, though not necessarily in the most coherent way.

There was Brendan, doing five things at once, working so hard; there was my mother bustling in and out with plates and cutlery; my father fiddling around with the barbecue to stop it tipping over; Kerry in conversation with Judy; Troy playing some game with the children. And I noticed something odd: they all seemed to be having a good time. Brendan brought me a plate of grilled chicken and salad and I ate it eagerly. I needed something to soak up the beer. I was so hungry that I barely noticed the very slight oddity that he had served me first. I looked over at Kerry and she sensed my looking at her in that way people do and she turned to me and smiled. I smiled back. We were being a happy family.

Chapter 6

I remember, when I was thirteen or fourteen, going with Bill to a house in Finsbury Park as his unpaid assistant. It was small, with poky rooms and brown furniture. We stood in the living room that had sheets over the floor and he gave me a sledgehammer and told me to smash it through the internal wall, into the kitchen on the other side. He had to tell me twice because it seemed impossible to me that I could do this. The wall looked so solid, the room so unchangeably square and drab, and surely you couldn't just break through structures like that, so casually? But he nodded and stood back, so I heaved the hammer, which was almost too heavy for me to lift, behind my left shoulder and swung it as hard as I could into the center of the wall, spinning with the weight of it, wrenching my arm. Plaster crumbled onto the floor and a crack appeared. I swung again and a hole opened in the surface, jagged and the size of my fist. Again and the hole widened. I could see the center of the kitchen, a draining board and sink with dripping taps, and beyond that a fractured piece of the small garden, with a bay tree at the end of it. And I felt all at once tremendously excited — to be opening things up like this, new vistas with each swing of the hammer, light suddenly flooding into the dreary room. I think it was what first made me think that I'd like to do what Bill did, though when years later I tried to say that to him he patted me on the shoulder and said, "We're just painters and decorators, Miranda."

Every so often at work I still had that feeling of euphoria, like a bubble of air in my chest, a wind blowing through me. I got it, for instance, with the roof garden in Clapham, which somehow took the lid off the whole house. And when we once uncovered a fireplace that was so vast you could stand inside it and look straight up to see a penny-size circle of sky at its top. Knocking walls down always fills me with fresh energy. And every so often I have the same elation in my personal life, too. It goes along with transition, change, spring, falling in love, traveling to a new country, even that feeling of newness that comes after an illness.

After that lunch, I came home and I made two resolutions: I was going to clean up my flat and I was going to start running. That was all. But I wrote them both down on the back of an envelope, as if I would forget otherwise, and then I underlined each of them twice. I sat back in the chair. I'd drunk three cans of beer and eaten two pieces of marinated chicken, a slab of charred salmon, three slices of garlic bread and a bowl of ice cream. If I was being really virtuous, I could go for a run right now, before it got too dark. Or maybe it wasn't healthy to run on a full stomach. And anyway, I didn't want to jog along the high street in my gray tracksuit trousers that had lost the elastic at the waist.

So I thought I'd start with the flat. I changed into some baggy trousers and a sleeveless T-shirt and put on some music. I rather like tidying my flat, which is on the first floor and very small — just my bedroom, the living room, with a table up against one wall, a galley kitchen whose windows overlook a patchwork of narrow gardens, and the bathroom. Clean surfaces, dishes all put away, a vacuumed carpet, washed floor, neat piles of paper on my desk, laundry in the basket, clothes back in the wardrobe, the gleaming bath, the pens in a mug on the mantelpiece, the smell of bleach, polish, lavatory cleaner, soap. My bare feet were gritty and my arms and forehead slick with sweat by the time I'd finished, and it was late. Afternoon had become dark evening, and now that I'd stopped racing around, I could feel the air had the slicing chill of a cloudless October night.

Some of my friends don't like living alone. It's what they're doing until they no longer have to. But I do. I like the feeling I get when I close the door behind me and go upstairs and everything's quiet and waiting. I don't need anybody's permission to lie in a bath for two hours, or go to bed at half-past eight or listen to music late into the night, or pour myself a glass of wine and watch a trashy quiz show. I even like eating alone, though I'm not like Troy. I have a very limited and conservative repertoire. Sometimes I eat the same thing several nights a week — for a bit it was scrambled eggs on very buttery brown toast. Then it was Greek salad, which I've perfected: not just tomatoes and cucumber and feta cheese, but avocado, fennel and sun-dried tomatoes as well. And there were a few weeks when I would add a tin of octopus chunks to a bowl of tinned chickpeas. I went off that one quite quickly. When friends come around I either cook chicken breasts with garlic, rosemary and olive oil you just have to put it in the oven and wait for half an hour or we get a take-away. Usually it's a take-away.

Maybe one of the reasons that Brendan had got on my nerves when we were going out was that he had so quickly made himself at home in my flat. As if it were his home, too. But I told myself not to think of Brendan anymore. Things were going to be different now.

At a shop called Run Run Run in Camden High Street, I bought a rather lovely silky blue singlet, a pair of white shorts, black suede shoes and a book called *Run for Your Life*. It was written by a man called Jan who appeared on the back of the book wearing a headband, like a member of Duran Duran. Then I went to the off-license and bought a bottle of white wine, cold from the fridge. Nothing that was so transparent could possibly have a significant number of calories in. And I bought a bag of expensive crisps that the packet said had been fried in an especially healthy kind of sunflower oil. I fastened the chain on the inside of my door and lay in the bath with a bowl of the crisps and a glass of the wine and read my running book. It was very comforting. The first chapter seemed to be aimed at people who were even less fit than I was. It suggested starting your running schedule with a brisk walk for ten minutes and then running very gently for a hundred yards followed by another ten-minute walk. It said that the training runner should never get seriously out of breath. At the first sign of any kind of discomfort, just stop. The fatal thing was just to set off and go for a run. "Better to start too slowly and build up," said a piece of text in italics, "than start too quickly and give up." That sounded fine to me. I flicked through a few pages. It looked like I could skip a few stages and still avoid breaking into a sweat.

The writer recommended the aspiring runner to think of all the exercise they do in the course of their normal working life. According to him, even getting up from your desk to go to the water cooler counted for something. I did far more than that. I carried ladders and planks around. I painted ceilings while holding myself at contorted angles. I held cans of paint for minutes at a time. This was going to be a doddle. I set my alarm clock half an hour earlier and the following morning I ventured out in my new singlet, shorts and shoes. I rather wished I had bought a mask as well. I walked for five minutes. No problem. I ran hard for about a hundred yards and then the pain began, so I followed Jan's advice and stopped. I walked for a few minutes more and then started to run again. The pain began more quickly this time. My body had started to realize what was being done to it. I slowed down to a walk again and headed for home. Jan said the important thing in the early stages was to avoid causing sprains or pulled muscles by excessively ambitious exercise. I got back to the flat having achieved that without much difficulty.

"Hello? Miranda? I just wanted . . ."
I picked up the phone. "Hi Mum."
"I didn't wake you, did I?"
"No. I was about to leave."
"I just wanted to thank you for yesterday. I was going to ring last night but then Kerry and Brendan stayed so long . . . It all went well, didn't it?"
"It was very nice."
"Doesn't Kerry seem happy?"
"Yes."
"Do you know what? I think it's a miracle."
"Mum —"
"A miracle," she repeated. "When I think how . . ." I closed my eyes and the words slid into each other. I was going to be good.

"Hi Miranda. It's me, Kerry. Miranda? Are you there?" There was a silence, then a man's voice in the background, though I couldn't catch what he said. Kerry giggled, then said, "We just wanted to say how are you, and it would be nice to meet again sometime. What's that? . . . Oh, Brendan says hello from him, too. . . ."

I pressed the button to erase the message.

I ran three times that week and I didn't notice any discernible difference. My lungs still hurt as soon as I jogged more than fifty paces; my legs still felt like lead and my heart a stone jolting around inside my rib cage. On hills, people often walked briskly past me. But at least I persevered and I felt good about that.

On Friday evening, I went out to a party given by my friends Jay and Pattie. I danced and drank beer and then wine and then some strange schnapps from Iceland that Pattie found at the back of her cupboard when most of her guests had left and we were at the lovely stage of the night, when you don't need to make an effort anymore. A dozen or so of us sat around in their dimly lit living room, which was strewn with beer cans and fag ends and odd shoes, and sipped cautiously at the schnapps, which made my eyes water. There was a man I'd met, his name was Nick. He sat cross-legged on the floor in front of me and after a bit he leaned against my knees, relaxing his weight. I could feel the sweat on his back. I waited a few minutes, and then I put my hand on his hair, which was short and soft and brown, like an animal's fur. He gave a little sigh and tipped his head back so I could see his upside-down face. He was smiling faintly. I leaned forward and kissed him quickly on his smile.

When I left, he asked me if I'd like to see him again.

"Yes," I said. "Okay."

"I'll call you."

"Do that."

We looked at each other. Beginnings are so very lovely, like smashing that first small hole in the wall and glimpsing a world on the other side.

Chapter 7

Nick did call two days later. There seems to be a strict code about when you call, the way there used to be a code about on which date to kiss for the first time. If you call on the same day, you're virtually a stalker. If you call the day after, you're maybe a bit desperate because, since the first day is out of the question, the second day is really the first day, so you're calling on the first day. If they're going to call, people call on the third day. If you wait longer than the third day, you might as well not call at all. The person will have got married or emigrated. Personally I've never paid any attention to the code. Life is too short. If it had been me, I would have called the moment I got home.

So Nick called and it was all pretty simple. We arranged to meet the next evening at a bar in Camden Town. I was five minutes early and he was a few minutes late. He was wearing faded jeans and a checked shirt that hung loosely under his leather jacket. He was unshaven and his eyes were very dark brown, almost black.

"You're a decorator," he said. "Pattie told me. And I can see some paint in your hair."

I rubbed my hair self-consciously. "There's nothing I can do about it," I said. "However much I check, there's always a spot somewhere around the back I've missed. It falls off in the end."

When I meet people, they get improbably excited by the fact that I'm a woman doing the work I do. You'd think I was defusing bombs. Still, it gives me something to talk about. And it's a bit like being a doctor. I get asked for my advice. People ask me about how they should do up their homes.

Then Nick asked me what I wanted to do after.

"After what?" I said, pretending not to understand.

"Well. I mean — do you want to always be a decorator?"

"You mean, instead of getting a profession?"

"I guess so," he said uncomfortably.

"Yes," I said simply. "This is what I want to do."

"Sorry — that probably sounded really patronizing."

Yes, it did, so I just asked Nick what he did. He told me that he worked for an advertising company. I asked if they'd done anything I would have seen. Lots, he said. He said that they were the ones who'd done the commercial with the fluffy talking pig. Unfortunately I hadn't seen it. I asked what he was working on now and he replied that they'd recently won a huge account with an oil company and he was working on a report in preparation for the campaign.

But it didn't matter. What mattered were the things going on underneath the conversation, the things we weren't saying. After what seemed like a short time I looked at my watch and was surprised we'd been talking for over an hour.

"I've got to go," I said. "I'm having dinner with this old friend of mine. Laura," I added, to make it clear that I wasn't off to meet a man who might be a boyfriend or an ex-boyfriend or someone I might be considering as a boyfriend.

"I'm sorry," he said. "I hoped that we could have dinner. Or something. Not tonight, obviously. What about, I don't know, Thursday?"

I had arranged to see Troy on Wednesday that week, so Thursday sounded fine. I walked out of the bar thinking, yes, I was sure, almost sure at least, that something at least was going to happen. I had another thought as well, almost a scary one: Maybe

71

this was the best hit. Probably for the next few days or weeks we would have the excitement of a new object in our lives, exploring it, finding out about it. We would ask each other questions, tell carefully edited stories from our earlier lives. We would be so nice to each other, so concerned and thoughtful and just endlessly curious. And then what? Either it would fade away or just end quickly and we would lose touch and become a memory. Somehow it never subsided into pleasant friendship. There was no way back to that. Or we would become a couple, and even then we would have to subside into some sort of normality in which we got on with our jobs and had anniversaries and had joint opinions about things and we would complete each other's sentences. It could be good. People say so. But it could never have the sheer possibility of the beginning. I felt wistful and it seemed to suit the early evening. On one side of the road the cars and shop fronts and people walking home from work were painted in gold from the last of the sun. On the other side of the road they were lost in deep shadow.

When I saw Laura, she knew straight away that something was up, which it wasn't, not really.

"You don't need to say anything," she

said. "I can tell just by looking at you." I tried to tell her not to be ridiculous. It had only been a drink. I thought he seemed nice but I couldn't tell yet.

I was more convinced than I let on. Thursday was good as well. We ate at a place just around the corner from my flat and the evening went by almost without my noticing, until we were the only people left in the restaurant and the chef was out from the kitchen with a glass of wine chatting with us. Twenty minutes later we were in the doorway of my flat, kissing each other. I pulled back from him and smiled.

"I'd like to ask you up," I said.

"But . . . ?"

"Soon," I said. "Really soon. It was such a nice evening, I had a great time, I really like you. I'm just not . . ."

"Sure?"

"Ready. I'm sure, Nick."

"Can I see you tomorrow?"

"Yes, of course . . ." Then I remembered. "Fuck. Sorry. I've got to . . . You won't believe it but I've got to go around to my parents. Things are a bit complicated with them. I'll tell you about it. But not now."

"What about the day after tomorrow?"

"That would be so lovely."

I arrived at my parents' house feeling sulky. It had been bad enough but then my mother had phoned me just before I left asking if I could dress up. I pulled off my trousers and top and put on the blue velvet dress that I've had for so long its hemline's gone wavy.

"You look lovely, dear," said my mother, as she let me in.

I growled something in response. At least she hadn't asked me how I was. My parents were also decidedly dressed up. Troy was there as well. He looked exactly the same as usual, in corduroy trousers and a faded green sweater that should have looked fine. Troy is a rather beautiful young man, or should be. But something was always just slightly off.

"It's good to see you, Miranda," said my father. "We're seeing a lot of each other, aren't we?"

"So where are the lovebirds?" I said.

"Miranda," said my mother in a tone of rebuke.

"I didn't mean anything by that," I said.

"They should be here any —" my mother said, and before she could finish the sentence, the door rang and she smiled at me. "Why don't you go?" she said to me, pushing me toward the door.

74

I opened the door and there were Brendan and Kerry on the doorstep, entangled, laughing, in love. They gave me another of their group hugs as they spilled into the house. When I saw them in the light of the living room, they looked startlingly smart. Kerry was wearing a purple satin dress I'd never seen before. It clung to her hips and breasts. When she looked at Brendan, it was with a sort of dazed carnal pleasure. They looked like a couple who had been in bed together about eight seconds earlier. Brendan was wearing an expensive-looking shiny suit and a large colorful tie decorated with some sort of cartoon character I couldn't recognize. He was carrying a shopping bag that clinked. He removed from it two bottles of champagne, glistening with droplets of water. He placed them on the table. There were already six tall glasses there. He picked up one of the glasses and lightly tapped it with his finger so that it rang like a little bell.

"Without further ado," he said. "I'm so glad you're all here. Kerry and I wanted you to be the first to know." I felt a lurch in my stomach. "Yesterday, I took Kerry out to dinner. And I regret to say that I caused a certain sensation just before the dessert course. I knelt down beside her and asked if she would marry me. And I am very glad to report that she said yes."

Kerry smiled shyly and held up her hand to reveal a ring. I looked at my mother. Tears were spilling from her eyes. She moved toward them with both arms outstretched, and after they'd hugged, I stepped forward as well.

"Kerry," I said, "I'm so happy for you."

"Hang on, hang on," said Brendan. "That can wait. I just wanted to say one more thing. I spent most of my life moving from foster parent to foster parent. I was a lonely little boy, and I didn't know what it was like to belong to a family, to be loved and welcomed and accepted for what you were." As he spoke, two huge tears welled up in his eyes and rolled symmetrically down his cheeks. He didn't wipe them away. "When I first came here," he continued, "when I met you, Derek and Marcia, I felt I had come home. I felt at home. What more can I say? Thank you. And now I've brought some champagne so that you can toast our happiness."

It was all chaos. Brendan opened the champagne in between hugs from my mother and handshakes from my father. Troy gave a shrug and said it was really good and wished them luck. My mother hugged

Kerry so tightly I thought she would do her damage. When the champagne was poured and distributed, my father gave a cough. Oh God, I thought. Another speech.

"I'm not going to say too much," he said. "It's all been rather quick, I must say." He smiled at my mother, a shy smile that made him look like a boy. "But then, if I remember rightly, some other people in this room acted rather impulsively when they first met." My parents met at a wedding of a friend in 1974 and were married two months later. "Sometimes we should trust our instincts. And one thing I know: I have never seen Kerry look so happy and so beautiful. Brendan, I think you're lucky to have her."

"I know," he said, and we all laughed.

"What I really wanted," said my father, "is to drink to the happy couple. Can we call them that?"

"The happy couple," we all said and clinked each other's glasses.

I looked at Kerry. She was almost crying. My mother was definitely crying. Brendan was blowing his nose on a handkerchief and wiping his shiny cheeks. Even my father looked suspiciously near to tears. I made myself a promise. I would make this work. Or, at least, I would let it work. I felt a prod at my elbow.

"A penny for your thoughts," said Brendan.

"Congratulations," I said. "I'm very glad for you."

"That's important to me." He looked around. Mum and Dad and Kerry and Troy were in a group at the far end of the room, talking, laughing. Brendan leaned closer to me.

"When I made the announcement, I was looking at you," he said. "You looked shocked."

"Surprised," I said. "It's been sudden."

"I can see it's difficult for you," he said.

"It's not difficult at all."

"When I was talking, I was looking at your mouth," he said.

"What?"

"You've got a beautiful mouth," Brendan said. He moved closer still. I could smell his breath, sour against my face. "And I was thinking that I've come into that mouth."

"What?"

"It's funny," he said, in a low voice. "I'm marrying your sister and I was thinking of my semen in your mouth."

"What?" I said again, too loudly.

The others stopped talking and looked around. I felt something on my skin, hot, feverish.

"Excuse me," I said, my mouth feeling clammy. I put my glass down and walked out of the room quickly. I heard Brendan saying something. I went into the lavatory. Just in time I pushed my head toward the bowl and vomited in spasms, again and again, until there was nothing left but hot fluid that burned my mouth and throat.

Chapter 8

"Are you sure you're all right to do this? Miranda?"

"What? Yes, quite sure. It'll be fun."

My mind was elsewhere entirely. In bed with Nick the night before, all night. Sleeping at last, then waking in the hours before dawn, dazed with tiredness, and feeling for each other in the darkness. And in the morning he was still there, a stranger's face on the pillow. Miraculous.

I blinked and smiled at Kerry. My lips were sore, my body tingled.

"There are four of them I've arranged to see," she was saying. "And I've worked out how to do it most efficiently. It'll only take an hour or so. Maybe less. You can't tell from the estate agents' details, can you?"

"I can take you out for lunch after, if you like."

"That would be lovely. I said I'd meet Brendan. We can just call him and he'll join us wherever we decide to go. He wanted to come this morning except he'd promised

Dad to help him with moving all their furniture before the workmen arrive tomorrow morning and tear the house to bits. He couldn't do it this afternoon because we've got this man coming to look at my flat for the second time."

"Let's see what time we're through with this," I said, backpedaling. "Maybe I'll just have to dash off anyway, come to think of it. I've got a loft extension waiting."

"It's Sunday," she protested. "You work too hard." Happiness had made her generous. She wanted everyone else to be happy, too. "You look tired."

"Do I?" I reached up and touched my face gently, the way Nick had done. "I'm fine, Kerry. Just a bit of a late night, that's all."

We'd gone to see a film. It wasn't much good, but that didn't matter. We'd leaned into each other, his hand on my thigh, my head pressed against his shoulder. Every so often we'd turned our faces to each other and kissed, just lightly: a promise. He'd bought a tub of salty popcorn but neither of us ate much of it. We'd both known it was tonight, and the film was just about waiting in the dark, emptying our minds of the other things. For me that meant trying to forget what Brendan had said to me the evening before. The way he'd leaned forward and whispered it to me. Smiling and saying that thing. I mustn't think of it; I had to get it out of my mind, where it was buzzing like a fat, unclean fly. So I gazed at the images flickering across the screen, glanced at Nick, every so often closed my eyes.

When we wandered into the foyer, it was dark outside. Nick lifted my hand and kissed the back of it. "Where now?"

"My flat's nearer than yours," I said.

We got a bus there and sat on the top, right at the front. I pressed my forehead against the window and felt the vibrations and looked at the people on the streets beneath me, walking with their heads bent against the gusts of wind. I felt nervous. Soon, I would be making love with this man who was sitting beside me now, not speaking, whom I'd only met twice. What then? Sometimes sex can feel casual and easy, but sometimes it seems momentous and full of problems, almost impossible. Two people with all their hopes and expectations and neuroses and desires, like two worlds colliding.

"This is our stop," I said.

He stood up and then pulled me to my feet. His hand was warm and firm. He smiled down at me. "All right?"

It was all right. Just fine. And then, after we'd made ourselves a sandwich out of one of those half-baked baguettes that I had in my cupboard, with goat cheese and tomatoes, and drunk a glass of wine each, we went back into the bedroom and this time it was better than all right. It was lovely. Just thinking about it now, in Kerry's car, made me feel liquid with desire. Then we had a bath together, legs tangled up in the small tub, my foot pressed against the inside of his thigh, grinning like idiots at each other.

"What are you grinning at?"
"Mmm? Oh, nothing."
"Here. This is the first one." Kerry pulled up and squinted at the sheet of paper dubiously. "It says it's a two-bedroom maisonette, retaining many period features."
"Does it say it's next to a pub?"
"No, it doesn't."
"Let's go and see, anyway."
It's dangerous buying houses. You know before you set foot inside whether you like them. It's almost like a relationship, when they say it's the first few seconds that count, that instant, prerational impression. You have to fall in love with the house you buy. Everything else — whether the roof's sound, the plumbing good, the rooms nu-

merous enough — is almost irrelevant at the start. You can knock down walls and install a damp proof course, but you can't make yourself fall in love. I was here as the expert; as the voice of caution.

Kerry knocked and the door flew open as if the woman had been standing with her eye pressed to the spy hole, looking for our approach.

"Hello, come in, mind the step, shall I show you round or do you want to do it yourself except there are a few details that you might miss, here, come in here first, this is the living room, sorry about the mess . . ." She was large and breathless and spoke in a headlong rush, words spilling over each other. She careered us from room to tidied room, over frantically patterned carpets. The walls were covered with plates they'd collected, from Venice, Amsterdam, Scarborough, Cardiff, Stockholm, and for some reason the sight of them made me feel sorry for her. She pulled open doors with a flourish, showed us the airing cupboard and the new boiler, the second toilet that was crammed into a space that had been carved out of the kitchen, the dimmer switches in the tiny master bedroom, and the spare bedroom that looked more like a broom cupboard and had clearly been built by

cowboys. I pushed the wall surreptitiously
and saw it shake. Kerry made polite murmurs and looked around her with bright
eyes that transformed everything into her
beatific future. She was probably already
putting a cot in the spare bedroom.

"Does the pub bother you?" I asked the
woman.

"The pub?" She acted surprised, wrinkled
her brow. "Oh that. No. You hardly hear it.
Maybe on a Saturday night . . ."

As if on cue, the first burst of music
thumped through the wall, the bass notes
shaking in the air. She flushed but then carried on talking as if she hadn't heard anything. I glanced at my watch: it was eleven-
thirty on a Sunday morning. We did the rest
of the tour anyway, making vaguely enthusiastic remarks about the view from the bathroom window, the wedge-shaped garden.
The more you don't like a place, the more
you have to pretend you do. But I don't
think the woman was fooled.

"What do you think?" asked Kerry as we
left. "If we —"

"Definitely not. Not for half the price."

"It's falling down," I said as we left the
second house.

"But —"

"That's why it's so cheap. That's why the sale fell through. You might be able to afford to buy it, but you'd have to spend the same again. I'm not even sure you could get it insured."

"It's such a nice house."

"It's a wreck. She'd got someone in to plaster and paint over the worst bits in the hall, but there's damp everywhere, probably subsidence. You'd need a structural engineer to check it over. The window frames are rotting. The wiring is primeval. Do you have the capital to do it up?"

"Maybe when Bren, you know, finds a job. . . ."

"Is he looking?"

"Oh yes. And thinking hard about what he really thinks is right for him. He says it's a chance to begin again, and make the life he really wants for himself." She blushed. "For us," she added.

"In the meantime, he's got nowhere to sell, and it's just what you get from your flat, and your income."

"Mum and Dad have been very generous."

"Have they?" I tried to suppress the stab of resentment I felt when I heard that. "No more than you deserve. But don't blow it on that house."

★ ★ ★

You have to be able to imagine what isn't there, and imagine away what is, see underneath things, impose your own taste on top of them. The third place was filthy and smelled of cigarettes and years of unopened windows. The walls were brown and stained, or had faded flowery wallpaper covering them. The carpets were an unlovely purple. The living room needed to be knocked into the kitchen–dining room, to create a huge open space downstairs. The plasterboard needed to be ripped away from the fireplace.

"You could have a huge sun roof over the kitchen, and maybe open it out even farther into a conservatory. It'd be fantastic."

"Do you think so?"

"With that garden, definitely. It must be about sixty feet long."

"It's big for London, isn't it? But it's just nettles."

"Think what it could be like!"

"Did you see the state of the kitchen?"

"He lived there for years without doing anything at all to it. But that's the joy of it — it's ready for you to do whatever you want."

"It's more spacious than I thought we could afford. And all the cornices and moldings and proper sash windows . . ."

"It looks pretty solid to me, as far as I could tell. I'll help you with it."

"Really? You'd do that?"

"Of course."

"And you think it's the right place for us?"

"It's your choice. You've got to want it, and what I think doesn't matter. But you could make it really lovely."

Kerry squeezed my arm. "I can't wait to tell Brendan."

I pressed the button on the answering machine.

"Hello, Mirrie. I hear you've just chosen our new home for us. That's very sweet. But a bit strange as well, don't you think? I guess we've just got to get used to that though, haven't we?"

I pressed the ERASE button. My hands were shaking.

Tony, Laura, Nick and I went to the pub together. That was the stage we'd jumped to, going out as a couple, in a foursome. Everyone was very friendly to each other, wanting to get along. Nick bought us all a round, and then Laura did, and then, out of the blue, just when things were going so well, I found myself talking about Brendan.

"I should be happy," I said. "I mean, Kerry's over the moon."

"Who are we talking about?" asked Nick amiably, putting a crisp into his mouth and crunching it.

"Brendan. Kerry's boyfriend," I said. "Or rather, her fiancé. They've only known each other a couple of weeks and they've got engaged."

"That's romantic."

"It makes me and Laura seem a bit staid and dull," said Tony cheerfully, and Laura shot him an angry look that he blithely did not notice.

"But there's something really, really wrong about him," I said. "He gives me the creeps."

"That's all right. *You* don't have to marry him."

"Didn't you go out with him though?" said Tony. Laura shot him another look. I think she may even have jabbed him under the table.

"Not really," I said.

"How do you go out with someone 'not really'?"

"Not for long, I meant. It wasn't anything." Most of me knew that I shouldn't be having this conversation, so I don't know why I then said: "I finished it with him. It wasn't the other way around whatever he goes around saying."

Nick looked puzzled and seemed about to speak, but Tony got there first.

"So what's the problem?"

"Well, for an example, he said this thing to me, when they announced they were going to get married."

"What thing?"

"It was sick. He said . . ." I stopped dead. I could feel a flush burning its way up my body. Sweat broke out on my brow. "He said something gross."

"What? Go on!" Only Tony didn't seem to be feeling any discomfort. Laura was glaring at me and Nick was looking down at the table, fiddling with his beer mat.

"It was stupid. I don't know why I mentioned it."

"Come on, Miranda. Otherwise I'll just have to imagine it!"

"I don't want to say." How prissy did that sound? "Let's drop it."

"It was you who started it."

"I know. I shouldn't have done. It's just stupid family stuff."

"Gross, as in sexually suggestive?" Tony persisted.

"He just said I had . . ." I hesitated, then said, "He said I had a nice mouth."

"Oh." There was a pause. Nick put another crisp into his mouth. Tony stared at me. "Well, that's not so bad, is it?"

"No," I said weakly. "Just leave it now. Forget it."

"So before me, it was this guy Brendan."

"Yes. Not really. It just lasted a couple of weeks or so. I drifted into it. It was a mistake really. Not even a big mistake, just a small one. It's just weird that he's turned up again like this . . ." Why the fuck were we lying in bed talking about Brendan? "Who was before me then?"

"A woman called Frieda, but that was quite a long time ago. . . ."

And so we were off into safer dangers, telling each other about past loves, giving each other our secrets the way new lovers do. This one adored me, this one meant nothing, and this one broke my heart . . . I once heard a discussion on the radio, where a man said you could only fall in love three or four times in your life. I lay there with Nick's arms around me and wondered how many times I'd been in love. I wondered, was I in love now? How do you know when you're in love?

A few days later, they arrived unannounced, ringing my doorbell when I'd just sunk into a hot bath after a sweaty day up a ladder. I cursed, pulled on an old toweling robe and opened the door, letting in the damp evening air. Kerry had an eager smile on her face, and Brendan was brandishing a bunch of flowers.

"Is this a bad time?"

"I was just having a bath." I pulled my robe tighter and clutched it at the neck.

"We can make ourselves at home while you finish," said Brendan. "Can't we, Kerry?"

"No, it's okay. Come on in."

I stepped back reluctantly and they followed me into the living room. Kerry sat on the sofa but Brendan stood squarely in the middle of the room, gazing around proprietarily.

"You've changed where the furniture is."

"A bit."

"I liked it better the way it was before. Don't you want to put the flowers in water?"

"Yes. Thanks." Actually, I wanted to jam them into the overflowing trash bin.

"Have you eaten?" he asked, as if I was the one who'd come barging in, not him.

"No. I'm not really hungry. I'll have a snack later." I took a deep breath, then said, "Do you want a coffee? Or something alcoholic?"

"Wine would be nice," he said.

I took the bottle from the fridge that Nick had brought around the last time he came.

"Shall I open it for you?"

"I can do it fine."

He held up his hands in mock alarm. "Whoa! Of course you can, Mirrie. I was just being polite."

I stabbed the corkscrew into the cork and twisted it down crookedly. When I pulled, only half the cork came out. Brendan watched me, smiling sympathetically, as I gingerly extracted the crumbled remains of the cork from the bottle and poured three glasses. He held his up to the light and carefully picked out a few bits from the wine before drinking.

"We should have brought a bottle around ourselves," said Kerry. "Because actually, we have a favor to ask."

"Yes?" I said warily.

"Well, something amazing's happened. You know that man who was coming around a second time to look at my flat on Sunday?"

"Yes."

"He's made an offer. Only a bit less than what we were asking."

"That's brilliant," I said.

"He seems really keen. And he's a first-time buyer. He's not in a chain at all."

"But he is in a hurry," interjected Brendan.

"Ah," I said. I had a horrible, horrible feeling that I knew where this was going.

"He seems to think," said Kerry, "that he can exchange and complete in a matter of a week or two. He says his solicitor told him that as long as she can do the search immediately and there's no problem with the survey, then he could be in by the end of next week."

"It has been known," I said dully.

"But Bren's already given up the place he was renting and we can't move into our new flat by then," said Kerry. "Though the owner's in an old people's home and our solicitor promises she'll do it as quickly as possible."

"So," said Brendan, smiling at me. He poured himself a second glass of wine and took a slurp of it.

"So if that happens, which maybe it won't anyway, we're in a bit of a fix," said Kerry. "And we wondered if we could come and stay at yours. Only for a few days, a week or two at the very most."

"What about . . . ?"

"Of course we'd go to Derek and Marcia's," said Brendan. "Except their house is going to be a complete bomb site for the next few months. Well, you know better than us the nightmare that can be to live in.

They might even have to move out for a bit themselves."

"Would it be possible, Miranda?" asked Kerry.

I wondered why Kerry wanted to stay with me in the first place. If it had been the other way around, I would have tried to keep a safe distance between Brendan and his ex-girlfriend, not put them in the same small flat as each other, even if — or especially if — that ex-girlfriend was my sister. Maybe I just had a more suspicious nature than she did. Or maybe she was asserting to herself, and to me and Brendan, that she knew she had nothing to fear. I looked at her but I couldn't read her expression.

"My flat's so small," I said hopelessly. "I haven't even got a spare bedroom."

"You've got your sofa bed," said Brendan.

"It might not even happen," said Kerry. "And we won't get in your way. We'll keep everything tidy and cook for you, and you'll hardly notice us before we're gone. A week."

"Haven't you got friends with a bigger place? Where you'd be more comfortable?"

"Miranda, you're my sister." Kerry had tears in her eyes. She darted a look at Brendan and he took her hand and stroked it. "You're *family*. It's not such a big thing we're asking. Mum and Dad were certain you wouldn't mind. I thought you wouldn't mind. I thought you might even be *pleased* to have us here. It didn't occur to me that . . ."

"Perhaps Mirrie is still finding it painful," said Brendan softly.

"What!"

"We shouldn't have asked you," continued Brendan. "It wasn't fair. Maybe you're not ready for this."

I squeezed my wineglass so tightly in my hand I thought it would break.

"But you do kind of owe it to Kerry, don't you?" His voice was still soft and insinuating. "After what happened. Mmm? Mmm?"

"Sorry?" said Kerry.

I stared at Brendan. There was red behind my eyes and I thought of throwing my wine into his face, of smashing my glass against his cheek, of kicking him in the legs, punching him as hard as I could in his belly, pushing him violently out of the door.

"Miranda?" said Kerry. "Just a few days?"

I turned to her and tried to focus on her reproachful face. I thought of lying in my bed and knowing Brendan was a few feet away, on the sofa, with my sister. Of getting up in the morning and seeing him sitting at the kitchen table, as if he belonged there. Bumping into him on my way to the bathroom . . . But maybe I could stay with Nick for a night or two, or even with Laura. Maybe go away for the weekend, somewhere. Anywhere.

"All right," I said. "One week."

Kerry gripped my hand and Brendan came toward me with outstretched arms. If he touched me, I would scream, vomit, become violent. I ducked out of reach.

"I'm going to have that interrupted bath now," I said. "Finish your wine."

The water was tepid but I lowered myself into it anyway. I closed my eyes and sank beneath the surface, where I waited for my heart to stop battering itself against my chest. When I came up for air, I heard a knocking at the door, Brendan calling my name.

"What?"

"The phone for you. I answered it. Hope you don't mind."

"Who is it?" I asked, reaching for a towel.

"Someone called Nick," said Brendan. "He seemed a bit surprised to get me."

I yanked open the door and marched through to the living room. "I'll take it in my bedroom. You can put it down out here."

"Is this Nick your new boyfriend?" When I didn't answer he put his arm around Kerry and pulled her close to him before saying,

"That's wonderful news, Mirrie. We're so glad for you."

I pulled sharply at my bedroom door and it shut with a bang. I picked up the phone. "Nick?"

"I just wanted to hear your voice. How are you?"

"All the better for speaking to you," I said.

Then I heard breathing. There was someone on the other line. I waited until there was a small click. A few moments later, I heard the front door shut.

Chapter 9

I leaned over the dishes of curry and cleared my throat.

"There's something I want to say. It's nothing serious," I added, seeing his suddenly wary look. "I just felt that when we were talking with Laura and Tony, things came out wrong."

"It's not a big deal," Nick said.

"I know it isn't," I said. "But I've been thinking. I want to be completely straight with you."

"Weren't you being straight?"

"I was, but it came out in a confused way that felt wrong. So I want to tell you about it in a clear way. It's really very simple."

I took a sip of wine and then gave him a basic digest of what had happened with Brendan and Kerry and my family.

"You see," I said. "He was someone I had no strong feelings about, except maybe that by the end I thought he was a bit of a creep. But now he's with my sister and everybody's going on about how she's happier than she's ever been, so, you know . . ."

"So maybe you're starting to wonder if you made a mistake."

"What do you mean?"

"Breaking up with him."

I pulled a face.

"Oh God, not for a single second. I broke up with him assuming I'd never see him again and now he's part of the furniture."

Nick cut a piece of tandoori chicken with his fork and ate it with deliberation.

"So why did you go out with him if he's a creep?"

"We only saw each other a few times. Then I stopped going out with him."

"It's strange to think of you with someone like that."

"Have you never started going out with someone and then gradually realized that you didn't like them that much after that?"

"I don't know," said Nick.

"You've never been attracted to someone and then once you've got over the attraction found that there was nothing left?"

"I'm just wondering what you'll think when you get to know *me*," said Nick.

"I think I know," I said. "That's why I'm going to such trouble to explain it to you."

"You don't need to explain anything to me."

"But —"

"Let's go home."

Afterward we lay side by side, the room dark except for the glow of the streetlights around the curtain edges. I lay with my head on Nick's chest, stroking his stomach softly down to the edge of his soft pubic hair. His breathing was slow and regular and I thought he might be asleep, but then he spoke.

"What did he say?"

"What?" I said.

"Brendan," Nick said. "What was it he said? I mean, what did he *really* say?"

I raised myself on an elbow and looked down at his face. "You can ask me anything, you know —" I said.

"That's why I'm asking."

"I was going on to say that some things aren't good to know. Sometimes you can feel contaminated by knowing something."

"But once you mentioned it, I had to know. It's hard not to think about it. It can't be so bad."

I felt a chilliness on my skin, like I'd once felt cold while suffering from a fever.

"He said . . ." I drew a deep breath and said it in a rush. "He said he was thinking how he had come in my mouth. I felt — well,

I left the room and threw up. So now you know. Now you know the truth."

"Jesus," he said. There was a silence, and I waited. "Did you tell anybody?"

"I'm telling you."

"I mean, why didn't you tell someone? They'd have thrown him straight out."

"Would they? I don't know. He might have denied it. He might have said I'd misheard. He'd have thought of something. In any case, I couldn't think clearly. I felt like I'd been punched in the face and the stomach simultaneously. So was that worse than anything you'd imagined?"

"I don't know," he said, and then we didn't speak. I didn't fall asleep straight away though and I'm not sure if he did. I murmured something to him but he didn't reply and there was just the sound of regular breathing. So I just lay there beside him looking at the lights outside, the car headlights sweeping across the ceiling.

When my mother walked into the bar, I suddenly realized that it wasn't just Kerry who had changed. She looked lovely and somehow younger than I was used to thinking of her. Her hair was brushed up on top of her head and she was wearing a belted mac that swished as she walked, and dangling earrings, dark red lipstick. She smiled, raised a gloved hand as she crossed the room. When she bent to kiss me, I smelled perfume, face powder.

Out of the blue, I remembered an episode from my childhood. We had gone for a bike ride and I had struggled along way behind the others. I had tried as hard as I possibly could but they had got farther and farther away from me. They would wait and I would catch up slowly and then they would leave me behind again as I pedaled stolidly through tears of rage and exhaustion. At the end of the ride, my father finally took a look at my bike and saw that there was a problem with the brake and it had been jammed down against one of the wheels for the entire journey. Maybe it's too convenient a metaphor for times when things just seem too hard: pedaling with the brake on. Now I wondered if my mother had spent years with the brakes on and that, with Kerry in love, she was released and pedaling free.

"I've got a bottle of white for us," I said.

"I really shouldn't," she said, which in mother-speak meant "thank you very much."

"Don't worry," I said. "There's a special deal here. You order two glasses and they give you the bottle. You know that I can never resist a bargain like that."

I filled her glass and she clinked it against mine, inevitably toasting Kerry and Brendan. I tried not to mind; tried to banish the five-year-old Miranda who wanted to be toasted and made a fuss of.

"Kerry's told me about your help with the flat-hunting and letting them stay and everything," she said. "I know she's not good at expressing her gratitude. She's probably embarrassed. But it means so much to her. And to me as well."

"It was really nothing," I said.

"I feel so happy about Kerry that I can hardly bear it. I keep my fingers crossed all the time. And I wake at night and just pray and pray that it will be all right."

"Why shouldn't it?" I said.

"It seems too good to be true," my mother said. "As if someone's waved a wand over her life."

"It's not a fairy tale. He's not a knight in shining armor," I said.

"I know, I know. But I have always thought with Kerry that all she needed was self-confidence and then she could do whatever she wanted. That's what Brendan's given her."

"It's scary, isn't it," I said, swirling my

amber wine around in its glass. "All the different things happiness depends on. You want it to be less fragile than that."

"Well, I never thought that way about you," said my mother. "Whatever the ups and downs, I knew you'd be all right."

"Oh," I said dully. Somehow that didn't make me feel cheerful.

"It's just Troy now," said my mother. "But I can't help feeling it's going to be okay now. Like we're getting into a virtuous circle." She tipped the last of her wine down her throat and I poured her another glass. She waited until I was done, then took a breath and said: "Talking of Kerry and Troy, it seemed like a good moment to talk about things that your father and I have never discussed properly with you."

"What things?" I said, with a creepy ominous feeling.

She took one of the little paper napkins that came with the wine and started twisting it and folding it as if she was going to make a paper airplane.

"Obviously, we all know that Troy is wonderful but he's always going to need financial help. You know that we have been paying money into a trust fund for him."

"He may get a job," I said dubiously. "It's a matter of finding the right area."

"I hope so, Miranda, I hope so. But that's not our immediate problem. Now Kerry and Brendan will be getting married in two months' time and it's going to be a very modest ceremony. But the two of them will be as poor as church mice for a while. Derek has talked with Brendan and he's very impressed with him. He has a large number of plans. All sorts of plans. But for the moment they will need help with their flat and other things. We have our own property problems, as you know, but still, we want to help them as much as we can. We are going to help them with buying the flat, in a small way."

"I'm glad," I said. "But why are you telling me?"

"You're doing so well," said my mother, squeezing my hand. "You always have done. I sometimes think it's hard for you to realize how difficult it has been for Troy and Kerry."

"I'm a jobbing decorator," I said. "I'm not a stockbroker."

My mother shook her head. "You're doing wonderfully. I've been talking with Bill. He thinks the world of you."

"I wish he'd pay me more, then."

"That will come, Miranda. The sky's the limit for you."

"So what are you saying?"

"You're so generous, Miranda, and I know you won't give this a second thought, the way some people would. It just seems clear to your father and me that Troy and Kerry need, will *always* need, help in a way that you won't."

"So what are you saying?" I repeated. I knew what she was saying.

"All I'm saying is that we're allocating special resources to Troy and Kerry and I hope that you agree with us about the need for that."

What she meant — of course — is that she was taking money from the slice of the family pie that was notionally in some sort of way allocated to me and giving it to Troy and Kerry. What could I say? *No, don't help my brother and sister?* There was a little dormouse-size Miranda in a corner of my brain giving a howl of rage and misery, but I put a metaphorical gag in her mouth.

I wanted to cry. It wasn't the money, or I don't think it was. It was the emotions behind the money. We never grow up enough not to need our parents looking after us, taking care of us. I smiled broadly. "Sure," I said.

"I knew you would," my mother said fervently.

"I guess I'll need to find a rich husband," I said, still smiling.

"You'll find whatever you want," said my mother.

Chapter 10

They arrived before I was expecting them, so I was still in my dressing gown, drinking coffee and eating a custard pie that I'd bought a few days ago on my way back from work. It wasn't a very healthy breakfast, but the crust was already a bit stale and if I didn't eat it now I would have to throw it away. Anyway, I'd been running. I'd puffed my way through five miles on the heath on a glorious late October morning, sharply cold, but bright, too, with soggy brown leaves underfoot. The run, all that pain, balanced out the custard pie. I had planned to paint my toenails, clear the living room a bit, and ring up Nick to arrange to meet him for lunch. That way, I could welcome them and then have an excuse to rush off.

But then the bell rang, in three assertive bursts. Before I could answer it, I heard the scrape of a key in the lock. I'd given Kerry a spare key, but I felt a twinge of resentment. I felt they ought to have let me admit them like guests on their arrival. The scraping went on, and I heard a muffled swear and then some giggles. I stuffed the last morsel of custard pie into my mouth, stood up, tightened the belt on my dressing gown and opened the door, pulling Brendan in with it, holding on to the key that was still in the lock. We were about three inches apart. He was wearing a thick coat that belonged to my father, a long, speckled scarf that looked like one I'd given Troy last Christmas. In his left hand he carried a large nylon bag. I could see pajamas, a dressing gown, bath foam. His eyes were bright, his dark hair glossy. His mouth looked redder than usual.

"Hi," I said curtly, standing back to let him in, but he simply took a step toward me, as if he was a partner in some dance, and stood looking down at me. The upturned collar of his coat brushed against my jaw. I felt his breath on my cheek.

"Hey there, Mirrie," he said. He lifted a thumb and before I could stop him had tenderly wiped a crumb from my upper lip. Then his head bent down, his red lips were on my cheek. I smelled mint and, underneath it, something sour.

I turned away and wiped the spot where his lips had been, then retreated farther into the hall. Brendan followed. Behind him, Kerry stood, in a bright red duffle coat. Her

110

cheeks were flushed, her fair hair was tied in a little girl's pigtails. She carried a box: bran, herbal tea, vitamin tablets, alfalfa beans, organic elderflower cordial. She had to put the box on the floor before she hugged me.

"Don't close the door," she said. "We've got loads more to get out of the car. And Mum and Dad and Troy are bringing the rest over."

"Don't worry," said Brendan. "Just essentials."

"I'll put some clothes on and then I'll help you with them."

"Why don't you make us some coffee instead?" said Brendan. "And we haven't had breakfast yet, have we Kerry? We were in such a rush."

"*You* were in such a rush. I don't know where you get your energy from."

He smirked, then said, "Just some toast and jam would be fine. Or do you have tahini?"

"What?"

"Kerry and I are trying to eat healthily." He put out his large hand, hair on the knuckles, and caressed the top of Kerry's head. "We want to have a long life together, don't we, sweetie?"

"We did this questionnaire on the Internet," said Kerry. "You had to say how much you exercised and what you ate and then it told you when you'd die. I'm going to live until I'm ninety-two. Brendan's going to live to ninety-six."

"I've only got jam," I said.

I took my time getting dressed. I sat on my bed for a few moments, breathing deeply, practicing being calm. I dressed, brushed my hair unnecessarily, made my bed. The phone rang, but someone picked it up in the other room before I could get to it.

The outside door was still open when I came out of my bedroom, and now my parents and Troy were there as well. There was a small television on one of the chairs. On the kitchen table were a computer with its printer, a portable CD player and a pile of CDs beside it, a bedside lamp with its wire trailing onto the floor. Three large and bulging holdalls stood by the door. For me, the detail that I found almost horribly intimate was the heap of shoes, his and hers, mixed together. Tennis rackets stood against the wall. An exercise bike blocked the entrance to the bathroom. There was a clutter on the kitchen surfaces: two electric toothbrushes, contact lens cleansing fluid — did Brendan wear contact lenses, and how had I failed to notice that while I was going out with him? — anti-dandruff shampoo, a makeup bag, another toaster, an electric iron, a framed photograph of Brendan and Kerry sitting on a wooden bench with their arms around each other, piles of holiday brochures, a tangled wind chime that Kerry had had since she was a teenager. How had they managed to accumulate so much so quickly?

I stood for a moment on the threshold of the room and looked at them all. Brendan was grinding coffee beans and Kerry was making toast and jam for everyone and a comforting burnt smell filled the air. Mum was dressed more casually than I was used to, in an old pair of corduroys and a plaid shirt. Her hair was loose and brushed behind her ears and for a moment I was taken aback at how carefree she looked. She was carrying a bright bunch of dahlias. Brendan came up to her and put his arm around her and she laughed and leaned against him and held the flowers under his nose. I looked at my father but he didn't seem to mind in the slightest. He was beaming at the room. He was unshaven and there were circles of sweat under his armpits, jam on his chin.

Troy was sitting on the floor on a folded-up duvet, with his back against the sofa. He was fiddling with a puzzle I'd given him last Thursday, a set of polystyrene shapes that

— so it said on the box — fitted together into a cube. I looked at his face as he concentrated. He looked thin and pale and tired. There were bruises under his eyes, as if he'd been crying. But he seemed peaceful as well. Troy is the only person that I know who can be happy and sad at the same time, carrying two kinds of weather around inside him. He slotted in the final shape — yes, it really did make a cube — and gave a smile of satisfaction before taking it apart again. Tenderness rose in my throat and I suddenly wanted to burst into tears.

"Hello everyone," I said. I kissed my parents on the cheek and ruffled Troy's hair.

"Coffee's up," said Brendan cheerily. "Afraid I've finished the beans though."

"Where do you want to put everything?" I asked Kerry. "There's nowhere really to hang your clothes."

"Dad's giving us one of those rails," she said. "Just for the smarter stuff and my work clothes. We can stand it behind the sofa. The rest we can just keep in the bags."

I couldn't manage anything more than a weak, acquiescent shrug. I watched Mum stuffing the dahlias into a tumbler and tried to swallow back a spasm of self-pity. She hadn't given me flowers when she last came around.

"Here we are," said Brendan. "Milk, no sugar, right?" He gave a sort of wink as if he had got a quiz question correct.

I sat down next to Troy and watched Kerry put cereal boxes into cupboards. Brendan lifted a heap of books off a wide shelf and inserted the tiny television. "We can watch it in bed," he said. "Is your sofa bed comfy, Mirrie? I've never slept in it."

"How are you?" I asked Troy. I could see how he was: subdued, all the energy gone, so his face looked blanched and his body limp.

A burst of music filled the room.

"Mozart," said Brendan, stepping back from the CD player. "We love Mozart, don't we Kerry?"

"All right," Troy said. "Fine." He picked up the polystyrene pieces again and started fiddling.

"Here we are, mate." Brendan squatted down beside him. "You need blood sugar." He put his hand under Troy's chin and lifted up his face. "You're tired, aren't you? Couldn't sleep?"

"Not much," said Troy.

"That's no good. Have some toast and jam. Later we can all go for a brisk walk. That'll help with insomnia. Mmm?"

"I don't know," said Troy. He looked away

115

from Brendan and bit into the toast. "I don't know if I feel like a walk."

"I ought to warn you," I said. "I've got to go out quite soon. Sorry. It was an arrangement I made before I knew when you were coming."

"What a pity," my mother said. "You can't cancel?"

"Who are you meeting?" asked Brendan.

"No one you know."

"Miranda," said my mother. "I know you don't mean to, but that sounded a bit rude."

It took an effort not to say something back to my mother that really was rude.

"He's called Nick," I said.

"Nick?" Brendan raised his eyebrows.

"Yes."

"How very strange. I just spoke to him on the phone. When you were getting dressed. Sorry — I should have said at once. He rang and I said you'd ring him back but he didn't seem to know about your prior arrangement. Mmm? On the spur of the moment, I invited him over to supper here. With all of us. I knew you wouldn't mind. We thought we could make a party of it, like a mini-housewarming, and Derek and Marcia's kitchen's only got three walls now, so we can't go there, can we?"

I closed my eyes and then opened them again. He was still there, smiling at me.

"I can't . . ." I said. I didn't know what to say next. I clenched my fists so that my nails dug into my palms.

"He said he'd love to come."

"We've got to meet him sometime," said Mum. She was placing Kerry's and Brendan's shoes in pairs against the wall.

"Troy can cook," said Brendan.

"I don't know if I feel like cooking."

"You seem to have got it all sorted," I said.

"You don't need to do a thing," said Brendan. "We're going to spoil you. Our treat, Mirrie."

Chapter 11

I went out anyway. I couldn't stay in the flat. My flat, though it didn't feel like mine anymore, with Brendan's shaving cream in the bathroom, Kerry's television on my bookshelf, their music playing, their soy milk in the fridge, their night things slung over the back of the sofa.

I strode over the heath, feet scuffling up leaves, breath curling in the clear air. A beautiful day and I'd met someone I liked and I should be happy and all I could feel was this sensation eating into my stomach lining like acid. I couldn't stop myself thinking of Brendan sitting on my lavatory, lying in my bath, eating food a few feet away from me, nuzzling up to Kerry, to my mother . . . His hair in my brush, his hand on my shoulder, his breath on my cheek. I shuddered and walked even faster, trying to burn off the anger and disgust.

I must be polite and friendly, for Kerry's sake, I told myself, kicking a little heap of conkers out of my path and watching them roll bumpily away from me. Just a few days, a week or two, then they'd be in their own house, busy decorating it and planning their wedding, and I'd hardly have to see them. Even as I persuaded myself this was true, I heard his voice telling me about my beautiful mouth, remembered his damp lips on my cheek, and felt instantly nauseous.

My mobile rang in my pocket. "Hello?"

"Miranda, it's me."

"Nick. I was going to call you."

"I'm round at Greg's just now. I'm looking forward to this evening, though it's a bit daunting meeting your whole family at once. Shall I bring anything?"

"You don't have to come you know."

"Don't you want me to?"

"It's not that. It'll just be a bit oppressive, you know, all the family and Kerry and Brendan have just moved in with half of their belongings and it's chaos."

"Brendan sounded very friendly."

"Oh did he?"

"No, really. I think he was making a big effort with me."

"It might be better to meet my family another time . . ."

"What are you so worried about?"

"Nothing."

"It's Brendan, isn't it? You don't want me to meet him."

"I was just thinking about you."

"I said I'd come and I'm coming." There was a pause, and he added stiffly, "If that's all right with you, that is."

"Why wouldn't it be?"

"Good. Seven o'clock then?"

"All right."

Troy and I went shopping for the supper. Mum had said she would bring the pudding, so we only needed to buy stuff for the main course. Troy couldn't make up his mind what to cook, so we drifted up and down the aisles. He picked up bags of lentils and beans and weird kinds of exotic rice and stared at them and put them back. His brain seemed flooded by all the choices, the colors and the bright lights.

"Pasta," I said. "Let's cook something with pasta."

"Maybe."

"Or something with rice."

"Rice?"

"Rice, yes. Good idea?"

"I don't know."

"Or we could cheat. Let's buy a ready-made meal and pretend we've cooked it ourselves."

I randomly picked out a pack of cod in cheese sauce from the freezer and held it up. "A couple of these," I said. "We could put them into a bowl and nobody would know. Anyway, who cares if they do know? It's not a big deal."

"That looks disgusting."

I tossed it back into the freezer. "You decide then."

He gazed around him, at all the shelves, at the overloaded carts. "I don't feel like cooking really. I'm not in the mood."

"We've been here for half a fucking hour," I said, slowing the shopping cart viciously around on its wheels. "All I've put in the trolley are some coffee beans and a bunch of bananas. I'm just going to buy something, right? Anything."

"Right," he said, staring at me so helplessly that all the heat went out of me.

I put my hands on his thin shoulders and squeezed them. "It's okay, Troy," I said. "Everything's fine. Leave it to me."

Kerry and Brendan had stayed behind to tidy up the flat, but when Troy and I returned in the late afternoon, the light fading and the rind of a moon already on the horizon, the mess had hardly been touched. For a blessed moment I thought they'd gone out, but then I heard the rumbling pipes and voices coming from behind the closed bathroom door. They were having a bath together. A very long bath, which continued as I helped Troy crush the garlic, chop the vegetables. We worked in comfortable silence. Every so often the pipes would rumble again as more water was used, or there would be a squeal of pleasure. I glanced across at Troy. It sounded to me as if sex were going on in there, sporadically and splashily. I put on some music, quite loud, and returned to the sink. My shoulders ached and I felt sweaty and lumpy. I wanted to have a bath, too, before Nick arrived, wash my hair and put on different clothes and some makeup. I looked at my watch and considered banging on the door, but restrained myself.

When they finally emerged, wrapped in towels, they were pink and damp. Fragrant steam billowed out behind them.

"I'm just going to take a quick bath myself," I said, laying down the sharp knife and leaving them rummaging in their bags for clothes.

There was no hot water. An unreasonable anger rose up in me. I washed my face in the sink and cleaned my teeth, but just as I was about to go into my bedroom to find something to wear the doorbell rang. Shit. Brendan flung the door open on Nick and my parents smiling awkwardly at each other on the threshold.

"Nick," said Brendan, holding out his hand. "Come in. We've all been wanting to meet you."

"Hi," I said to him. I thought about going over and giving him a kiss, but instead hovered by the cooker. "You've probably worked it out already, but the chef here is my brother Troy." Troy turned from the hob and lifted a wooden spoon in the air. "And my parents, Marcia and Derek. My sister, Kerry." Who, I now saw, was looking gorgeous, in a red velvet dress with a choker that made her neck long and slender. "And Brendan."

Everyone said hello and shook hands. I pulled the duvet and the coats off the sofa, but nobody sat down. I cleared my throat.

"Good day?" I said brightly to Nick across the room.

"Fine," he said.

"It was lovely weather, wasn't it?"

We stared at each other, appalled.

"Drinks," cried Brendan. He took the two bottles of wine I'd brought out of the fridge and opened them both with a flourish. "Get those crisps, Kerry. It's always nerve-racking, meeting the parents, isn't it?" he said. "When I first met Marcia and Derek I was petrified." He gave a happy shout of laughter.

"Were you?" asked my father. "We certainly didn't notice that." He turned to Nick. "Miranda tells me you're in advertising."

"Yes," said Nick. "And you're in packaging."

"Yes."

"I once thought about advertising as a career," said Brendan into the pause. "But then I worried about having to advertise things I didn't agree with."

"Well . . ." began Nick.

"Like one of those multinational petrol companies," said Brendan. Nick gave me a sharp glance, obviously suspecting I'd told Brendan about his commission. "For instance. That would be impossible. Mmm? I want to work with people. That's where my real interests lie. Here's your wine."

"It's a bit like being a lawyer," said Nick. "You can't just pick the things that you agree with."

"You mean that even bad companies deserve good advertising," said Brendan, taking a sip — no, a large gulp — of wine. "That's an interesting thought."

★ ★ ★

We sat around the small table, everyone pressed against their neighbor, forks scraping against unmatching plates, the third bottle of wine opened and poured. Nick ate slowly and was quiet, but Brendan wolfed down his helping and asked for more.

"You'll have to teach me how to cook it," he said to Troy. He turned companionably to Nick. "Has Mirrie ever cooked for you?"

"Once."

Brendan grinned. "Let me guess. Chicken breasts with garlic and olive oil?"

"In fact, I mentioned it to Kerry," I said.

"Right," said Nick. He smiled at me affectionately.

And I'd said, when I produced it . . .

"And when she put it down in front of you, she went like this" — Brendan's voice climbed higher, he raised his eyebrows — "*Da-daaa!* Make the most of this, mister." Even I could hear that it sounded a bit like me.

He laughed. I looked across the table at Nick. He was smiling, a bit. And Kerry. Everybody. I stared down at my plate. I thought that Brendan was being repulsive, but I wondered if — for Nick — Brendan's repulsiveness would rub off on me as well.

In which case, should I hope that Nick would be charmed by him?

"You okay?" It was Kerry, next to me, laying her cool hand over my sweaty one. Her smell of soap and perfume in my nostrils.

"Fine." I took my hand away.

"Mirrie?"

Suddenly they were all looking at me.

"I'm fine," I repeated.

"We're family," said Brendan gently. "Family. It's all right."

I turned on him. *"I finished it with you,"* I heard myself say. *"I was the one who finished it."*

The room was silent, except for the sound of Nick's fork, scraping on the plate.

"What was that about?"

We were walking along the street toward the underground, having made a hurried exit.

"I don't know. It doesn't matter. It was just me being stupid."

"Is that all?"

"I just felt — oh, I don't know. Stifled."

"Nobody was being nasty to you. You just flared up."

"You don't understand, Nick. It's all the things that lie between the lines. Things that aren't spoken but I know are there."

126

"That sounds a bit paranoid to me."

"Yeah? Well, that's because you're not in my family."

"Brendan was trying to be kind."

"Right. That's what he wanted you to think. He wants to get you on his side."

"Christ, Miranda, you should listen to yourself."

"Oh forget it." I rubbed my eyes. "I made a fool of myself, I know that. I feel stupid, ridiculous. I don't really want to have a postmortem over it."

"Very well." His voice was cool.

We reached the underground station. A warm and dirty wind blew up from below. I felt I could hardly breathe. I took Nick's hand.

"I'm sorry," I said. "Can we let it go now?"

"I can," he said. "Can you?"

Chapter 12

"Go on, Miranda," said Kerry. "It'd be so easy for me to set up; you could be on a plane tomorrow evening! Go on." She paused, then added almost bossily, "I think you need a break."

"I'm fine," I said snappishly.

"I'm only trying to help you," she said. "We're all a bit concerned." I clenched my fists and told myself to stay calm.

I opened my mouth to say no, but then I thought, why not? Why not escape for a few days? Long nights, deep baths, pavement cafés, room service, new sights, new faces, language a babble of sounds in my ear, sun on the nape of my neck, oysters, carafes of wine . . . And when I returned from work, no Brendan. When I staggered into the kitchen in the morning, no Brendan sitting at the table with his dressing gown flapping open, chomping vigorously on the last slice of bread. Calling me Mirrie. Whispering things into my ear. It had only been one night and one day and already I felt as if I could barely breathe. Just now I had sent him to the shops to buy some toilet rolls, and for the few minutes he was gone I felt as if a boulder had been lifted off my chest.

"All right," I said. "Just two or three days. After all, I might as well make use of having a travel agent for a sister."

"Good. It's just what you need, and I'm sure you'll feel much better when you come back."

"I could do with a few days off," I said. This was the way we were going to play it then: Miranda has been overworking.

I was busy calculating to myself. If I left tomorrow evening, or the next day, to be more realistic, and was away for the rest of the week, then when I returned maybe they'd be gone. Kerry said that everything seemed to be going smoothly with their house purchase.

"Where do you fancy going then? It can't be too far if it's only for a short time." She stood up and collected her briefcase from behind the sofa. "Look, I brought these back on the off chance. We do these mini-breaks and there are always spaces at this time of year — I could get you one for a quarter of the price." She spilled several brochures onto the table. "What about Prague? Or Madrid? Or here's one for a few days in Normandy, by the sea. It might be a bit cold now. I'd go further south, if I were you."

"Italy," I said, picking up a brochure and opening it.

"Rome?"

"I've been to Rome. I want to go somewhere I've never been before."

"There's Florence, Venice, Siena or Naples. Four days. Or look, there's a really nice hotel in Sicily, on a cliff overlooking the sea."

I looked at the glossy pictures. Pink and gray churches, canals with gondolas, hotel rooms with large beds.

"Hang on," I said. I picked up the phone and dialed.

"Nick, it's Miranda . . . yes . . . yes, I feel much better, thanks. Sorry about it all, I don't know what came over me, tired I guess . . . Listen . . ."

It rained. It was raining when we arrived at the airport and queued for the water bus that would take us to the city. The sky was steel gray. Rain pounded onto the roads like arrows, sending up shoots of water. Our clothes were drenched after thirty seconds. Rain poured down our necks. Nick's hair was plastered to his skull. It rained all the way on the boat, and our first view of the city was a blur — a ghost city rising from the water. It was a five-minute walk from our stop to the hotel, and we lugged our bags, full of light clothes and no waterproofs, along a narrow canal where all the boats were tethered to the side, covered in tarpaulins.

It rained every day. We ran to churches and art galleries, and in between we sheltered in little cafés drinking double espressos or hot chocolate. I'd dreamed of long slow walks through the labyrinth of canals, leaning together on bridges to watch the boats go by, sex under thin sheets with the shutters closed against the sunlight. We spent too much money on lunches, which were meant to have been picnics of bread and cheese or slices of pizza, because it was better to sit inside for a couple of hours with the tourists' three-course menu and a jug of house wine. Nick bought me a leather wallet and a glass thumb ring. I took photographs of him standing damply on the Rialto Bridge. At night we ate in tiny restaurants and went to bed with the sound of rain clattering against the small windows of our room. He flossed his teeth for five minutes every morning and every evening. He snored in his sleep. He loved chocolate and ice cream.

Every so often, the rain momentarily stopped and the sun half appeared through a gauze of clouds. The puddles glistened and the swollen canals rippled in the light, and the stones steamed. It was the most silent, beautiful city I had ever been in, and I found myself wishing, once or twice, that I was here alone, not worrying about our relationship, not having to make an effort. I would have walked and walked along the deserted paths, not speaking, storing everything up. I wouldn't have minded the rain.

They were still there when I got back on Sunday afternoon. Indeed, they seemed more firmly installed than ever, their belongings spreading along shelves, their laundry in the washing machine, toothbrushes in my London underground mug. In two thick piles on the table were wedding invitations: Saturday, December thirteenth, at four P.M. They were making lists of who to invite, of decisions to make, tasks to be done. There was an air of bustle and excitement about them.

I unpacked and went to see Laura, but she had her parents there so after half an hour I came back. I said to Brendan and Kerry that I had a headache. I made myself scrambled eggs and a cup of tea and took them into my room, shutting the door behind me. I sat in bed, hearing the television next door, the phone ringing and being answered, water running, laughter, the springs on the sofa bed creaking. I poked at my scrambled eggs until they went cold and unappetizing, and stared at my bookshelves and the piles of paper on my desk. Was I imagining things, or did it all look a bit different, as if someone had been tampering with my stuff? I turned off my light and lay in the dark. Brendan laughed very loudly, as if he wanted to be heard. As if he wanted me to hear him.

The next morning, though, they left early to go to the house they were buying. They said they wanted to measure up for curtains and bookshelves, before Kerry went to her office at ten. I decided to arrive at work later than usual, so that I could spend some time alone in my flat.

Later on, I went over and over it in my mind, everything I did in that lovely, quiet, empty hour before leaving. I tidied the kitchen–living room, pushing the duvet and sheets into the tall corner cupboard, folding up the sofa bed, cramming scattered garments into bags, washing plates and glasses from the night before. I opened the windows wide to air the room and rid it of its unfamiliar smell, swept the tiles, vacuumed the carpet. Then I had a long bath and washed my hair. I pulled the plug and cleaned the bath out before sitting down to breakfast in my dressing gown, a towel wrapped like a turban around my head. I ate the remains of the muesli with yogurt and drank a big cup of coffee. I even heated the milk for the coffee. Then I got dressed, cleaned my teeth, picked up my overalls and left, locking the door behind me. I know I did all of that. I clearly remember.

I was still working on the big house in Hampstead. Bill dropped in at lunchtime and took me out for a salad. I finished at half-past five, cleaned my brushes, and drove home. I wasn't seeing Nick that evening, and Kerry had said something about going to a movie, so I thought maybe I would be able to spend time on my own, which I was craving. I could get a take-away and listen to music perhaps. Read a book. Mooch.

It was nearly six-thirty when I pulled up outside my flat. There were no lights on, and the curtains were still open. My heart lifted. I ran up the stairs and even as I pushed the door open I heard it. The sound of dripping, tinkling. A tap running. Except it wasn't the same sound as a tap running; it was bigger, more complicated. Then I stepped inside.

There was water everywhere. The kitchen floor was an inch deep in it and the carpet was sodden when I stepped on it. There was water pouring from beneath the bathroom door. I opened it and stepped into the flood; the remnants of the book I'd been reading in the bath that morning floated by the toilet bowl, along with a mushy roll of toilet paper. There was a steady waterfall cascading over the rim of the tub. The hot tap was half-on. I waded across the room and turned off the tap, then plunged my arm, still in its jacket sleeve, into the water to find the plug. I felt ill and sick and consumed with anguish and then I thought about the flat below and I felt worse. I found a dustpan and started sloshing water off the floor, into the emptying bath.

It took forty-five minutes to get the worst of the water off the bathroom floor. I laid newspapers everywhere to soak up the rest and started on the kitchen. Then the bell rang.

He was yelling before I'd even got the door open. He sploshed across the carpet, still shouting at me. His face was quite purple. I thought he might have a heart attack or a stroke or he might just die from his head exploding.

"I'm so sorry," I kept saying. I couldn't even remember his name. "So sorry. I don't know how . . ."

"You'll sort this out, do you hear? Every last thing."

"Of course. If you give me the details of your in—"

At that moment Brendan and Kerry appeared, arms wrapped around each other, faces glowing from the night air.

"What on earth —" began Kerry.

"You may well ask." I whirled on Brendan. "Look at what you've fucking gone and done. You stay here, you clean out my fridge, you drink my coffee and my wine, you take up every inch of space so I can't move without bumping into you. You have bloody baths in the middle of the day and then . . ." I was spluttering with rage. "Then you go and leave the plug in and the water running. Look! Look!"

"And that's nothing compared to downstairs," said my neighbor grimly.

"Miranda," said Kerry. "I'm sure —"

"Whoa!" said Brendan, holding up his hands. "Calm down, Mirrie."

"Miranda," I said. "Miranda. There's no such name as Mirrie."

136

"Don't get all hysterical."

"I'm not hysterical. I'm angry."

"I haven't been here today."

"What?"

"I haven't been here."

"You must have been."

"No. Now sit down, why don't you, and I'll make us all some tea. Or maybe a drink would be better." He turned to my neighbor. "What about for you, Mr. . . . er . . . ?"

"Lockley. Ken."

"Ken. Whisky? I think we've got whisky."

"All right then," he said grudgingly.

"Good."

He pulled the whisky bottle and four tumblers out of the cupboard.

"You must have been here," I said to his back. "You must."

"I went to look at the house with Kerry, then I went shopping. Then I met Kerry for lunch." Kerry nodded. She still looked shaken by my outburst. "Then I went to Derek and Marcia's to see Troy." He put his hand on my shoulder. "No midday baths, Mirrie."

"But . . ."

"Did you have a bath before you left, maybe?"

"There's no way I left the plug in and the tap running. I don't do things like that."

"It's so easy to do. We've all done something like that at one time or another." He turned to Ken. "Haven't we, eh? I'm sure Miranda will make sure everything's dealt with. And she's in the building and decorating trade, so maybe she can help you with the painting and stuff. Mmm?"

"I didn't do it," I said hopelessly.

"Miranda," said Kerry. "No one's blaming you. But you were the last to leave. And you had a bath, didn't you?"

"But I . . ." I stopped. A tremendous weariness came over me. "I remember cleaning out the bath."

"Don't worry," he said gently. "We'll help you sort this mess out."

"I don't understand." To my horror, I felt tears sliding down my cheeks.

"Miranda! Listen . . ." Kerry's voice was sharp.

"Ssssh," said Brendan. He actually took her by the forearm and pulled her aside. I saw her flinch. Her mouth hardened for an instant.

"There, there," he cooed into my ear. "There, there, Mirrie. I'm here. I'm here."

I closed the bedroom door and picked up the phone.

"Laura!" I said. I kept my voice low, so

they couldn't hear me. "Listen Laura, this thing's happened. I need to speak to someone about it . . ."

"Are you telling me," said Laura when I'd finished, "are you seriously saying that Brendan crept back into your flat and *on purpose* flooded your flat?"

"Yes."

"Why on earth?"

"Because he's weird; he's got this thing about me."

"Oh come on. I've let the bath run over loads of time," she said. "It's really easy to just forget about it."

"But I don't do things like that."

"There's a first time for everything. It's a more likely explanation than yours, isn't it?"

"I remember cleaning out the bath. Vividly."

"There you are then. You put the plug back in, hosed down the tub, then left the water running a bit."

I gave up trying to persuade her. It was starting to seem possible even to me, and I'd been there and knew it hadn't happened. And anyway, it was just too tiring.

Chapter 13

The couple who lived in the house in Ealing had hired two skips and they were already almost full. When I left, I peered into them. Among the jumble of old rugs, chipped plates, broken furniture, I saw a computer that looked quite new, a laser printer, two telephones, a large oil painting of a greyhound, several cookery books, a standard lamp, a wicker basket. I should be used to it by now. I often see people throw away TVs still under guarantee, year-old cookers and perfectly functioning fridges. In my job, we're always ripping out new things and substituting the even newer. Last year's fashions are replaced with this year's. Whole kitchens disappear into skips, bathtubs and beds and cupboards, garden sheds and miles of shelving. Recycling centers are mountains of obsolescence. It gives us extra work, I suppose. The people we do jobs for are always talking about beginning again, as if the stainless steel and glass that we're installing everywhere at the moment won't soon be replaced by old-fashioned, newly trendy wood. Everything comes around again. Every decade falls out of favor and then reemerges in a slightly different form, like the flares on my trousers, which Bill is always laughing about because they remind him of when he was young in the seventies.

I surreptitiously reached in and pulled out a cookery book. I'd rescue that at least. Recipes from Spain. I put it in my holdall, along with my paint brushes.

At home, Brendan was making a great fuss about washing up a few bowls and Kerry was standing over the stove, stirring something. She looked sticky and irritable.

"We're cooking for you tonight," she said.

"Thanks."

I took a beer from the fridge and retreated to the bathroom. What I needed was hot water on the outside of my body and cold alcohol on the inside of my body. I was lying in the bath feeling pleasantly woozy when the door opened and Brendan came in. I sat up abruptly and hunched my knees against my body. As if he were alone, he took a piss into the lavatory, which was next to the bath. He zipped himself up, rinsed his hands and turned to me with a smile.

"Excuse me," I said sharply.

"Yes?" He stood over me.

"Get out."

"Sorry?"

"Get the fuck out of here. I'm in the bath."

"You should have locked the door," he said.

"You know there isn't a lock," I said.

"There you are then."

"And you haven't flushed it. Oh for God's sake."

I stood up and reached for a towel. Brendan took it from the rail and held it just out of reach. He was looking at my body. He had a strange expression, a triumphant smirk. He was like a little boy who had never seen a naked woman before.

"Give me the fucking towel, Brendan."

"It's not as if I haven't seen your naked body before." He gave me the towel and I wrapped it around me.

The door opened and Kerry came in. She looked at Brendan and then she looked at me. Her face sharpened with disapproval.

"What's going on?" she asked.

"Miranda didn't lock the door," Brendan said. "I didn't know she was in here so I barged in."

"Oh," said Kerry. "I see." She stared at me and I felt myself flush. I pulled the towel tighter around me.

"There isn't a lock," I said, but she didn't seem to take any notice.

"Supper will be ready soon," she said after a pause. "Brendan? Can I have a word with you?"

"Oops," said Brendan, and gave a wink in my direction. "Trouble from the missus, eh?"

As I got dressed I told myself that this wouldn't go on for long. I just had to get through it and then I could get on with my life.

Kerry had done all the cooking and Kerry isn't really someone who has ever bothered about food. She had made macaroni cheese with peas and bits of mince added. It was stodgy and oversalted. Brendan opened a bottle of red wine with a flourish. Kerry loaded much too much onto my plate. Brendan poured too much wine into my glass. Maybe getting drunk was a good idea. Brendan lifted his glass.

"To the cook," he said.

"To the cook," I said, and took a very small sip.

"And to you," said Kerry, looking at me. "Our host."

They both clinked their glasses on mine.

"It's a pleasure," I said, because they seemed to expect me to say something.

"That's good, in the circumstances," said Brendan.

"What do you mean?"

"There's something we've got to ask you," said Kerry.

"What?"

"Well, our flat has fallen through."

Suddenly my face felt like a mask of hardened clay.

"What happened? You were about to exchange, for God's sake. You said it would be a matter of days before you could move in."

"They were pissing us around," said Brendan.

"In what way?"

"You don't want to hear the details," he said.

"I do."

"The main point is that we walked away."

"*You* walked away," said Kerry with sudden sharpness.

"Whatever." He waved his hand in the air as though that were a trifle. "I'm afraid that we'll have to trespass on your hospitality for a little more."

"Why did you walk away?" I persisted.

"Lots of things," said Brendan.

"Miranda? Is that all right?" said Kerry. "We feel terrible. We're desperately looking for somewhere else to move to in the meantime."

"Don't worry about it," I said drearily.

I didn't say much for the rest of the meal. The food had started to taste like wallpaper paste and it took all my concentration to eat it without vomiting. Kerry made me have a second helping. She had bought a frozen lemon meringue pie for pudding and I ate half of a small slice and then said I had a headache and I had to go to bed.

When I got to my room I threw the window open and took several deep breaths as if the air in my room were contaminated. I had the most terrible night. I was awake for what seemed like hours making feverish, deranged plans for the future. I could get married to Nick. At around three in the morning, I seriously considered emigrating and started to rank countries according to how far they were from north London. New Zealand seemed especially tempting. This dissolved into a dream in which I was going away and had to catch a train. I had so much to pack that I was never able to escape from my room. Then I was staring into the darkness of my room and wondering if something had woken me up and then I cried out. I couldn't stop myself. I had made out a shape in the semidarkness, and befuddled as

I was I could recognize Brendan looking down at me. I fumbled for the light and switched it on.

"What the fuck?" I said.

"Sshh," he said.

"Don't *sshh* me," I hissed, shocked and angry. "What are you doing?"

"I er . . . I was looking for something to read."

"Get the hell out . . ."

He sat down on the bed and actually put his hand over my mouth. He leaned down and spoke to me in a whisper. "Please don't shout," he said. "You might wake Kerry. It might look strange."

I pushed his hand away. "That's not my problem."

He smiled and looked around the room as if it were all a bit of a game. "I think it is, really," he said.

I pulled the duvet up over my shoulders and forced myself to speak calmly and reasonably. "Brendan, this is all wrong."

"You mean about you and me?"

"There is nothing between you and me."

He shook his head. "You know, Miranda, I was once looking at you. It was the second time we slept together. I took my clothes off more quickly than you did and got into the bed. *This* bed. I lay where you're lying now

146

and watched you. When you unclipped your bra, you turned away from me, as if I wasn't about to see your naked body, and when you turned around you had a funny little smile on your face. It was beautiful and I wondered if anybody but me had ever noticed it before. You see, I notice things like that and I remember them."

At that moment in the midst of all the confusion, all my anger and desperation and frustration, I was able to think with an absolute cold clarity. If I had been in love with Brendan, this would have been tender and beautiful. But I wasn't in love with him and I felt physically repulsed. I felt as if he were a parasite that had crawled into my flesh and I couldn't rid myself of him.

"This is quite wrong," I said. "You've got to leave."

"None of this matters," he said. "Didn't you hear what I said? There's this secret smile you have. I've seen it. I know you in a way that nobody else does. We share that. Good night, Miranda."

The next morning I woke and it was like an awful dream I'd emerged from. And then with a lurch I remembered him standing over me and what he had said and that it hadn't been a dream. My mouth felt as if it were full of dry fluff. I had a headache and a stabbing sensation behind my eyes. I showered, dressed and drank a black coffee. Nobody else was up. Before I left for work, I returned to my bedroom. I looked at the bookshelves, trying to determine by sheer force of concentration whether anything had been moved. I reached for an old novel I had been given as a girl. It's my special emergency hiding place. Tucked inside the book was some money. I counted it out. Seventy-five pounds. I replaced it. I tried to think of something to do. I remembered something I had seen in a film once. I tore a small strip of paper an inch long and maybe a quarter of an inch wide. When I closed the door I wedged the piece of paper in the crack, exactly at the height of the lower hinge. As I left, I asked myself: How can I be living in such a way that I have to do things like that?

It kept coming into my mind all day and I tried and failed to push it away. Partly I regretted having done it, because it felt as if I had poured corrosive liquid onto my body and was watching it bubble and steam as it ate away at me. And what good would it do me, whatever I found out? If I found the paper still in place, would that reassure me? If I found it lying on the floor, what would that prove? Kerry might have popped in to borrow my deodorant or run the vacuum cleaner over the floor. But was that what I wanted? Was I looking for ways to get even more angry and suspicious?

When I got back to my empty flat and ran to my room, I found something I hadn't even considered. The slip of paper was held fast in the door, but now it was a full foot higher than where I had left it that morning.

Chapter 14

"Nick," I began.

"Mmm?"

We were walking across the heath, our feet kicking up crackly amber leaves. The trees were almost bare now, the sun pale and low in the sky. It wasn't yet four o'clock, but the clocks had just been turned back and it got dark early now. My cold hand was in his warm one, my breath steamed in the air. We'd met in a bistro near his flat for lunch — a bowl of pumpkin soup with crusty bread, a glass of wine each and later on that evening we were going to a party thrown by a friend of his who I hadn't met before. Then I was going to stay the night at his place, though he didn't know it yet. I had my toothbrush and a spare pair of knickers stuffed into my bag.

"I was wondering . . ."

"Yes?"

I slowed down.

"Well. You know Kerry and Brendan need to stay with me a bit longer?"

"You want to come back to my flat rather than the other way round? Is that it?"

"There's that, yes, but . . ."

"I was going to say the very same thing. We need a bit of privacy, don't we?" His hand tightened on mine.

"What if I came and stayed with you? Just until they move out."

I looked up at him just in time to see the smallest frown, a momentary tightening of his mouth.

"Forget it, it was a bad idea," I said, at the same time as he said, "If you're really desperate . . ."

"I shouldn't have asked."

"Of course you should ask," he said, too heartily. "You know how small my flat is, and it's a bit early in our relationship isn't it, but I was going to say that if —"

"No. Forget I ever asked."

He wouldn't forget. And I wouldn't forget either — that flicker of dismay and disapproval, that small pause into which all our doubts flooded. I knew then what I'd known anyway, since Venice at least, that it wasn't going to last. It wasn't going to be a big affair after all, but a nice interim fling. We'd fallen for each other, with that lovely rush of happiness that almost feels like coming down with the flu. We'd spent sleepless nights together,

and days apart thinking of each other, remembering what the other had said, had
done, longing for the next time we could hold
each other. For a week or so, we'd maybe
thought that the other might be the one for us.
But no, it would be over. Not today, not this
week, but soon enough, because the tide that
had rushed in on us was ebbing again, leaving
only a few odd items of debris behind.

Tears stung my eyes and I started walking
more briskly again, tugging Nick after me. I
knew it wasn't really him I was going to
miss, so much as being with someone.
Rushing home from work, full of anticipa-
tion. Planning things together. Waking up
and feeling energetic and light-footed.
Being wanted. Being beautiful. Being in
love. That's what I didn't want to end. I
blinked fiercely, trying to ward off self-pity.

"Come on," I said. "It's getting too cold."

"Miranda, listen, if you need to stay . . ."

"No."

"Then it would be fine . . ."

"No, Nick."

"I don't know why you've suddenly got
all offended, just because I didn't immediately —"

"Oh don't," I said. "Please don't."

"What?"

"You know."

"I don't." He pursed his lips.

I was filled with a sudden foreboding that if we went on pulling at each other's words like this then everything was going to unravel right now and I'd be alone by nightfall.

"Let's go and have a bath together," I said. "All right?"

"Yes."

"Can I stay the night?"

"Of course. I want you to. And if you need . . ."

"I put a hand across his mouth. "Sshh."

"Laura?"

"Miranda? Hi." There was music in the background and Tony's voice calling something. It made me feel homesick for my flat where Kerry and Brendan were now sitting, eating supper in front of a video. I'd told them I was going out to see friends, but it hadn't been true, and instead I was crouched in a chilly little café down the road, drinking my second bitter cup of coffee, wishing I'd put on warmer clothes.

"Is this a bad time?"

"Not at all. We were about to eat, but that's fine."

"I've got a favor to ask."

"Tell me."

"It's quite a big favor. Can I come and stay at yours?"

"Stay?" There was a violent crunching sound, as if she'd stuck a piece of carrot or apple in her mouth. "Sure. Tonight you mean? Is everything all right?"

"Yes. No. I mean, everything's all right. Kind of all right. And not necessarily tonight, maybe tomorrow or the next day. But just for a few days . . ."

"Hang on, you're not making sense, I can hardly hear you anyway, and the pan's boiling over. Wait there." There was a pause, then the music was turned down. "Right."

I took a breath. "Kerry and Brendan's flat has fallen through, God knows why, as a result of which they can't move out, so I've got to." I heard my voice rise. "I've *got* to, Laura, or I'll do something violent. Stab him with a kitchen knife. Pour scalding —"

"I get the picture," said Laura.

"It sounds mad, I know."

"A bit. How long for?"

"Just a few days." I swallowed and clutched my mobile. A young woman with a shaved head came and wiped my table, lifting the two coffee cups and then putting them back down again. "I hope. I've no idea. Days or a week or so. Not more." That was what Brendan and Kerry had said to

154

me. Now the flat was filling up with all their things and I was leaving instead of them. A small howl of rage rose in my chest. "Will Tony mind?" I asked.

"It's got nothing to do with him," said Laura defiantly. "But of course you can come. Tomorrow, you say?"

"If it's all right."

"Really fine. You'd do the same for me."

"I would," I said fervently. "And I'll keep out of your way. And Tony's."

"It's all a bit drastic, Miranda."

"It's like an allergy," I said. "I just have to avoid him and then I'll be all right."

"Hmmm," said Laura.

I didn't want another cup of coffee and it was too early to go back home. I wandered up the high street until I came to the all-night bagel place. I bought one filled with salmon and cream cheese, still warm in its paper bag, and ate it on the pavement, while people milled past me. Sunday evening and probably they were on their way home, a hot bath and something cooking in the oven, their own bed waiting.

"I thought it would be better this way," I said to Brendan and Kerry. "You need to have time on your own."

Kerry sat down at the kitchen table and

propped her chin in her hands and stared at me. She didn't seem so radiantly happy anymore. Her face had a pinched, anxious look to it, the way it used to have in her bad old days, before Brendan came along and made her feel loved.

"It's not possible, Miranda," she said. "Don't you see? We can't let you leave your own home."

"I've arranged it already."

"If it's what Miranda wants," said Brendan softly.

"Is it so terrible for you, having us here then?"

"It's not that. I just thought it was the obvious solution."

"Have it your own way," she said. "You always do anyway." Then she stood up and left the room, banging the door shut behind her. We heard the front door slam.

"What are you playing at?" said Brendan, in a horribly amiable tone of voice. He came and stood over me.

"What do you mean?"

"You don't get it, do you?" he went on. "You can't win. Look." He picked up a tumbler still half full of lime juice and banged it hard on the table so the liquid splattered across the table and shards of glass spun onto the floor.

"Oh shit," I said. "What do you think you're doing now?"

"Look," he repeated and sat down and started squeezing the broken glass in his hand. "I'll always win. I can stand things you can't."

"What the fuck . . . ?"

"Mmm?" He smiled at me, though his face had gone rather pale.

"You're mad! Jesus!" I grabbed hold of his fist and started to pull it loose. Blood seeped out between his fingers, ran down my wrist.

"You have to ask me to stop."

"You're a fucking lunatic."

"Ask me to stop."

I looked at the blood gushing from his hand. I heard the front door open again, Kerry's footsteps coming toward us. She started to say she was sorry that she'd stormed out like that and then she stopped and began to scream wildly. Brendan was smiling at me still. Sweat ran down his forehead.

"Stop," I said. "Stop!"

He opened up his hand and shook the glass out onto the table. Blood puddled into his outstretched palm and overflowed onto the table.

"There you are," he said, before he passed out.

At the hospital they gave Brendan twelve stitches and a tetanus jab. They wrapped his hand in a bandage and told him to take paracetamol every four hours.

"What happened?" asked Kerry for about the tenth time.

"An accident," said Brendan. "Stupid, eh? It really wasn't Mirrie's fault. If anyone was to blame it was me."

I opened my mouth to speak. "It wasn't . . ." I began. "It didn't . . ." Then I ground to a halt, choked by all the things I couldn't say because no one would believe me and I didn't even know anymore if I believed myself. "Fuck it," I said, mostly to myself.

Brendan was smiling in a drowsy and contented way. His head was on Kerry's shoulder and his bandaged hand lay in her lap. His shirt was covered in splashes of blood.

"You two girls should make up," he said. "It was a stupid argument anyway. It's very nice of Mirrie to give us her flat for a while you know, Kerry."

Kerry stroked his hair off his forehead. "I know," she said softly. She looked up at me. "Okay," she said. "Thanks." Then she looked back at Brendan as if he were a war hero or something.

"These things happen in families," said Brendan and closed his eyes. "Tiffs. I just want everyone to be happy."

I left Kerry with him, holding his un-wounded hand, and went home to pack.

Chapter 15

Moving out had seemed like an essential response to an emergency, like pulling the communication cord on a train. But like so much in my life, it hadn't been properly thought out. I remembered a friend of mine who had been at a dinner party. He'd got into a flaming row with someone and finally shouted "Fuck off!" at the other person and stormed out. As he slammed the outside door behind him and walked down the steps to the pavement, he realized that he had just stormed out of his own flat. He had to turn around and ring humbly at his door to be readmitted.

Now I was outside, and feeling foolish. I had exited at high speed without a plan. On my second evening at Laura's I sat up late with her, drinking a bottle of whisky that I had brought home with me, along with half a dozen bottles of wine, some fresh ravioli and sauce from the deli near where I was working and a couple of bags of prepared salad. Tony was spending the evening doing something laddish, so I made a meal for just the two of us. It was good spending time with her like that. It took me back to when we were at university, staying up all night. But we weren't at university anymore and we both had lives to lead. I wondered how long it would take before her patience started to wear thin. I poured some more of the whisky for both of us.

"You know," I said, "I associate whisky with moments like this." I was starting to slur my words a bit, but then so was Laura. "When I think of whisky and me and you, I think of very late nights and one of us would be crying and then the other one would start crying as well and we'd probably be smoking, too. Like that time when I was on my bike and a taxi ran into me, remember?"

"Sure," said Laura, taking a sip, and flinching with the expression of pain that people display when they have taken a bigger gulp of whisky than they meant to. "Why was it always whisky?"

"Why not?" I said. "Am I mad?"

"Is this still to do with the whisky?" said Laura.

I took another sip and shook my head. "Look at the facts," I said. "I break up with Brendan. Next thing, he's engaged to my sister. I can't bear the very sight of him.

Next thing, he's living in my flat. Them living in my flat is awful. Next thing, I've moved out. So after days of maneuvering, the result is that a man who makes me want to throw up when I'm around him is living in my flat and I've become a vagrant."

"You're living here," said Laura. "That's not being a vagrant."

I put my arms around her and hugged her.

"That's so lovely," I said, overflowing with emotion.

To an onlooker we would have looked like two drunks outside a pub after closing time.

"I must say, I'm curious," said Laura.

"What about?"

"This Brendan. You make him sound so appalling that I'd actually quite like to see him. It's like one of those exhibits in an old circus. Do you dare see the bearded lady?"

"You think I'm exaggerating."

"I want to see him in action," Laura said with a laugh. "I want to see what it takes to make you vomit."

The next day I was at work early, wanting to give Tony and Laura a bit of time together. I went back to the Hampstead house, because the owners kept changing their mind about what they wanted. They'd decided that all the lights in the living room were wrong — they didn't want sidelights after all, but soft halogen spot lights on the ceiling. The Venetian red in the bedroom was too dark; in fact, it was too red. Maybe they should have gone for the pea green color after all. . . . The man of the household, a Sam Broughton, had arranged to come back to the house at lunch to discuss the fine details, and I spent the morning painting doors and skirting boards, laying licks of glossy white over graying wood.

Sam Broughton had just arrived from the City, insistent that he only had twenty minutes to spare, if that, and we were walking through the house, me with my notepad, when my mobile rang.

"Sorry," I said to him. "I'll turn it off after this. Hello?"

"Miranda? Thank God you're there."

"I'm just in the middle of a meeting, Mum. Could you call back in a —"

"I wouldn't have called except it's an emergency."

I turned away from Broughton's impatient face, his overdone glances at his watch, and looked out of the window at a sodden squirrel immobile on the branch of a chestnut tree outside. "Tell me."

"I've just had a phone call from Troy's tutor and she says that Troy's not come in."

"That's not really an emergency, Mum."

"He's not come in for days." She paused. "Most of last week."

"That's not good."

"It's like before. Pretending he's going there and then not turning up. I thought he was getting better." I heard her gulp. "I'm worried, Miranda. I called our house and he's not there, or at least there's no reply, and I don't know where he is or what he's doing and it's cold and raining outside." Another gulp.

"What do you want me to do?"

"I'm stuck here. I can't really get away — and anyway, the dental surgery's miles away. I tried your flat but there was just an answering machine. So I thought you could just pop over and see if you could find him."

"Find him?"

Behind me, Broughton cleared his throat angrily. His polished brogue tap-tapped on the newly varnished floorboards.

"It's much easier for you to get away and Bill wouldn't mind. And if something's happened . . ."

"I'll see if I can find him," I said.

"I can't bear all of this anymore," said my mother. "I've had enough of being strong. It's too much for me. What's wrong with us? I thought it was all going to be all right."

"It will be all right," I said, too loudly. "I'll go now."

I ended the call and turned to Broughton. "I have to leave," I said.

His glare deepened. "Do you realize how expensive my time is?" he said.

"I'm very sorry," I repeated. I wanted to say that my time was valuable as well, to me, at least. But I didn't. I was thinking of Troy, out there in the rain.

I went to my parents' house first. The workmen weren't there, though the ground floor looked like a building site — well, it *was* a building site. The kitchen was half exposed to the weather. There was yellow London clay everywhere. I went from room to room, calling him. In his bedroom I opened the curtains and shook out the crumpled duvet, to make it look more welcoming if he returned. A book about the migration of birds lay open on the floor. I marked it with a scrap of paper and put it on his pillow.

I didn't really know where to look. Where would I go, if I were him and hanging around waiting for the end of the day? I walked onto the high street and peered into cafés, record shops, the local bookstore. I tried the library, but it was closed; it's only open two days a week now. I looked into the mini-arcade, where several boys — other truants, I assumed — were playing the fruit machines in the smoky, bleeping gloom. Troy hated places like that. They made him feel trapped.

I walked to the park and wandered around in the rain. There weren't many other people, just a couple of winos sitting on a bench and a young mother striding furiously past, pushing a buggy from which came a yell like a siren. No Troy. I went to the playground in case he was taking shelter there, but it was deserted. Pigeons hopped through the puddles. I went to the little snack bar that sells ice cream on sunny days, but there was just one woman in there.

Really, he could be anywhere. I rang Mum at work and she'd heard nothing. I rang Dad, who was in Sheffield on business, but his voice kept breaking up until it eventually crackled into silence. I rang my flat in case Troy had somehow found his way there, but after two rings the answering machine clicked on and my own voice told me no one was there to take the call. I left a message anyway, one of those that go: "Troy? Troy? Are you there? Can you hear me? If you can hear me, pick up the phone. Please pick up the phone. Troy?" I heard the note of fear in my voice.

When you're looking for someone, you see them everywhere. Out of the corner of your eye, and then you turn and it's an old man. In the distance, but as they get closer it's nothing like them after all. Ahead of you, and they turn around and it's a stranger's face. I walked for an hour, telling myself reasonably enough that I shouldn't worry too much. In the end, wet and chilly, I went back to collect my car from outside my parents' house and, on the chance that he'd returned, went in.

The hall doorway was slightly open and through it I could see Troy seated on the old sofa. His hair was plastered to his skull, and he was draped in a thick tartan blanket, under which he was naked. He thought he was alone and he looked so shrunken and desolate, sitting there, that I could hardly bear to approach him. He lifted his head and looked up and gave a half smile at someone I couldn't see, and a figure moved across to block him from my view. I pushed the door fully open and stepped into the room.

"Troy," I said. "Brendan. What's going on?"

I don't know what I was thinking, but my voice was sharp. I pushed past Brendan and knelt by Troy, clutched him by his narrow shoulders.

"Troy? Are you all right?"

He didn't reply, just looked at me, through me. He had the appearance of one of those people you see on the news, who's just been pulled out of wreckage, off a sinking ship.

"Sweetheart," I said as if he were a baby. I wanted to cry. "What happened?"

"I've run your bath," said Brendan. "Nice and warm. And I'll bring you hot chocolate while you're in it. Okay, mate?"

Troy nodded.

"And I better ring your mum, all right?"

"I'll take you up to your bath," I said.

I left Troy in his bath and went to the kitchen, where Brendan was standing amid the builders' wreckage microwaving a jug of milk for Troy's chocolate. It was a clumsy process because he could only use his unbandaged hand.

"I got Marcia's message on your answering machine. Clearly she doesn't know you've moved out," he said. The microwave bleeped and he took the jug out, stirred in the cocoa and sugar and whisked it till it frothed. "There." He took a little sip and added more sugar. "So I thought I should go and look."

"Where was he?"

"Down by the derelict warehouses. I don't know why I went there — I just had a feeling he was there, like an instinct. I *knew*. I think some people have that gift, don't you?"

I shrugged.

"Who knows what might have happened if I hadn't been there? I think I was meant to save him. It was fate. And so I've made a decision." He poured the drink into a mug. "I'm going to put off looking for a job until Troy's all right. Troy will be my job."

"Oh no," I said. "I don't think that's a very good idea. Not at all. In fact, if you ask me —"

"I'm not," he said calmly.

"Well, I'm going to tell you anyway. Troy doesn't need you. The very opposite. What Troy needs, apart from anything else, is you out of his —"

"I'll take him his chocolate," Brendan cut in. "You don't really need to stay if you're busy."

"I'll wait," I said furiously. "I'm not leaving him."

"As you like," he said.

Chapter 16

"I thought you were getting better. I thought things were getting back to normal at last." My mother was pacing the room in an agitated fashion. Her hair was half loosed from its bun and hanging down in strands over her face. She was wearing a jumper back-to-front.

"What does 'better' mean, exactly?" asked Troy. "And what's 'normal'? No one's normal."

He was sitting on the same sofa I'd found him on the previous night, in the same slumped position, as if there weren't a bone in his body.

"Oh for God's sake," snapped my mother.

"Calm down, love," said my father, who was standing with his back to the window. He'd come home early from Sheffield and was still wearing his suit. He hadn't shaved though, and the knot of his tie was pulled loose. It wasn't exactly a total psychological collapse but it gave him an odd raffish look.

" 'Calm down'? Is that all you've got to

say? Every time something goes wrong, that's your advice. Why don't you say you'll make us all a nice cup of tea?"

"Marcia . . ."

"I want someone else to take charge here, not always me."

I glanced across at Troy. The sun was shining through the window onto his silky hair, and he seemed quite tranquil. He felt my eyes on him and looked up, raised his eyebrows and gave a little smile.

"Tea would be nice actually," he said. "And I'm quite hungry. I haven't had anything to eat all day."

I stood up. "I'll get us all something in a minute," I said. "Toasted cheese sandwiches?"

"Thank God Brendan was here," said Mum fervently. I flinched. I'd been there, too, hadn't I? "If he hadn't found him —"

"I'm in the same room, Mum," said Troy. "You can talk to me."

"What have I done wrong?"

"What's it got to do with you?"

"Exactly," said my father. "We're not going to get anywhere if this becomes about your feelings of guilt. This is about Troy."

My mother opened her mouth to say something, then changed her mind. She sat down on the sofa and took Troy's hand.

"I know," she said. "I was so worried. I kept thinking . . ." She stopped.

"I wasn't going to kill myself or anything," said Troy.

"So what were you up to?" asked Dad. "Skipping lessons, wandering around."

Troy shrugged.

"I wanted to be left alone," he said eventually. "I couldn't bear everyone fussing over me all the time. People looking at me to see how I am."

"You mean me," said my mother. "I'm the one who fusses. I know I fuss. I try to stop myself and stand back, but I can't help it. I feel if I could just help push you back onto the tracks, everything would be all right for you."

"You should trust me."

"How can we trust you," said my father, "when you skip lessons and lie to us?"

"It's my life," said Troy mutinously. "I'm seventeen. If I want to skip lessons, that's my choice. If I fuck up, it's my fuckup, not yours. You treat me like a little child."

"Oh," said my mother. It sounded like a moan.

"If you want to be treated like an adult, you've got to behave like one," said my father. He rubbed his forehead, then added, "It's because we love you, Troy."

172

My father never says things like that.

"I'll make us those sandwiches," I said, backing into the windy, half-wrecked kitchen.

When I came back in, carrying a tray loaded with toasted sandwiches oozing melted cheese and four mugs of tea, my mother had red eyes and had clearly been crying. She said, "Troy says he'd like to stay with you for a while."

"Oh," I said. "Well, I'd love that, Troy. It'd be great. The snag is, I'm not living there at the moment. Brendan and Kerry are."

"Not for long though," said Troy. "I can stay there with them for a couple of weeks or so and then you'll be back. Right?"

"You know how much I want you to stay," I said, "but can't you wait just for a week or so?"

"Why?"

I stared at him helplessly. "Are you sure you'll be all right with Kerry and Brendan?"

He shrugged. "They'll fuss too much as well. It'll be better with you."

"So wait."

"I need to move now."

"I'll be around," I said. "Just call me when you need me, okay?"

"Okay."

The following day I took time off work and went with Troy to the aquarium. We spent two hours there, noses pressed against the glass. Troy loved the tropical fish, glinting like shards of colored glass, but my favorite were the great flat fish with their stitched upside-down faces. They looked friendly and puzzled as they floated through the water with their bodies waving. Afterward I drove him to my parents' house to pack his stuff. Brendan and Kerry were going to collect him in a few hours' time. I hugged him hard.

"I'll come and see you there very soon," I said. "A day or two."

In fact, hardly an hour passed without me discovering something that I'd forgotten. I actually had to carry a piece of paper and a pen around with me so that I could keep a list. I could buy more knickers but I couldn't buy everything. Three more T-shirts. Nail clippers. Conditioner. Woolly hat. Checkbook. Street map. It was just ridiculous. So after work the next day, I went to my flat with the shopping list. Inside, I found Brendan and Troy playing cards in the main room. They looked at me in some surprise. Brendan said something but I couldn't hear

174

him over the music. I marched across the room and turned it down.

"I can hardly hear it," said Troy. "You'd have to put a stethoscope against the speaker to hear that."

"I just popped in to collect some stuff," I said.

"That's fine," said Brendan. "Go ahead."

The very idea of Brendan airily telling me to go ahead in my own flat made me want to boil a kettle of water and pour it over his head. I couldn't speak. But then I did speak. "How are you doing, Troy?"

"Pretty well, aren't we?" said Brendan. Troy smiled at me and raised his eyebrows.

I went into my bedroom. Unsurprisingly, this was where Troy was sleeping, and in only a day my room had started to look the way his bedroom always looked. The bed was unmade, there were clothes on the floor, books lying open, a funny sweaty smell. I was as quick as I could possibly be. I threw some things into a carrier bag I'd brought with me. I pushed the door gently closed and climbed up and reached for the book where I had hidden the money. I counted it and felt my skin crawl as I did so. Sixty pounds. I counted it again. Sixty. Couldn't he just have taken it all? What was he doing with me? I put the rest of the money in my purse. I went back out into the main room.

"I had some money in my bedroom," I said.

Brendan looked around cheerfully. "Yes?"

"Some of it's gone. I wondered if anybody had borrowed it."

Brendan shrugged. "Not guilty," he said. "Where was it?"

"What does that matter?"

"It might have got lost or fallen down the back of something."

"It doesn't matter," I said. "Also, I can't find my Tampax."

"Kerry may have borrowed them," Brendan said. "She's having her period."

"Borrowed them?"

"Yes," said Brendan. "It's anal sex only at the moment."

I couldn't quite believe what I'd heard. I felt bile rise, sour and sharp, in the back of my throat.

"Sorry?" I said.

"Only joking," said Brendan, grinning at Troy, whose face had gone as blank as a stone. "Miranda likes it when I tease her. At least I think she does. It's your deal."

I started going over it all in my head and I tried to explain it to Nick. I told him how I'd put the slip of paper in the door and how it had been in a different place when I checked it. I took a sip of wine. We were sitting in a wine bar on Tottenham Court Road, just around the corner from his flat.

"I'm finding it rather complicated," I said. "You know in films where they leave a slip of paper and then they see it lying on the floor and they know someone's been there."

"Yes," said Nick. "It happened in *The Sting*. Robert Redford did it because these gangsters were after him."

"Really?" I said. "I think I saw it on TV years ago. I can't remember that bit. I'm terrible about films. I forget them completely." I took another gulp of wine. It felt like I was drinking more than Nick was. He was sitting there being all calm and sober and I was talking and drinking. "The difficult thing for me was the slip of paper being back but in an obviously different place. Do you see what I mean?"

"No," said Nick.

I found it hard to work out myself. I really had to stop and think about it. It hurt my brain.

"The thing is," I said, "most people wouldn't notice the piece of paper at all. And maybe, like five percent of people would spot the paper and they would make a huge effort to put it back exactly where it had been left in order to disguise that they'd opened the door. But of that five percent about five percent — do you see that? Five percent of the five percent — a tiny, Machiavellian group would deliberately put the piece of paper in an obviously *different* place. They're calling your bluff, do you see?"

"Not really," said Nick.

I could see that Nick's attention was wandering, that he was becoming impatient, but I couldn't stop myself. I didn't want to stop myself. In a way I wanted to test him. If you like someone — or love them — you don't mind them being obsessed with something. You don't even mind them being boring. Perhaps I wanted to see how tolerant he could be to me.

"Brendan is playing with me. He put back that piece of paper deliberately so I would know that it had been put back. But also so I would know that he had put it back and he had not tried to conceal that he had been in my room." I took another sip of wine. "He was sending me a message. He was saying: *You were suspecting that I was looking in your room, I know that you were suspecting me. I want to show you that I know. I also want to show you that I don't care that you know. Also, I have actually been in your room and you don't*

178

know what I've actually been up to. That's another thing. I left seventy-five pounds hidden in a book. It's my secret stash."

"Can't you just go to the bank machine like other people?" Nick asked.

"That's no good," I said. "Sometimes the bank machines run out of money. You should always have some cash hidden somewhere. Now, any normal thief would just have taken all the money. But Brendan just took fifteen pounds. He was teasing me. He's trying to get into my head."

"Into your head?"

"And now here I am. He's living in my fucking flat and I'm sitting here pissed in this bar."

There was quite a long silence now. I felt like a comedian who was doing his act and nobody was laughing. There was just silence out there in the audience.

"I can't do this," Nick said, finally.

"What do you mean?" I said, except I knew.

"Do you mind if I'm honest?"

"No," I said, knowing that when someone said they were going to be honest, they never meant they were going to be especially nice.

"Do you know what I think?"

"No, I don't."

"I don't think," said Nick. "I *know*. You're still in love with Brendan."

"What?" I said. This I really hadn't expected.

"You're obsessed with him. He's all you talk about."

"Of course I'm obsessed with him," I said. "He's like a worm that's infesting me. He's tormenting me."

"Exactly. It was lovely, Miranda."

"Was," I said dully.

Now, finally, he took a sip of wine. "I'm sorry," he said.

I wanted to shout at him. I wanted to hit him. And then suddenly I didn't. I fumbled in my purse and found a twenty-pound note and put it by my empty glass. I leaned over, a bit unsteadily, and kissed him.

"Bye-bye, Nick," I said. "It was really the wrong time."

I walked out of the bar. Another of these sudden exits. I had meant to be staying the night with Nick. That was what I had promised Laura. Another broken promise.

Chapter 17

The next day, I lay for a while on Laura's sofa before making myself get up and face the morning. Outside, it was windy and still half dark. I was cold, I was tired, my hair needed washing. My tongue felt too thick in my mouth. I hadn't run for days now and my limbs felt stiff with disuse. I shut my eyes and listened to the companionable murmurs coming from Laura's bedroom and felt as if I were sliding down a slope, unable to stop myself. Anything I grabbed hold of came away in my hands.

I thought about the day ahead. I had to go to the bloody house in Hampstead again and paint a red wall green. In my lunch hour I had to collect Kerry from her work and look at yet another overpriced flat. And I'd come back here as late as possible, so Laura and Tony didn't start getting irritated by my presence. I sighed and, with an immense effort, threw off the duvet.

I got to Journey's End, the travel agent's

where Kerry worked, a bit early and shouldered the door open, grateful to be out of the blustery weather. Kerry's boss, Malcolm, was at the nearest desk, trying to persuade an overweight man in a loud suit that it was safe to travel to Egypt, and a couple of other customers milled around by the brochure stand, looking at pictures of sun and sea and laughing young people with white teeth and blond hair. Kerry was at the far end of the room talking to another man in a long overcoat, and although he had his back turned to me I saw it was Brendan. I stopped in my tracks, a few feet from them.

"I'm overdrawn already," Kerry was saying, pleadingly.

"Forty quid should see me through."

"But . . ."

"Kerry." His voice was soft and heavy. It made me shudder just to hear it. "Do you begrudge me? After everything I've done."

"You know it's not that, Bren . . ." And she started fishing around in her purse for money.

"No? I'm surprised, Kerry. Disappointed."

"Don't say that. Here. This is all I've got."

"How can I, now?"

"Please, Bren. Take it." Kerry held out a handful of notes and at the same time looked up and saw I was there. Her cheeks flushed and she looked away, back at Brendan.

"I must say, you look a bit washed out today," he said as he took the money and stuffed it into his pocket. "Mmm?"

I saw Kerry flinch as if he'd slapped her. She put a hand half across her face, wanting to hide.

"You look lovely in that coat," I said.

Forty-five minutes later, Kerry and I were drinking coffee in a shabby little café in Finsbury Park.

"Do I?" She fiddled with the collar self-consciously. "You don't think it makes me look pasty?"

"It's November. We're all a bit pale. You look great." I spoke cheerily, as if she were a convalescent in a hospital ward.

"Thanks," she said, with a humility that made me want to shake her.

"Anyway, you'll soon be on your honeymoon, soaking up the sun — where is it? Fiji?"

"Yes." She made herself smile with an effort.

"Fabulous."

There was a pause and I picked up my empty coffee cup and pretended to drink the dregs. "Has Brendan decided what he's going to do?"

"You mean, what kind of job?"

"Yes."

"He says he's going to put Troy right first."

"That sounds like a really, really bad idea to me."

"I don't know really." She sounded listless.

"Even Troy wants to be left to himself more," I said. "That's why he's moved out."

"I know." She bit her lip nervously. "I told Brendan that, more or less."

"Are you two all right?"

"Of course," she said curtly. "Why shouldn't we be?"

"Anyway, he should start thinking of you two; that's where his first priorities lie. What's he done before?"

"Well," said Kerry. "Lots of things, really." She chewed the corner of a nail. "He studied psychology for a bit, and then he did some kind of job connected with that which didn't work out. He's too much of a maverick. And he was involved in various business ventures, you know. He takes risks with things. And he traveled of course."

"Of course," I said. "I see."

I tried to remember things he had said. And out of memory's darkness came a name, spoken over a barbecue in my parents' garden. I held on to it: Vermont. That was it. Harry Vermont and the dot com company. When Kerry had left, I picked up my mobile and dialed directory inquiries.

At half-past eight the next morning I was sitting in a large warm office with huge windows that would have overlooked the Thames if they had been on the other side of the building. Instead, they looked out on public housing with boarded doors and windows. If "boarded" is the right term for those huge sheets of metal. Harry Vermont offered me coffee, but we were both in a hurry and anyway, when it came down to it, it didn't take very long. I told him that I knew Brendan Block.

"Oh yeah?"

"You and Brendan set up a dot com business, didn't you?"

"What?"

"I wanted to find out about the work you did together."

He took a cigarette from a packet on his desk and lit it. He took a drag from it.

"The work we did together?" he said sarcastically.

"Is there a problem?" I said. "Can you talk about it?"

"Yeah," he said. "I can talk about it."

"Did you lose much money when your dot com business collapsed?" I asked brightly, then popped a piece of crumbly Stilton into my mouth. It was Bill's birthday and we were all around at his house for lunch. Outside, it was misty and cold but inside it was beautifully warm, and a large fire burned in the hearth. Judy and Bill are good cooks, much better than my parents, and they'd produced a vast game pie, lots of red wine, and now cheese and biscuits. Kerry was at the other end of the table, trying to persuade Sacha to be her bridesmaid; and Sacha, who's twelve but looks twenty-one and only wears hugely flared jeans and hooded tops, was saying that she wasn't going to wear a peach satin dress for anyone. But Dad and Bill were listening to me, and Troy was sitting opposite Brendan. I couldn't tell if he was listening or not because he was in one of his unreadable moods.

"Too much," said Brendan and laughed ruefully, a man of the world.

"What about the others?" I said. I drained my glass and plonked it back on the table. I raised my voice so that Kerry and Judy looked across at us. "Did everyone lose money? Like that Harry person you told us about once, what was his name?"

Brendan looked momentarily confused.

"Vermont, that was it, wasn't it?" I said.

"How on earth did you remember that?" My mother laughed, pleased with me. I was taking an interest, being polite.

"Mitch and Sacha — clear the plates away," said Judy. The children rose grudgingly.

"Because I remember thinking Vermont like New England," I said.

Bill refilled my glass and I took a large mouthful and swallowed. Mitch took away my cheese plate and dropped the buttery knife in my lap.

"Poor old Harry," said Brendan. "He was wiped out."

"What does he do now? Do you keep in touch with him?"

"You can't drop friends just because they go through bad times," he said sententiously.

"I talked to him," I said.

"What?"

"He said he met you briefly, but you never actually worked together and he's never done anything in the packaging business. Anyway, you didn't get the job."

I took a large gulp of wine.

"Coffee?" asked Bill again.

"Lovely, Bill," said my mother. There was an edge of panic in her voice.

"Well?" I asked Brendan.

"You went and talked to Harry Vermont?" Brendan spoke softly. "Why, Miranda? Why didn't you talk to me about it?"

Everyone was looking at me. I gripped the edge of the table.

"You never worked together," I said. "You never lost money. You hardly knew him."

"Why would you do something like that?" He shook his head from side to side in wonderment, taking in the whole watching room. "Why?"

"Because you weren't telling the truth," I said. A sick feeling rose up in me. My forehead felt clammy.

"If you'd asked me, I would have told you, Miranda," he said.

"Harry Vermont said . . ."

"Harry Vermont let down everyone he worked with," said Brendan. He sat back a bit, addressing everyone now; his tone was one of sorrowful resignation. "He wanted the glory but not the responsibility. But I forgave him. He was my friend."

"He said . . ."

"Miranda," hissed my mother, as if everyone couldn't hear every word. "That's quite enough now."

"I wanted to find out —"

"Enough, I say." She slapped her hand on

the table's surface so cutlery rattled. "Stop it. Let's have coffee."

Judy glared at Bill and nodded at him. They both stood up and went out. In the kitchen, someone dropped a glass.

I thought about standing up and making a run for it, but I was wedged between the table and the wall and Troy would have had to stand up to let me out. So instead I said, "You were deceiving us." I turned to the table. "He was deceiving us," I repeated desperately.

Brendan shook his head. "Maybe I didn't tell you the whole ugly story, because he was my friend and I felt sorry for him. I was protecting him, I guess. But I wasn't deceiving you. No, Miranda." He paused and smiled at me. "You do that though, don't you?"

Outside in the hallway, I could hear the grandfather clock ticking. Through the French windows, I saw the bare branches of the copper beech tree waving in the wind.

"Like the way you deceived Kerry."

"Let's stop this," said Troy. "I don't like it. Please stop."

"What?" Kerry's voice came at the same time, sharp with fear. "What do you mean?"

"I'm sure Kerry forgave you though. Because that's what she's like, very forgiving. Mmm?"

"What are you talking about? Tell me." I saw Kerry's face across from me.

"You were only seventeen, after all."

"Brendan, I'm sorry if I . . ."

"And how old were you, Kerry? Nineteen, I guess."

"When I what?"

"You know, when Miranda went off with your boyfriend. What was he called? Mike, wasn't it?"

The silence deepened around us.

Brendan put his hand over his mouth.

"You mean you didn't know? Miranda never said? I had no idea. I just thought — if she told me so early on in our relationship, and so casually — I just assumed you all knew, too, and it was one of those family things . . ." His voice trailed away.

I opened my mouth to say I'd never told him, he'd read it in a diary that was private. But I didn't, because who cared how he knew. It was true.

"Kerry," I said at last. "Let's not do this here. Can we go somewhere and talk?"

She stared at me. "I get it," she said. "Now you're trying to do it all over again."

Chapter 18

I left the house, though Judy tried to hold me back at the door, and I got in my car and drove to the bottom of the road where I pulled in at a bus stop. I felt cold to the bone, but sweaty at the same time, and my hands were trembling so badly that I could barely turn the ignition off. There was a nasty taste coating the inside of my mouth: game pie, blue cheese, red wine, dread. For a moment, I thought I would be sick. I sat for a while, just staring ahead but barely seeing the traffic that flowed past me as the day started to turn dark, as if the color were running out of everything, leaving the world gray.

A loud horn sounded behind me, and I glanced in the rearview mirror to see a bus waiting. I started up the car and edged out into the road. But I didn't know where to go. For a while I drove as if heading home, but that was the last place in the world I could be right now. Anyway, it didn't feel like home any longer. I'd loved it, it had been my haven. Not anymore.

I could just go back to Laura's. But I wanted to be alone, desperately. So I just kept on going, not turning left or right, heading east out of London, past shops selling old fridges, mobile phones, catering equipment, BB guns, cheap videos, garden gnomes, floor tiles, wind chimes. . . . It grew poorer; there was graffiti on the bridges overhead, dank little cafés, queasy looking butchers still open with slabs of meat swaying in the window, and at a traffic light a young man in combat gear banged on my window and mouthed orders at me to give him money. After I'd passed a flyover and several arterial crossroads, it grew more prosperous again, and houses thinned to detached properties with gardens in front and behind. Lights were beginning to go on. Streetlamps glowed in the graying dusk. At last there were fields, large trees with scarcely any leaves left on them, a river running by.

I took a random left up a small road, then left again up a smaller lane, and stopped the car in the entrance to a field where cows were standing in the far corner. In an hour or so it would be dark, and when I opened the door I could feel the cold biting through my jacket. I wasn't dressed for outside, wasn't wearing the right shoes, but it didn't matter. I started to walk along the lane and welcomed the sting of the wind, the way my hair whipped against my face. For several minutes I just walked, fast so my calves ached. And then I started to think and to let myself remember.

When Kerry was nineteen, she was pretty but she didn't think she was, so of course people rarely noticed her. At least, boys didn't. Michael wasn't her first boyfriend, but he was the first she really let herself fall in love with, and maybe he was the first she had sex with. She never said and I never asked, at first, because I was waiting for the right intimate moment, and later because there never would be that right moment. It was in the summer holidays, just before she went to university, and in the meantime she was working in the local café, washing dishes and serving customers chocolate fudge brownies and coconut flapjacks. He was about three years older than her, studying civil engineering at Hull, but home for the holidays. He saw her a few times and then one day he leaned over the counter and asked her for a cup of tea and if she'd like to go out for a drink.

Maybe it was because he knew nothing about her, had no part of the world in which she was always on the sidelines, or maybe she was just ready to get carried away — anyway, she was very taken up with him. She seemed proud of herself as well, because he was older than her, and not exactly handsome but extroverted and rather a charmer, and he made her feel more worldly and glamorous than she'd felt before. She visibly bloomed, in much the same way, I thought, pounding along the lane with the darkness falling, that she had bloomed with Brendan.

And then . . . I had spent too many years trying not to think about this, and I had to wrench my mind around to contemplating the forbidden memory. It didn't go on for that long between Kerry and Michael, and after a few days it seemed obvious that she was keener than he was. Or that's what I said then, and after. At first, he'd taken no notice of me. I was five, maybe six years his junior. I had homework and a meager allowance. And I was a virgin. I don't think I flirted with him exactly, but I remember a look he gave me one day — a suddenly appraising look, right over the head of Kerry, and I remember even now how I was filled with a rush of triumph and violent self-loathing. All at once, I couldn't stop thinking about him, just because he'd looked at me like that, public-private. I glowed with secret, guilty pleasure.

He kissed me, outside Kerry's bedroom, very quickly, and I let him and told myself it didn't matter, didn't count, I'd done nothing. We had sex, one afternoon after school, on my bed, while Kerry went around the corner to buy cigarettes for him. I couldn't tell myself that didn't count. It took about two painful, horrible minutes, and even before we'd begun I realized I was making the biggest mistake of my life. I was no longer able to stand the sight of his shallow, self-satisfied face. I kept out of his way completely after that. If he was coming around, I went out. If the phone rang, I never answered it. I waited for the flooding shame to subside. He and Kerry stayed together a bit longer, but gradually he stopped calling her and then he didn't return her calls either. A week or so later, when he'd gone back to Hull, Kerry started university. I felt sure he would have left her anyway; I tried to find ways of justifying my actions but never succeeded. I didn't know and didn't want to know how much Kerry minded. I couldn't believe what had happened. Sometimes, I still couldn't believe it. I'd never told anyone about it. Except for my diary. I had written it down almost as a way of getting it out of my head, turning it into an object that could be thrown, or hidden, away. But I never could throw my diary away. It would have been like throwing away a piece of myself.

What I wanted to know now was this: Had I done it because he was going out with my older sister? I came to a stile going over a fence and sat down on it, feeling the dampness of the wood through my trousers, the moistness of the soil through my thin shoes. I put my head in my chilly hands, pressed my thumbs against my ears to seal me into my own interior world. Because if I had done that, what did that make me and what was happening now? What strange ugly replica of that event was being played out again, but now in full view and everyone witnessing it? In my mind, I heard my mother's hissed commands, Troy's whimper. I saw them all looking at me. Kerry's white face. I saw Brendan's smile.

More to the immediate point, what was I going to do now? I opened my eyes and stood up. I saw it was cloudy dark, with no moon. Here I was, on some remote lane in the middle of fields and woods, and I had no idea of what to do next. A part of me just wanted to run away so I didn't have to deal with any of this. But you have to run *to* somewhere, make a decision to drive the car along this road to that town, where you eat that food and sleep in that bed and get up in the morning. . . .

So in the end, I returned to the car and got in it and turned on the ignition and drove back the way I'd come. I was so cold that even when I had the inefficient heating full on, I couldn't warm up. I bought milk and cocoa powder and digestive biscuits at the corner shop a few minutes from Laura's flat. When I let myself in, I could hear the sound of taps running in her bathroom, so I made myself a large mug of hot chocolate, with lots of sugar in it, and sat on the sofa with my legs curled up under me and drank it very slowly, trying to make it last.

Chapter 19

I plucked up the courage and rang my own flat and Brendan answered. My heart plummeted. I was tempted just to put the phone down but Brendan would have been able to discover who called and then he would have rung back or thought of something else and it would all have gone wrong. For me, that is. Again. So I said, "Hello."

"Are you all right, Miranda?" he said.

"What do you mean?"

"It must have been painful for you."

"Whose fault is that?" I said and then cursed myself immediately. I was like a boxer who had deliberately let his guard down. The punch in the face duly arrived.

"Miranda, Miranda, Miranda," he said in a horrible, soothing tone. "I wasn't the one who betrayed Kerry."

"You learned that by reading my diary," I said. "And then you lied. You said I told you about it."

"Does it really matter how I learned about it? But maybe it's all for the best, Miranda.

Secrets are bad for families. It's cleansing to get them out into the open."

For a moment I wondered if I was going insane. It wasn't just what Brendan was saying that made me want to gag. I felt as if his voice were physically contaminating me, even over the phone, as if it were something alive and slimy, oozing its way into my ear.

"I was ringing to say I'm coming round tomorrow to pick up some of my stuff." I paused. "If that's all right."

"Do you know what time?"

I was going to ask why it mattered but I just couldn't be bothered. I would just get sucked back into some sort of argument and come off worse. "I'll come over on my way back from work."

"Which will be when?" he said.

"I guess about six-thirty," I said. "Does it really matter?"

"We always like to have a welcome ready for you, Miranda," he said.

"Is Kerry there?"

"No."

"Can you ask her to call me?"

"Of course," he said affably.

I put the phone down, rather hard, and then looked guiltily up at Laura. Breaking her phone would not be a helpful contribution to the household. She looked at me with a concerned expression. She was being nice to me yet again.

"Are you all right?" she said.

"You don't want to know," I said. "It's just that I feel like I virtually have to make an appointment to visit my own house. I'm sorry. You'll notice I said you don't want to know and then told you." She smiled and gave me a little hug. "You know, it's important that you and Tony start having children as soon as possible."

"Why?"

"Because I'll need to do about eight years of baby-sitting to pay you back for what you've done for me."

She laughed.

"I'll hold you to that," she said. "But don't mention that to Tony for the moment. Whenever the idea of children gets mentioned, his face closes down."

Laura and Tony were rushing around the flat getting ready to go out. They had obviously had an argument, because Laura was being curt and efficient and Tony sulky. I was going to have a maudlin, self-pitying Sunday evening alone. I had it all planned. A couple of glasses of wine. A sandwich for dinner, made out of avocado and precooked bacon and a jar of mayonnaise that I'd bought on my way home from work. More wine. A bath. Bed. Drunken stupor. Various sobbing and howling at moments yet to be decided.

I must have looked like a child on a poster because I heard some muttering behind me, Laura hissing, and then Tony asked me if I wanted to come with them.

"What, me?" I said, feeling embarrassed and pathetic. "No, no, my gooseberry costume's in the wash. I'll be fine."

"Don't be stupid," said Laura. "We're going to a party. There'll be loads of people. You'll have a good time. You won't be in *our* way." This last sentence she said to Tony rather than me. Turning away from her, he raised his eyebrows in a complicit gesture that I tried not to notice.

"It's not right," I said.

"Shut up," said Laura. "It's a friend of mine, Joanna Gergen. Do you know her?"

"No."

"Well, she knows about you."

"Have you told her I'm insane?"

"I've told her you're my best friend. She's having a flat warming. It'll be fun."

They were insistent, and in the end I let myself be persuaded. I had a thirty-second shower and then took another forty-five seconds to throw on my black dress and then I sat in the back of their car as we drove across London and I tried to apply mascara and lipstick in incredibly adverse conditions.

Joanna had a flat off Ladbroke Grove that must have cost . . . well, I made myself not think about how much it cost. I was not at work. I was going to have an evening that was an escape from my wretched normal life. Joanna, who had expensive blond hair and a shamefully lascivious scarlet dress, looked a little surprised when she opened the door and saw me standing behind Laura and Tony like someone who had come to a fancy dress party as a fifth wheel.

"This is Miranda," said Laura.

Joanna's face broke into a smile. "You're the woman who's been kicked out of her own flat?" she said.

Laura looked apologetic. "I just said that you were my best friend and that you'd had one or two problems," she said.

It didn't seem to matter and it broke the ice. Joanna escorted me in and started telling me in too much detail about what she'd done to the house and how long it had taken. She obviously knew other things about me as well.

It was an improbably good party, though. It was a large flat with a garden you could walk out to through French doors in the kitchen. The garden was flickering with candles in jam jars. There was a salsa band — a real-life salsa band in the living room — and the bath was full of ice and bottles of beer. Apart from Laura and Tony, there was nobody at all I knew, which I've always found kind of fun. A party crammed with strangers is like going to another planet for the evening. I was struggling with the top of a bottle when a man next to me took it, used his lighter to get the top off and handed it back to me.

"There," he said.

"You're looking a bit too proud of yourself," I said.

"I'm Callum," he said.

I looked at him suspiciously. He was tall, with dark frizzy hair and with that funny form of hair growth about the size of a postage stamp just under the bottom lip. He caught me looking at it.

"You can touch it, if you want," he said.

"Is there a word for it?" I asked.

"I don't know."

"Is it difficult to do?"

"Compared with what?" he asked. "Brain surgery?"

"A beard."

"It doesn't seem that hard."

"My name's Miranda," I said.

"I know," he said. "You're the woman who's moved out of her own flat."

"It's not that big a deal. It's just a pathetic, sad tale."

"It sounded pretty funny the way I heard it," said Callum.

"Well it isn't," I said. "It's sad."

I went into my Ancient Mariner mode, telling him the full story. While I was talking, he steered me toward the food table and loaded up a plate for me with a slice of pork pie and two kinds of salad. I'd told the story to numerous people but the odd thing was that this time it did come out funny. Partly it was because Callum was about five inches taller than me and was looking down at me with a quizzical expression, his hair drooping over his forehead. Also, it's hard to remain dignified and solemn while simultaneously telling a story, drinking from a bottle of beer, holding a plate and trying to eat from it.

"What you should do," said Callum when I had finished, "is chuck them out."

"I can't do that," I said instantly.

"Then treat this like a holiday, except that it's in the place where you already live. You've got house sitters, so you can go out and have fun in London."

The conversation meandered into other

areas. He already knew what I worked at and, like most people, he was too impressed by the fact that I went up ladders and sawed pieces of wood for a living. In the end he asked me for my phone number and I told him I didn't have a phone number, that was the whole point, hadn't he been listening? He laughed and said that he was a friend of Tony's and he would ring me there.

I felt a bit ashamed when I saw Laura and Tony hovering, obviously wanting to be on their way. I was meant to be the depressed one and I'd apparently had a better evening at their friend's party than they had. In the car back I remembered what Callum had said.

"I'm going to chuck them out," I said.

Laura looked around with a puzzled expression. "What?" she said.

"I've got too caught up in all of this," I said. "I haven't been thinking straight. Now I'm going to act like a normal person. I'll find somewhere for Kerry and what's-his-name to stay, even if I have to put them up in a hotel."

"You can still stay with us, you know," said Laura. "Can't she, Tony?"

"What?"

"Can't she stay with us?"

"You're the boss."

"Oh for God's sake."

I intervened. "No. You've been lovely. I feel like I've been trapped in a room with the heating on and the curtains closed and something rotting somewhere. I'm going to pull back the curtains and open the window."

"What about the thing that's rotting?" asked Laura.

"I think that was just in my imagination. You know, if other people want to be weird, that's their problem. I'm going to get on with my own life."

"It's good to hear you talk like that. Why the sudden change?"

I laughed. "Maybe it was talking to Callum. I'd been thinking I was in a Greek tragedy. Maybe I'm just in a situation comedy."

Chapter 20

I fastened the laces of my trainers and drank a glass of water before opening the front door. It was half-past six in the morning, still dark outside and much colder. There was a glint of frost on the pavement, and car windows were iced up. For a brief moment, I allowed myself to think that this was masochistic. Instead of torturing myself like a medieval nun, I should go back to bed, or at least, sofa bed. It would still be warm from my body. I set aside that thought, pulled the door shut behind me and set out on a run that would take me up the small roads to the park.

It had been a long time. At first I felt chilly and stiff but gradually I settled into a rhythm. And as I jogged past the newsagent that was just opening up its metal shutters, past the deserted primary school, past the recycling center, I watched the dawn turn to day. Lights came on in houses, streetlamps turned off, cars spluttered into life along the roadside, the sky that had been dark gray became gradually lighter and streaked with pink clouds. The postman was doing his rounds. A woman walking three huge dogs straining at their leads was pulled past me. I thought of people turning over in bed to stop their alarm clocks, children stretching and yawning and wriggling down under their duvets for the last snatch of sleep, showers running, kettles boiling, bread toasting. . . . All of a sudden I felt a small stab of happiness, to be running along the empty London streets as the sun rose on a glorious late autumn day.

I stopped at the bottom of the road on my way back to pick up a pack of streaky bacon and some white bread. In the flat, no one was stirring yet, so I had a quick shower and pulled on trousers and a jersey that was old and warm and raspberry pink. I put on the kettle for coffee and started to grill the bacon. Laura's door opened and her head poked around. She looked half asleep, still like a young girl, with mussed hair and rosy cheeks. She sniffed the air and murmured something unintelligible.

"Coffee and bacon sandwiches," I said. "Do you want it in bed?"

"It's Monday morning!"

"I thought we should start the week well."

"How long have you been up?"

"An hour or so. I went running."

"Why are you so cheerful all of a sudden?"

"I'm taking my life in hand," I said. "This is the new me."

"God," she said, and withdrew her head. A moment later she had joined me in the kitchen, wrapped in a thick dressing gown.

She sat at the kitchen table and watched as I put the rashers between thick slices of bread, and boiled milk for the coffee. She nibbled at her sandwich cautiously. I chomped into mine.

"What are you up to today?" she asked.

I slurped at my coffee. Warmth was spreading through me.

"I had an idea in the night. I'm going to ring round the people who I know are going to be out of the country for a bit. There are quite a few, because our customers often want us to do work for them while they're not there. I'll ask if they want a responsible couple to house-sit for them. There's at least one family who's got loads of pets that someone would have to feed twice a day anyway. Maybe they'd be glad of Kerry and Brendan staying. I'm sure I can find someone like that — it's much better than looking in the classifieds. So" — I poured myself another cup of coffee and topped it up with hot milk, then took another sand-wich — "I'm going to find them somewhere else to live because they're obviously not going to do it themselves, are they, and then Troy can be with me like we'd planned. And then I'm going to the reclamation center with Bill and then I'm going to do my accounts and then I'll go to my flat and collect a few things and tell them when they've got to be out by. There."

"I feel tired just thinking about it."

"So I'll be out of your hair soon."

"I like you being here."

"You've been fabulous, but I feel in the way. I want to leave before you're wishing me gone."

"Shall I cook us supper?"

"I'll buy a take-away," I said. "Curry and beer."

Laura left for work and I cleared up breakfast, put a clothes wash on and vacuumed the living room. I promised myself that I'd buy her a big present when I left.

I went to Bill's office, just a few hundred meters from his house, and started making phone calls. The family with pets had already arranged for a friend to house-sit. The young woman who lived in Shoreditch didn't really want someone she didn't know living in her flat. The couple with the beautiful conservatory had changed their plans and weren't leaving for several months. But the two men with a small house on London Fields were interested. They'd call me back when they'd talked it through.

I started on the accounts while I was waiting. It didn't take long before the phone rang. They were going to America in eight days' time for three months, maybe for longer if everything went well. They hadn't thought of getting someone in, but since it came through a personal recommendation, and as long as the new kitchen was still done while they were away, and as long as Kerry and Brendan paid some rent, kept the house clean and watered the date palm and the orange tree that were in the bathroom, then that would be fine.

"Eight days?" I said.

"Right."

Their house was lovely, far more spacious than my flat, and overlooking a park. It had a circular bath and deep-pile carpets, and when we'd installed their kitchen it would have a stainless steel hob and quarry tiles and a large sunroof. There could be nothing that Brendan could find to object to, surely. In eight days I could be back in my flat. I'd paint my bedroom wall yellow and change all the furniture around. I'd clean windows and throw things out.

"That's great," I said. "Really, really great. You've no idea."

I called Troy on my mobile and told him. I could hear him smile.

I got to my flat a bit early. There was a light on in one of the windows, though I could see no sign of Kerry's car. I inserted the key in the lock, fumbling in the darkness, and pushed open the door. If no one was there, that would be a relief. If they were in, I could tell them about the house in London Fields and try to talk to Kerry. Yesterday I had felt that she would never forgive me, but today it looked different to me. Nothing had happened, except inside me.

I went up the stairs and there was a smell that made me mutter crossly to myself, because it was bad enough them forcing me out of my own home, the least they could do was keep it clean. Then I pushed open the living room door. It banged against something that clattered out of the way as I pushed harder.

What did I see? What did I feel? I don't know really. I never will know. It's jumbled up together in a foul twist of memory that I'll never lose.

Scuff-toed boots that I'd seen hundreds of

times before, but a foot above the floor, and then his canvas trousers, stained at the knee, and a buckled belt around the waist. A smell of shit. A chair on its side. Fear a thick eel in my throat. I couldn't look up. I had to look up. His face above me, tilted to one side, his mouth slightly open. I could see the tip of his tongue. Blue around his lips. His eyes were open, staring. I saw the rope that he was hanging from.

Maybe he was still alive. Oh God, maybe he was; please please please. I righted the chair and clambered onto it, half falling over, and there I was pressed up against his body, trying to hold him up to relieve the pressure of the noose on his neck and trying to undo the knot. Fingers trembling too much. His hair against my cheek. His cold forehead. The slump of his body, but people can be alive when they look dead, you read about it, bringing them back to life when all hope is gone. But I couldn't undo the knot and he was so heavy and smelled of death already. Shit and death and his flesh was cold.

I jumped down from the chair, leaving his body swaying there, and raced to the kitchen. The bread knife was in the sink, and I grabbed it and ran back to Troy. Standing on tiptoe on the chair I began sawing at the cord while still trying to hold his body. Suddenly he was free and we fell onto the floor together and his arms were over my body in a ghastly embrace.

I pushed him off me and hurled myself toward the phone. Jabbed the buttons.

"Help," I said. "Help. He's hung himself. Please come and help. Please. What shall I do?"

The voice at the other end was quite calm. It asked questions and I gabbled answers and all the time Troy lay an arm's length away and I kept saying, "But what shall I do, what shall I do?"

"The emergency services will be with you as soon as possible," said the voice.

"Shall I give him the kiss of life? Shall I pump his chest? Tell me what to do."

I looked at Troy while I was saying it. His skin was chalky white except where it was blue around the lips. The tip of his tongue protruded. The eyes were open and sightless. The noose around his neck was slack now, but there was dark bruising where it had been. My little brother.

"Hurry," I said in a whisper. "Hurry up."

I put the phone down and crawled across to where he lay. I put his head in my lap and stroked the hair off his forehead. I leaned down and kissed him on his cheeks, and on his mouth. I picked up his hand and cradled it between both my own. I did up the middle button of his shirt, which had come undone. In a minute I would pick up the phone and call my parents. How do you say, *Your son is dead*? I shut my eyes for a moment, drenched with the horror of it.

His sweater was draped over the back of the sofa. There was a book on the table, face down. The clock ticked on the wall. I looked at it: 6:25. If you could turn the clock back through the minutes and the hours until it was before Troy had stood on that chair with the noose around his neck and then kicked off, into death. If I'd arrived before, left my cheese-and-pickle roll and my accounts and my loitering in the warm office, and driven here instead. I ran my fingers through his hair. Nothing would ever be all right again.

The doorbell rang and I laid Troy's head gently back on the carpet and went to open it. While they were clustered around Troy, I picked up the phone.

"Mum," I said. Then before she could ask me how I was, or tell me any of her news, I said, "Listen . . ."

Chapter 21

Everything was disjointed, skewed, in a strange light, a foreign language. My flat didn't feel like my own flat anymore. It was like being out in the street when there has been an accident. People were bustling in and out who had nothing to do with me. There were three people in green overalls, who at first were very urgent and quick and shouting instructions, and then suddenly were slow and quiet because, after all, there was nothing to be urgent about anymore because we were all too late. I saw a policeman and a policewoman. They must have arrived quickly. I looked at my watch but I couldn't make out the time properly, as if the numbers were far away and in the wrong order. Someone handed me a mug of something hot and I sipped at it and I burned my lips. It felt good. I wanted it to hurt. I wanted it to make me feel something, to wake me out of this numbness.

I'd talked to my mother on the phone. That had been one of the first things I'd done. I'd thought of trying to break it to her gradually. It felt like the right thing to do. I'd wanted to say something like, *Troy is seriously ill. Very seriously ill.* I could have made it easier for her, except that I couldn't. He was too cold and dead, his eyes open. So I couldn't say anything to her except that Troy was dead and that maybe she should come but that they didn't need to because I could deal with things. I heard a gasp and then some fumbling attempts at questions. Dead? Was I sure? And then just a sort of moan. She started to say something about how she had thought Troy was better and I think I cut her short because I couldn't concentrate on what she was saying.

There was a hand on my arm, a female face looking into mine. She was a police officer, younger than me, pale-faced, purple spots like a rash on her cheekbones. Was I all right? I nodded. She wanted details. Troy's name. Age. My name. I started to get angry. How could they ask stupid questions at a time like this? Then I stopped getting angry. I realized that these were the questions that needed to be asked. Suddenly I saw the scene from her point of view. This was what she did for a living. She was called to events like this, one after another. The people in the green uniforms as well. They dealt with them and went home and watched TV. The policewoman was probably specially trained to deal with people like me. When she looked at me, she saw just one of a series of people that she had to deal with, people who weren't used to this. There had probably been someone a bit like me yesterday or the day before and there would probably be someone a bit like me tomorrow or the day after. She would look at me and wonder whether I was the sort to make trouble. Some people would be difficult, some would cry, some would just be numb and unable to talk, some would become manic, a few might turn violent. Which would I be?

There would be so much to organize, I thought. Forms to fill, envelopes to lick, people to be informed. At that moment it hit me, like a warm wet wave that ran through every cell. I had to open my mouth wide and gasp as if the air in my flat were suddenly hard to breathe. My head felt light and I started to sway and the woman's face appeared in front of me.

"Are you all right, Miranda?" she said. She took the mug out of my hand. Some of it had already splashed onto my trousers. It had stung and felt hot but now it was cold. "Are you all right? Are you going to faint?"

All I said was "I'm fine" because I

couldn't say what I really felt, which was that I had suddenly realized, like a hot wet wave, that this was the end of Troy's story. My head was buzzing with memories of Troy. A little boy on a beach standing on a sand castle, the tide washing around it. Running into a fence in the playground at primary school and losing one of his front teeth. The way he bit his lip when he was hunched over a drawing. When he used to get the giggles and roll around with them on the floor as if he were possessed. The other times, more common, when he went dark like bad weather and we couldn't reach him. When he was buzzing with ideas and it was as if he couldn't get them out fast enough, his eyes glowing with them. His very delicate long white fingers and his large eyes, almost too big for his face. There were all those conversations about him when he wasn't there, the Troy problem. It was one of the main things I remember about growing up, the pained expression on my mother's face when she looked at him. What to do about Troy? They had tried so many things. They had taken him to a therapist and to the doctor. They had tried leaving him alone, encouraging him, warning him, shouting at him, crying, behaving as if everything were normal. Thousands of memories, fragments of stories, but now they had all ended in the same way. All the roads from all those memories led to my flat and a rope and a beam and the thing that was Troy and also wasn't Troy anymore, lying on my floor with people he didn't know and who didn't know him clustered around him.

The policewoman appeared once more. She was clutching handfuls of tissues and I realized that I was sobbing and sobbing. The people in my flat were looking at me awkwardly. I pushed my face into the tissues, wiping the tears away and blowing my nose. I couldn't stop myself crying. We'd failed, we'd all failed. It was like for the whole of my life we had watched Troy drowning. We had done this and that, we'd talked and we'd worried and we'd made plans and we'd tried to help, but in the end he had just slipped below the water and it was all for nothing. Gradually my sobbing gave way to a few snuffles and then I felt squeezed out.

The police officer told me that she was called Vicky Reeder. A man in a suit was standing next to her. He was a detective called Rob Pryor. He asked me some questions about how I had found Troy. I was impressed by the calmness of my voice and my precision as I spoke. There was nothing I could say that wasn't obvious and the man nodded as I spoke. Afterward, he and a man in uniform looked up at the beam and at the chair lying on its side on the floor. I hadn't noticed that. The detective came back to me. He talked to me in a low respectful voice, as if he were an undertaker. I realized that I was now part of a particular tribe, the bereaved, who are slightly removed from normal life and have to be treated with respect and even a certain reverence. He told me that they would now be taking Troy's body away. This might be upsetting for me, and he wondered if I might like to step into another room for a few minutes. I shook my head. I wanted to see everything. I made myself look at Troy. He was wearing his khaki trousers and a navy blue fleece. He was in old familiar boots and above them I could see his jaunty red-and-blue striped socks. I thought of him pulling them on this morning. Did he know that he would never pull them off again? Had he already decided this morning or was it a sudden impulse? If I had phoned him for a chat that afternoon, would it have made a difference? I must stop thinking like that. He was my brother and he had died in my own flat and I hadn't been there. I wondered what I had been doing at the moment when the chair tipped over and he flapped in the air for those last seconds. No. I must stop myself thinking like that.

One of the green-uniformed men from the ambulance unrolled a bulky plastic bag along the length of Troy's body. It was like a very long pencil case. One of them looked up at me self-consciously as if he was doing something indecent. It was all very crude. They lifted him, holding him by the feet and the shoulders, and lifted him the few inches across. The bag took some adjusting around him, the end of the cord around his neck had to be tucked inside and then the large zipper was pulled shut. Now he could be carried out to the ambulance without members of the public being alarmed.

At that moment I heard voices outside and my parents came through the door. They had walked up without ringing. They looked around as if they had just woken up and weren't sure where they were or what was happening. They looked old. My father was in his suit. He must have driven from work and picked my mother up on the way. My mother looked down at the bag and that was one of the bad moments again. She had an expression of shock and disbelief at the grossness of it, the thereness of it. The detective introduced himself and then he and my father moved away and spoke in a murmur. I felt a sort of relief at that. I could be a child again. My dad would sort things out. I wouldn't have to make the calls, fill out the forms. My parents could do that.

My mother knelt down for a moment by the side of the bundle that had once been Troy. She put her hand very gently on the place where his forehead would be. I saw that her lips were moving but I couldn't hear any words. She blinked several times, then stood up and came over to me. She didn't step over Troy's body but awkwardly edged her way around it, her eyes on it as if it were an abyss into which she might fall. She pulled a chair over to me and stood by me, holding my hand but not meeting my eye. When the ambulancemen picked up the awkward bundle on the floor, I looked over at my mother. She wasn't crying but I could see her jaw flexing.

My father said good-bye to Detective Rob Pryor as if he had helped him change a tire. I saw Pryor write something on a piece of paper and give it to my father and they shook hands and then everybody left and we were alone. It felt mad. Was that it? The authorities had come and removed Troy, taken him somewhere, and now what were we meant to do? Didn't they want anything from us? Did we have any duties? I still hadn't said anything to my parents.

"Troy," I said, and then stopped. There was nothing to say, and everything.

I expected that when I said that, my mother would start crying the way I had and I could hold her and we could avoid talking or thinking for a while, but she continued just looking puzzled. My father came and sat opposite me and looked very calm.

"Was this a surprise?" he said.

I almost screamed at him that of course it was a fucking surprise and then I thought of my mother and father and their lost child and I said "Yes."

"Should we have seen anything?" he said.

"We've been seeing things all his life," I said. *All his life*. The meaning of words had changed. Mum started to speak as if she were talking in her sleep. She spoke about Troy in the last few weeks, about how he had been bad but she thought it had been getting better. There had been worse times before and he had always recovered. She'd been trying and trying to think if there had been some signal or warning but she couldn't. She talked of Troy when he had been younger. These weren't reminiscences. They would come later. We had all the rest of our lives for that. She talked about what they had done for him and how they had failed and wondered over and over again if they should have done it differently. She didn't sound self-pitying or bitter. Just genuinely curious, as if I or my father could provide an answer that would satisfy her.

Dad was businesslike, in a mad kind of way. He made tea for us all and then he found some paper and a pen. He began to make a list of everything that needed doing and it appeared that there was a lot. There were people to be told, arrangements, decisions to be made. So many. A whole side of paper was covered with his precise, square handwriting.

On top of the horror, it was a strange situation. The three of us were sitting in my flat. My mother hadn't even taken her coat off. My father had made his list. There was so much to do but there was nothing to do. Nobody wanted to eat. Nobody wanted to go anywhere. There were people who would have to be told, but not yet. It was as if we needed to sit there together and hold the secret to us awhile longer before letting it out into the world. So there was nothing to do except talk in fragments, but if there was any awkwardness, I wasn't aware of it. I was still glowing with the awfulness of what had happened. I felt as if I'd jabbed my fingers into an electric socket and the current was just pulsing through me over and over again.

Hours went by like this and it was just before nine when I heard a noise downstairs and voices and laughter on the stairs and then Brendan and Kerry burst into the room, arm in arm, laughing. They were cheerfully startled to see us.

"What's up?" said Brendan with a smile.

Chapter 22

It was damp and weirdly warm. In less than four weeks it would be Christmas. Every high street in the city had its lights up, the Santa Claus, the swinging bells, the Disney characters. Shop windows glittered with tinsel and baubles. There were already Christmas trees outside the greengrocers' shops, leaning against the wall with their wide branches tied up with string. Some doors in the street where I lived had holly wreaths on them. The shelves in the supermarkets were loaded with crackers, mince pies, advent calendars, boxes of dates, vast tins of chocolates, frozen turkeys, bottles of port and sherry, little baskets of bath salts and soaps, CDs of seasonal music, humorous books, crappy stocking fillers. The brass band played "O Little Town of Bethlehem" outside Woolworth. Women in thick coats rattled collection tins in the cold.

What would we do this Christmas? Would we put up a tree in my parents' half-demolished house or in my living room, where nine days ago Troy had killed himself? Would we sit around a table eating turkey with chestnut stuffing and sprouts and roast potatoes? Would we pull crackers, put silly hats on our heads and take it in turn to read out the jokes? What would we do, what could we do, that wouldn't seem grotesque? How do you ever return to normal life, when something like this has happened?

Troy's funeral wasn't crowded. He'd been a lonely boy and a solitary young man. His few friends at school had fallen away after he'd left, although a couple of them turned up with the deputy head and his old physics teacher. His tutor came, too, and several family friends who'd known Troy since he was tiny. There was Bill and Judy and their kids, and my mother's sister Kath who'd come down from Sheffield with her family, and then there were the relatives my parents saw once or twice a year, and the ones they barely ever saw but exchanged Christmas cards with. A friend of Kerry's called Carol came, and Tony and Laura.

We were there, of course: Mum and Dad, me and Kerry. And Brendan. Brendan looked more stricken than anyone, with his red eyes, and a faint bruise on his forehead turning yellow. Even I had to admit that he'd been wonderful over the past week: inexhaustible, indispensable, solid. Wonderful in quotation marks, though. There was more to Brendan than I'd seen before. I didn't understand it, whatever "it" was, but he was good at it. Resourceful, energetic, committed to each moment, persuasive, cooperative, endlessly aware of other people's needs, feelings. He had a radar for what everyone around him needed just at that very instant.

He'd offered to make all the funeral arrangements himself, to take the burden off the family, but Mum had told him quietly that it helped her to be busy. He'd answered the phone, filled out forms, made pots of tea, gone shopping, shifted his and Kerry's stuff into my parents' house again, so I could move back into my flat. They were moving to the house I'd found in two days' time.

A week after the death, we talked about the wedding. Kerry wanted to postpone it but my parents said that love was the only thing that would get us through. Brendan nodded at that and held Kerry's hand, stroking it and saying in a wise, reflective voice, "Yes, yes, love will get us through," his eyes shining. At any other time it would have driven me insane with irritation. I still knew it was irritating, but now there were numb layers between the irritation and me.

"Here you are, better than tea."

Bill pushed a tumbler of whisky into my hand and stood beside me while I took a large, fiery mouthful. We had all come back to my parents' house and were standing in the drafty living room, drinking mugs of tea and not really knowing what to say to each other. What is there to say at events like these?

"Thanks."

"Are you all right?"

"Yeah."

"Silly question. How could you be?"

"If he'd died in an accident, or of an illness or something, that would have been one thing . . ." I said. I didn't need to finish the sentence.

"Marcia's going to spend the rest of her life asking herself where she went wrong, what she did wrong."

"Yes."

"That's what suicide does. The fact is, she did all she could. You all did."

"No. He shouldn't have killed himself."

"Well, of course not."

"I mean, I don't understand it. Mum

keeps saying she thought he was getting better. And he was getting better, Bill."

"You never know what's going on in someone's head."

"I guess."

I took another gulp.

"He was a troubled young man."

"Yeah."

I thought about Troy giggling, making stupid jokes, grinning up at me. I kept seeing his face when he was in his happy phases and energy seemed to shine out of him, illuminating him and making him beautiful.

Bill refilled my glass and took the whisky bottle across to Dad. I wandered out of the crowded living room, into the building site that used to be the kitchen, then through the hole in the wall where once there was a door and into the soggy garden. Ripped, splintered floorboards and pieces of the old kitchen units were heaped up against the fence. I leaned against an old bit of shelving. It was slightly misty, every outline just a bit blurred, but maybe that was the whisky.

After my conversation with Bill, I was in a state wide open for doubts to crash in. The autopsy had been straightforward: suicide by hanging. I thought of the last conversation I'd had with Troy on the phone that morning, when he'd sounded tired but quite cheerful. I'd told him about finding the house for Brendan and Kerry and we'd talked about our plans. I'd said how much I was looking forward to sharing the flat with him, and he'd said, a bit gruffly, that he was looking forward to it, too. My stinging eyes filled with tears again, though I had believed I was all cried out. I heard Brendan asking me, the day before, what time I would be collecting my stuff from the flat, and me replying it would be about half-past six. I let myself remember pushing the door open at the appointed time and seeing Troy's body hanging there; his chalky face and sightless, open eyes, the chair upturned by his feet.

I was hysterical, I told myself. Mad. I so badly wanted Troy not to have killed himself, so badly wanted not to have to blame my parents and myself for his death, so wanted not to have to imagine the despair that had led him to that moment, I was inventing gothic fantasies instead.

A few drops of rain fell on me. I drained my whisky and went back through the kitchen and into the living room. I hung back by the door, unwilling to talk about Troy and not wanting to talk about anything else. Kerry was standing with her arm through my father's. Her mascara had smudged and there were red blotches on her neck. Across the room, Brendan was on his own. Our eyes met. He looked away and his face crumpled. I suddenly felt that he was staging this just for me, a private drama. Tears coursed down his face, into his neck; he stuffed a fist into his mouth and doubled up as if he was muffling a great howl.

It was Laura who went up to him and put a hand on his shoulder. She just stood there like that while his bulky body shook. After a while he stood up straighter, and she took away her hand. I saw them talking. At one point they both looked over to me.

I turned away and went upstairs to find my mother, who had disappeared from the gathering. She was sitting in Troy's old room — Kerry and Brendan's room now, I supposed, for their bags were by the door. She was sitting on his bed, plucking at the sheets with her fingers and staring ahead into nothing. She looked tired. Her face was full of lines and pouches that I hadn't seen before. Even her hair was lackluster. I went and crouched beside her and put a hand on her knee. She looked up and gave me a small nod of acknowledgment.

"I thought I'd leave them to it," she said. "It's fine."

"I don't know what to do with myself really. Nowhere seems the right place to be."

"I know what you mean."

"Miranda?"

"Yes."

"He was getting better. He was."

"I know."

I crouched there for a little longer, then went back to the thinning crowd and the whisky bottle.

Laura took me home because I'd drunk far too much whisky to drive myself. She steered me upstairs to my flat and took off my coat, then sat me on the sofa and pulled off my shoes.

"There," she said. "Now: tea or coffee?"

"Shame to let the drink wear off," I said. "Whisky?"

"I'll make coffee," she said firmly. "And I'll run you a bath."

"That's nice of you. You don't need to. I'll be fine."

"It's nothing." She filled the kettle with water and plugged it in.

"We were going to share this flat," I said.

"I know. Do you want something to eat?"

"I've got a horrible taste in my mouth," I said. "What did Brendan say then?"

"Say?" She looked confused.

"You were talking with him. After he'd done his great weeping act."

"That's not fair, Miranda."

"You don't think so?"

"He's heartbroken but doesn't think he can show it in front of all of you. He has to be strong for the family."

"That's what he said?"

"Yes."

"Oh well, who cares?"

"He does," she said. "I know what you feel about him, but he cares a lot. After all, you're the only family he's got. He thought of Troy as his little brother."

"You, too," I said, infinitely tired.

"What?"

"He's got you on his side, too."

"It's not a question of sides."

"That's what he says, too, but he's lying. He's on one side and I'm on the other. Now more than ever. You can't be on both sides at once you know. And you can't be some fucking United Nations mediator. You have to choose." There was a pause. "You've crossed over, haven't you?" I could feel my speech thicken. My head was aching with the whisky and the wretchedness.

"Miranda, you're my best friend. Don't say things like that."

"Sorry," I said. But I couldn't let it go. "You liked him, didn't you?"

"I felt sorry for him."

She poured boiling water over the coffee grounds and stirred vigorously. I stood up and fetched the whisky bottle from the shelf.

"Look at that," I said. "How've I drunk all of that since the day before yesterday?"

I was almost proud of myself. It was an achievement, of a kind. I sloshed a generous measure into a dirty wineglass, closed my eyes and took a gulp.

"You'll feel lousy tomorrow," said Laura.

"One way or another," I said.

"Do you want me to stay the night?"

"No. You've been lovely."

"Are you going to work tomorrow?"

"Obviously. It's a working day."

"I'll ring you in the evening then."

"You don't need to."

"No, but I will."

"What would I do without you?"

I finished off the bottle. If I shut my eyes, the room tipped sickeningly, so I kept them squinted open though the lights were hurting my head. I padded into the bedroom and sat down on the bed, which had been Troy's bed for a bit. Although I'd changed the sheets, some of his things were still there — his watch on the bedside table, his jacket hanging from the hook on the door, his books scattered around the place. I fancied I could still smell him. I picked up a book he'd been reading about bread-making and held it against my chest.

"Oh dear," I said out loud. My tongue was thick in my mouth. "Oh dear, Troy. What shall I do now?"

Later, about two in the morning, I staggered out of bed and was sick, leaning over the toilet bowl and retching until there was nothing left in my stomach to vomit up. My eyes stung and my throat hurt and my head throbbed, but I felt a bit better. I drank three beakers of water and went back to bed. I couldn't get to sleep at once. Thoughts swarmed in my head. I heard Troy's voice, his last words: "See you later then." He wouldn't see me, but I'd see him. All the time.

Chapter 23

If I'd felt bad in the middle of the night, I felt unspeakably worse when I woke the next morning. I was going to die, and when I was dead I was going to be pickled and put in a large jar and put on display with a label identifying me as the first person ever to die of a hangover. It was hard to think because it hurt. It hurt to do anything.

At about half-past nine I made an attempt to get up and then lay down again. No hangover had ever been quite like this one. I had the usual symptoms, in a more intense form: the parched leathery tongue, the headache, which felt as if small rodents were eating my brain from the inside, the general feeling of being poisoned, a shivery creepy-crawly sensation over my skin. Additional bits of my body seemed to be hurting. Even my hair was sore. The particular innovation was that I still felt drunk, but it was like an evil stale parody of the previous night's drunkenness. All the good bits — if there had been any good bits — were gone. But the floor-swaying was still there. The room-revolving was present and correct. That was why I had to lie down again but even so it felt as if I were on a water bed. People didn't die of hangovers but they did die of alcohol poisoning. Could it be that? I remembered that I had a book about medical problems. There were a couple of snags. The first was that I didn't have a maid who could get it for me. The second was that I kept it with the cookbooks so when I finally staggered across my flat to get it, stomach heaving, I had to see things that made me think of food. I tried not to think of food but then the idea of a huge trifle came into my mind and I could only eject that by thinking of the smell of overcooked cabbage and then I thought of Troy and that was worse, the worst of all.

I took the book back to bed. There was no entry for alcohol poisoning but there was one for hangovers. The book recommended me to drink plenty of water, to go for a brisk run "even if you do not feel like it." If nauseous, and I felt very nauseous, I was to take something called magnesium trisilicate. Right, I decided, I was going to be positive. Previously I had wanted to curl up under the bedclothes and die, like a wounded animal retreating into its hole. Now I was going to adopt the opposite plan. I was going to attack the problem. I would not only get this drug, I would run to get it. And I would have a drink of water first.

Everything felt wrong. The water was too late for my arid mouth. It seemed to run over it without being absorbed. I could barely lift my legs to get my foot into my shorts. I pulled the T-shirt over my head. It hurt my head. It hurt my arms. I tied the laces of my shoes slowly, trying to think how to do it for the first time since I was about six years old. I clutched a five-pound note in my hand and shuffled out onto the pavement. The bright light, the cold air on my skin and in my lungs, made me gasp. I don't know if it was making me better in any way but there was a new clarity. In a way it felt good to be hurting and I wondered if this was a welcome continuation of last night. To be drunk, to ache, to be confused, to be in pain, perhaps anything would be better than opening my eyes and looking into the sun, truly facing up to what Troy had done to himself and done to us.

The chemist was only a couple of hundred yards away. I asked the pharmacist, a very tall Sikh, for the magnesium trisilicate. It had a sickly minty taste, but I sucked it desperately and headed back for home in an approximation of a jog. I had a shower, I put some grown-up clothes on and lay on my bed to think. There was a metallic taste in my mouth, and when I swallowed it felt to me as if there were something bristly stuck in my throat that wouldn't go down. My skin felt clammy. I felt sick but I wasn't going to *be* sick.

There was no doubt about it. I was in slightly less of a dreadful state. The day could now begin. What was the time? I reached the bedside table for the watch, Troy's watch, that was lying there. Quarter past ten. That was another thing. I knew why the watch was there. Part of Troy's problem was that there was never any balance, any compromise in his life, or even normal behavior. He was either completely wired, wildly funny, incredibly enthusiastic, or he was somnolent, slow, detached, often just fast asleep. Even in his good times he would have big sleeps in the afternoon, like a small child or a cat. He didn't just flop in a soft chair. He pulled the curtains, took his clothes off, got into bed. It was like nighttime. When he was medicated he was almost in a coma. He had been sleeping in my bed, and he had taken his clothes off and put his watch on my bedside table. His clothes were on his dead body but not his watch. He may have forgotten. He was depressed, after all.

There was another thing. I closed my eyes and made myself do it. I pictured my dear lost Troy hanging from that beam. The rope. It was easy to remember, shiny green, synthetic, rough. I remembered the strands as I'd cut it with the knife to bring him down. For the first time I thought of suicide as a human activity that needed organizing. You need to plan it, you need to obtain materials.

I felt clear-headed now. I got up and felt a wave of nausea and dizziness but it passed quickly. I didn't have the time to be ill. I had things to do. My flat was so small that there wasn't much to search. I couldn't remember having seen that rope before, but I had to make sure. Under the sink there was a bucket, some washing cloths, various bottles of cleaning fluid. In the cupboard there was the vacuum cleaner, a broom and a mop, a rolled-up rug, a shoe box containing screwdrivers, a hammer, nails, screws, a couple of plugs. I looked on top shelves, behind the sofa, under my bed, everywhere. There was no rope. It could be that he just found a length of rope and used all of it. Or bought the length he needed and used all of it. Or . . .

I phoned my mother. It was difficult not to begin every sentence I spoke to my mother and father or sister by asking how they were. We could spend the rest of our lives asking and thinking what to say in return. I just asked if I could come around and she said, "Yes, that would be good."

On the way, I thought of something else. A few months earlier I'd been stuck in a tube train on the Piccadilly line for more than an hour. An announcement came over the loudspeaker apologizing to all customers and informing us that there was a customer under a train at the next station. To which the obvious answer would be, *Well, tell him to get out from under it so that we can all be on our way.* But of course that is a euphemism for throwing yourself in front of the train and lots of unimaginable things happening to the person on their way to being underneath. I had a lot of time to think about it and one of the things I thought about was: Do you owe anything to anyone when you kill yourself? If you throw yourself under a tube train, the driver is only about three inches in front of you as you go under, with whatever god-awful scrapes and bumps and crunches that ensue. The tube driver takes early retirement after a suicide, mostly. And what about all the commuters who suffer half an hour of irritation? Do all the missed dental appointments, toddlers left standing outside schools, the burned meals, do they do some damage to your karma?

I let a thought come into my mind that I had managed to exclude until that moment. In my flat. Troy had killed himself in my flat. I wondered if even thinking this was an obscenity, but I couldn't stop myself. He had hanged himself where I might find him. His dead body hung there, rotating slowly until it came to rest, in the space where I slept and ate and lived my life. How could he do that? I wanted to think to myself that Troy could never have done that. I loved Troy. And surely, even when his fog of misery was at its thickest, he loved me. Would he have done that to me? Something I could never forget. I tried to tell myself that when you kill yourself you are beyond thinking of other people except that they will be better off without you. Or was it worse? I made myself consider the possibility that Troy's suicide, and the manner of it, and the place of it, was a statement to me: *There, Miranda, there. You thought you understood me. You thought you could help me. Well, here you are. Here is what I've come to. Do something to help me now.*

I expected my mother to start crying when she saw me but her mind seemed somewhere else. Even when she opened the door, she was looking over my shoulder as if she expected someone to be with me.

"I'm glad you came, Miranda," she said, but it sounded as if she were speaking lines someone else had written for her. "Your father's out."

"Where?" I said. Where did he have to go at a time like this?

"Where?" my mother said, foggily, as if she were on something.

"What about Kerry and Brendan?"

"They've gone out. Would you like some tea?"

"Love some. I'll just pop upstairs."

That's the good thing about your parents' house. It's still sort of your home, even if it's not the one you grew up in. You can go anywhere in it, open cupboards. I was going to do something terrible. I hardly knew why. It was as if I had an abscess in a tooth and I was getting a penknife and jabbing it into the abscess, flooding myself with more and more pain so that it would just overwhelm me and be gone, or I would be gone. My mother had gone to the kitchen and I ran up the stairs and into the spare bedroom where Kerry and Brendan were staying. I felt a tension like electricity in me. My ears were humming with it. I could hear my pulse, hear the blood rushing through my veins.

The arrangement in the bedroom was obviously temporary. They had barely unpacked. Kerry's dressing gown and nightie were tossed over the bed. A suitcase was half open, leaning against the wall, her clothes neatly folded. On the corner table there were a number of bottles, shampoo, conditioner, creams, scent, all of it Kerry's. I looked around. That was a funny thing. Kerry could have been staying here alone. I couldn't see a single object or item of clothing that belonged to Brendan. Next to the bed was another closed suitcase. I laid it flat on the floor, flicked the catches and opened it, revealing Brendan's clothes. It wouldn't take a minute. One by one I lifted shirts, trousers, underpants and turned them over so that I could replace them in the right order. The case was almost empty when I felt as much as heard steps running up the stairs. I didn't even have time to move from my knees when the door opened and Brendan appeared. For about a tenth of a second I had thought, Well, what does it matter? But at the look on his face, I thought: Oh fuck. At first he just looked surprised, and no wonder, with me rooting around in his case, his clothes arranged around me.

"Miranda?" he said. "What the . . . ?"

I tried to think of something but my brain had turned to thick soup.

"I'd forgotten something," I said randomly. "I mean, I thought you'd taken something by mistake."

Now his face turned angry.

"What the fuck?"

And then Kerry appeared behind him.

"Brendan?" she said. "What . . . ?" And then she, too, caught sight of me.

"The rope," I said. "I thought you'd taken my rope by mistake."

Chapter 24

"What?" said Kerry wildly. "What rope?"

"Jesus Christ," said Brendan. "Look at you!"

"What rope?" repeated Kerry.

She took a step forward so that she was glaring down at me. She had her hands on her hips and her face was scarlet. It was as if all her natural reserve, her anxiety and timidity, had been burned away by grief and rage. I could almost feel the emotion steaming off her. I got up from the floor and stood there, surrounded by Brendan's clothes.

"I don't know," I said. "I just thought . . ." I trailed off.

"You were going through Brendan's stuff, for God's sake. What did you think?"

"I was sorting out my flat," I said.

"And? *And?*"

"Let me get this straight," said Brendan. "You're going through my things" — here he kicked at his clothes with a foot, so they spread out on the floor — "to find some rope. Yes?"

"I was just confused," I said in a mumble.

"Confused?" said Kerry. "Do you realize that our little brother was buried yesterday? And now you come over here, you make a special journey, to poke around in Brendan's case . . ."

"It'd be better if I went now," I said.

Brendan took a step forward so that he was barring my way. "I don't think so, Mirrie."

"Let me through."

"You're not going anywhere until we've got to the bottom of this."

"We're all overwrought."

"Overwrought," yelled Kerry. For such a slight person she can make a very loud noise. "Over-fucking-wrought?"

"What's going on?"

My father had appeared in the doorway.

"Nothing," I said, hopelessly.

"I'll tell you what's going on," said Kerry. "She" — she pointed a finger at me — "she was going through Brendan's case."

"Miranda?" said my father.

"Looking for rope," added Brendan.

"Rope?"

"That's what she said."

Brendan squatted down and started folding up his scattered clothes and putting them neatly back in the case.

"I think I should go," I said.

"I think you should explain yourself," said my father in a voice tinged with disgust. He rubbed his face with his hand and looked around for somewhere to sit down.

"I was simply trying to get things in order," I began, then stopped.

"The rope," prompted Brendan. "Mmm? Secretly going through my belongings looking for some rope?"

I didn't have anything to say.

"What rope?" asked my mother, entering the room.

I sat down on the unmade bed and put my face in my hands, like a small child trying to keep the world out of my head. Kerry started telling my mother what she'd found me doing, stoking up her outrage all over again, and I stared through the crack in my fingers at a patch of carpet and the legs of the chest of drawers, trying to block out the words.

"I don't know you anymore," my mother said in a flat voice once Kerry was done.

"Please," I said. "I'm upset. We're all upset."

"What I want to know," said Brendan, "is what rope it was. I mean when you say rope, well, the word only means one thing to all of us now. Mmm? Only one thing."

There was a horrible silence in the room,

then he went on: "Is that what you mean by the rope — you mean, the *rest* of the rope. Mmm?"

"I don't mean anything."

"And yet you went to the trouble of coming over here to look for it."

"Shut up," I said, lifting my head from my hands. "Shut up shut up shut up! I feel as if I'm in court or something, and everything I say's being turned against me. Don't all look at me like that!"

"Why did you think it would be here? Mmm? Among my things? Is there something you want to tell us?"

"No," I said in a whisper.

"It's obvious," said Kerry sharply. "She's obsessed with Brendan. She's always been obsessed with him. I tried not to see it. I tried telling myself it didn't matter. I was generous about it, wasn't I? I thought she'd get over it. Even when she went on and on about their relationship, and wouldn't let go of it. When she wouldn't behave in an ordinary friendly way in front of him, but had to be all angry and bitter, or else too friendly. Even when she took her clothes off in the bathroom when he was in there, for God's sake, and I was in the bloody next room trying to behave nicely to her."

"Say 'you,' " I said, hysteria rising up in

me. "Don't say 'she' when I'm right in front of you."

Kerry talked over me. Everything she'd stored up was cascading out now. Her voice was high and hoarse. "Even when she started going all peculiar and flooding the bathroom and then accusing Brendan of doing it. Or tracking down old friends, like a spy, a bloody spy. I still thought it would be all right. Stupid of me, I see that now. Stupid, stupid, stupid. And don't think we don't all understand what it's about. It's not just about Brendan, it's about me. Her elder sister. She's always been jealous of me. She always wanted to destroy everything. Like she did with Mike. And now look at her. Look!" She pointed again. "Troy died. He killed himself. Our darling brother killed himself in her flat. Yesterday was his funeral. Does it stop her? No. No, it bloody does not. Because the morning after, the very next morning, she comes over here and starts snooping around. Even Troy dying doesn't stop her."

She started sobbing till her thin shoulders shook. Brendan went across to her and wrapped his arm around her waist.

"It's not about you, Kerry," he said softly. "Don't you see? When you say she's obsessed, that's probably exactly the right word. I've thought this for some time now. I blame myself for not doing anything about it. She's like a stalker. If she wasn't family, I'd be calling the police by now, asking for protection. I've read about things like this. I think there's even a name for it, though I can't remember what. She probably can't even help herself."

"No," I said. "Don't say things like that."

"Miranda," said my mother in her new, dull voice. "There are things that have to be said now. Things we've all been avoiding. I don't think I've even said them to myself, but now that Troy's dead, I can say anything. Perhaps you need professional help."

"You don't understand," I said. "No one understands." I turned to my father. "You don't think I'm obsessed, do you?"

"I don't know what I think anymore," he said. "But I know one thing."

"What?"

"You'll start off by apologizing to Brendan for the way you've behaved. Just because there's been a tragedy in this family doesn't mean that we're going to stop behaving like decent human beings."

"But I . . ."

"Whatever it is you're about to say, I don't want to hear," he said. "You apologize to

Brendan. Do you hear me? That's the least we expect."

I looked at his caved-in face. I looked at my mother's empty eyes. Then I stood up and faced Brendan. He stared at me, waiting. I clenched my fists together and dug my nails into my palms.

"I'm sorry," I said.

He bowed his head slightly, in recognition. "Mirrie, I'm sorry, too. I'm sorry for you. I pity you."

I turned away. "Can I go now?" I asked.

We all trooped downstairs together in silence. Kerry was still half sobbing. At the front door, I stopped.

"I left my bag upstairs," I said. "I'll get it and then I'll be out of your way."

I took the stairs two at a time, in spite of the pain hanging around inside my skull, and pushed open the door to Brendan and Kerry's room. I knelt down in front of the chest of drawers and pushed my hand under it, into the narrow space I'd been staring at from my position on the bed. And I pulled out the coil of green rope.

Chapter 25

Detective Inspector Rob Pryor was nice, like a normal person that you might meet in the real world. He had curly blond hair and a relaxed, almost lazy manner. He got me coffee from a machine just outside his office. He introduced me to colleagues. Vicky Reeder, the WPC who had looked after me, came over and said hello. Then Rob — he asked me to call him Rob, and I asked him to call me Miranda — took me into his office and shut the door. He showed me the view from his office. It was really just trees on the other side of the high wall that surrounded the police car park but he knew what kinds of trees they were. He seemed proud of his view, or maybe he was just being reassuring, because then he turned to me and asked how I was.

I said I was devastated, that we all were, and he nodded and said he understood.

"It's difficult to deal with," he said.

"It's funny," I said. "I thought you'd be puzzled to see me and that you'd just tell me to go away. But you're acting as if you were expecting me."

He gave a sympathetic smile.

"I wasn't," he said. "Not exactly, but it's not a complete surprise. When tragedies like this happen, people go over and over them in their head. They ask themselves if they could have done that or this to stop it. They get obsessed. They need someone to talk about it with. Sometimes they come in here and go over it with us without being exactly sure what they want. It feels so like a crime against them, they can't quite believe it isn't."

"So you think I'm using you as some kind of therapy?"

He took a sip of coffee. "You were the one who found your brother," he said. "That's a big thing to deal with."

"That's not it," I said. "I've got things to tell you."

He leaned back in his chair and looked at me warily. "What things?"

I told him my suspicions. I'd even brought the rope with me. I took it from my bag and placed it on his desk. When I'd finished, he gave a little shrug.

"As I said, these things take time to get over."

"Which means you haven't listened to what I've said."

"What have you said, Miranda?"

"I knew Troy," I said. "Better than anybody. He wasn't in the mood to kill himself."

"He was suffering from intense depression."

"He was in a good phase."

"Depression can be difficult to assess from the outside. Sometimes suicide can be the first visible symptom."

"This isn't just a feeling. There were all the other details I mentioned to you. There was the watch."

He looked at me with a questioning expression. "You're not serious about this, are you? So he forgot to put his watch on after his afternoon sleep. I do it all the time and *he* was depressed. You forget things when you're depressed."

"There's the rope."

"What do you mean, the rope?"

"I didn't have any rope. This was bought specially. Brendan said he knew nothing about it and then I found this in his luggage. As I told you, I was looking for it when I was found by my sister."

"You see, Miranda, I'm with your sister on this one. You don't want to go looking through other people's stuff without their permission. You'll get into trouble."

"I'm *in* trouble," I said. "They're all furious with me."

"What can I say?"

"It doesn't matter," I said. "The important thing is to sort this out."

"I don't understand," he said. "What is it you really believe?"

I paused. I wanted to express this calmly. "I think that, at best, Brendan encouraged Troy to kill himself. At worst he, well . . ." I couldn't say the words.

"Killed him? Is that what you're trying to say?" Rob's tone was harsher now, sarcastic. "And what? Staged it?"

"That's what I've been thinking about. I think it's worth looking into."

There was a long silence. Rob was gazing out of the window, as if something had caught his interest. When he turned back to me, I sensed a barrier between us.

"Troy took pills," I said. "He had terrible trouble sleeping. When he had taken his pills, he was out for the count."

Rob picked up a file from his desk. "Your brother had traces of barbiturate in his bloodstream."

"Exactly."

He tossed the file onto his desk again. "He was taking medication. There was nothing beyond what you'd expect. Come on,

Miranda. What would *you* do?" he said. "I mean, if you were me."

"I'd investigate Brendan," I said.

"You mean, just like that. Investigate?"

"To see what you find."

Rob looked irritably puzzled. "What is it with this guy, Brendan?" he said. "Have you got some problem with him?"

"It's a bit of a long story."

He was definitely wary now, glancing at his watch. "Miranda, I'm a bit pressed —"

"It won't take a minute," I said, and I gave him the quick version of the story of Brendan and me as the view from his window darkened behind him. It was one of those dark December days. When I finished, it was harder to make out his expression.

"So?" I said.

"You've had a tough time," he said. "Breaking up with a boyfriend."

"He wasn't exactly my boyfriend."

"And a death in the family. I'm really sorry, Miranda, but there's nothing I can do."

"What about this creep?" I said. "Doesn't he sound dangerous?"

"I don't know," Rob said. "One of the things I don't do is get involved in private disputes."

"Until a crime has been committed."

"That's right. I'm a policeman."

"Do you want more evidence? Is that it?"

"No, no," he said urgently. "Definitely not. You've done enough." He stood up, walked around his desk and put his hand on my shoulder. "Miranda. Give it some time. In a few weeks, or months, it will seem different. I promise."

"And you're not going to do anything at all?"

He patted a large pile of files on his desk. "I'm going to do a lot," he said.

Laura looked gorgeous. She'd just had her hair done at a place in Clerkenwell where you virtually have to take out a mortgage, but I had to admit it was worth it, streaked and tousled. It glowed like a beacon on this horrible gray day. It seemed to light up the bar. She looked smart as well. I'd met her straight from work and she was wearing a suit and a white shirt with a ruff down the front. I suddenly became self-conscious and looked around to see if I could catch my reflection in the window. I had an uneasy feeling that I didn't look particularly presentable. I didn't seem to have had the time for a few days. There had always been something more urgent. I'd been in a hurry to get to meet Laura, walking along Camden High

Street, and I'd been going over in my mind what I wanted to say to her, getting it right, when I passed two schoolgirls and noticed that they were giggling and one of them glanced at me. They were giggling at me. I realized I'd been thinking aloud, walking along muttering to myself, like those people you cross the street to avoid because you think you might catch their eye and they might turn scary.

In my sloppier moments, like when I was working hard, without the time ever to get ready properly, I tried to tell myself that I had a cute gamine look. I wondered if it had tipped over and I just looked like someone who had been released into the community.

I brought the bottle of wine over to the table. Now that was another issue. I was going to start keeping track of my drinking. I didn't think it was particularly excessive, but I was going to start thinking about it. Not now, though. I had other things to sort out first. As I poured the wine, Laura looked at me and with a flicker of a smile she took a packet of Marlboro Lights and a lighter from her bag.

"You've started again," I said.

"I used to love smoking so much," she said, taking a cigarette from the packet and placing it between her glossy red lips. "And then suddenly I thought: Why not? I'll give it up again when I'm old. You want one?"

She flicked the lighter and sucked the flame into the end of the cigarette and then ejected a dense cloud of smoke. I was very tempted. The smell of it brought back late nights in a fog of drink and talk and laughter and intimacy. But I shook my head. Things were bad enough already. I had to make one gesture toward healthy living, however feeble. It took an effort. Laura was breathing the smoke deep into her lungs and when she breathed it out she seemed to be savoring its taste on her tongue. I took a gulp of wine to take my mind off it.

"I'd hoped we could go for a walk," I said.

Laura looked through the window with an expression of distaste. "In this weather?"

"I wanted to breathe some cold air," I said. "Clear my head."

"You can do that on your own," Laura said. "I'm not dressed for that."

I had planned what I was going to say to Laura, so that it would seem coherent and sane, but it all came out wrong. I talked about Troy and Brendan and going to the police and it turned into a chaotic exercise in free association, hopping from one subject to another as ideas occurred to me.

By the time I was finished, Laura was on her third cigarette.

"This isn't like you, Miranda," she said.

I took a deep breath and tried not to get angry.

"I don't want you to make a judgment about my psychological state," I said. "Or at least, not yet. Just listen to what I'm saying. It adds up."

"You know what I've always admired about you, Miranda? You've always been wonderful about putting things behind you. When I had snarl-ups in my life, you were the one I'd come to and you'd give me this amazingly sensible advice."

"Now *I'm* the one that's coming to you."

"Listen to yourself," Laura said. "I'm so sorry about Troy. We all are. But listen to yourself. I know what it's like to break up with someone. I know what it's like to be dumped by someone. When Saul broke up with me, you remember what I was like. I couldn't get it out of my head. I kept going over it in my head wondering if he would still love me if I had done this thing or that thing differently. It makes me embarrassed to say it, but do you remember that I even came up with schemes to get him? Do you remember?"

"Of course I do, darling."

"You do, because I poured it all out to you. And what did you say to me?"

"It's a completely different situation."

"You told me to bite my tongue, not do anything I would regret and just let time pass and that you promised it would look different. I wanted to slap you and you were absolutely right."

"This isn't just a breakup and, as you know, *I* broke up with Brendan, but I don't want to get into that again . . ."

"For God's sake, Miranda. I've talked to Brendan. He's puzzled by all this, as much as I am."

"What?" I said. "Brendan? Have you been discussing *me* with Brendan?"

"Miranda . . ."

"You've gone over to him. That's it. I can tell. You think he's charming? A nice guy? How dare you? How dare you talk about me to him? What have you told him? Have you given away things I've said to you about him?"

"Miranda, stop this, this is me."

I stopped and looked at her. She was beautiful and slightly evasive. She took a drag on her cigarette. She was avoiding my eyes.

"You like him, don't you?"

She gave a shrug.

"He's just an ordinary, nice guy," she said. "He's concerned about you."

"That's it," I said. I rummaged in my purse and, dimly feeling I'd done all this before in a dream, found a ten-pound note and threw it down on the table. "There. I'll be in touch. Sorry. I can't say anything more. I've got to go. I can't be doing this."

And I walked out on Laura. Out on the pavement I looked around, stunned by what I had done. What did I do now? The damp cold stung me. Good. I walked and walked without knowing where I was going.

Chapter 26

There were sixteen days to go until Christmas and four days until Kerry and Brendan were to be married in the register office half a mile from my parents' house. Overnight, the weather changed. It was still cold, but it became grayer, wetter, foggier. I woke in the morning to darkness outside my windows and the sound of rain, and for several minutes I couldn't make myself get out of my warm bed. The hot-water bottle I'd made myself last night was stony cold so I pushed it onto the floor with my feet. I thought of having to scrape the ice from the van's windscreen, of hammering nails into floorboards in the empty and unheated house in Tottenham with bare, numb hands, and squirmed deeper under my duvet.

I heard the sound of mail being pushed through the letterbox and thumping onto the floorboards. In twelve days, it would be the shortest day of the year — and then they would start getting longer again. I tried to remind myself that there would be a spring on the other side of these dark months.

There was gray showing at the edges of the curtains. I forced myself out of bed, sliding my feet into my slippers and putting on my dressing gown, and collected the letters. I made a large pot of coffee, put two slices of stale whole meal bread into the toaster, turned on the radio for the company of someone else's voice. I spread honey on one slice and marmalade on the other, warmed up some milk in the microwave and poured myself a cup of coffee.

I sat at the table and opened my mail. There were nine Christmas cards, one of which was from someone I couldn't remember ever having met. He hoped we'd manage to meet up in the new year; another was from Callum, the man I'd met at the party I'd gate-crashed with Laura and Tony. It seemed ages ago, another life. I had thought then that things had got as bad as they could and would now begin to get better. I didn't know then what bad meant. I pushed away Callum's card, with the scrawled invitation to a party. I didn't think I'd be getting around to writing Christmas cards myself this year, or going to parties. There were two appeals from charities, a credit card bill, a bank statement, three catalogs. And there was an envelope with Kerry's writing on it.

I finished my cup of coffee and poured another one. I ate a triangle of toast and honey slowly. Then I slid my finger under the gummed flap and lifted out the letter inside. "Dear Miranda," I read. "Brendan and I thought it might be a good idea if you would be one of our witnesses on Friday. Please let me know as soon as possible if this is all right with you. Kerry." That was all.

I grimaced and a little corkscrew of pain wound itself around my right eye. That would be Brendan's doing. Getting me to stand beside the happy couple and sign my name by theirs. Pose for the camera. Smile at Brendan, my brother-in-law, part of my family. I felt nauseous and pushed away the toast. I managed a last sip of tepid coffee.

Perhaps I should just say no. *No, I will not be your fucking witness. No, I will not play your game. No, no, no, never again.* Perhaps I should simply stay away from the wedding altogether. They'd be better off without me anyway. But of course I had to be there because not being there would just be read as yet another hysterical gesture on my part: mad, obsessed, lovesick, hate-filled Miranda; the ghost at the feast. I had to be there because I was now Kerry's only sibling.

I sighed and stood up, tightening the belt of my dressing gown. I crossed the room to the phone and dialed.

"Hello?"

"Mum. It's me."

"Miranda." The flat tone I'd become used to since Troy's death.

"Hi. Sorry to ring so early. I really just wanted to speak to Kerry. About being a witness."

"She said she was asking you." There was a pause, then: "I think it is a very generous gesture on her part."

"Yes," I said. "Can I talk to her?"

"I'll go and call her. Before I do though . . . we thought, Derek and I, that we should have a small gathering for them before Friday. There'll be no party on the day. It doesn't seem right. Anyway, they'll be leaving almost at once for their week away. This would be just family really, to wish them well. We think it's important for them. Bill and Judy are definitely coming. Are you free tomorrow?"

It wasn't really a question.

"Yes."

"About seven. I'll get Kerry for you."

I said to Kerry that I'd be a witness and Kerry said she was glad, in a cool, polite voice. I said I'd see her tomorrow and she said "good," like a verbal shrug. I had a sudden memory, a bright shaft of sunlight shining through the dreariness, of Kerry and me swimming in the waves off the Cornish coast, both of us sitting in large rubber rings and letting ourselves be tossed onto the shore, over and over again until we were breathless with tiredness and cold, our skin tingling with the rub of the sand. We must have been about ten and eight. I remembered us laughing together, laughing at each other, squealing with gleeful fear. She used to wear her hair in neat plaits. She used to have a shy, close-lipped smile that made one small dimple appear in her cheek. She still did, I thought.

"I'm thinking of you," I said in a rush, wanting to fall to my knees and howl.

There was a silence.

"Kerry?"

"Thanks," she replied. Then, "Miranda?"

"Yes."

"Oh, nothing. See you tomorrow."

She put the phone down.

I drove to work through the fog. Houses and cars loomed up at me. People passed by like shadows. The trees were dismal specters lining the roads. It was one of those days that never get properly light and dampness clings like an icy second skin.

The house in Tottenham was quiet and cold. My footsteps echoed on the boards and the sound of hammers echoed around the room. I made too many cups of acrid instant coffee, just to be able to fold my hands around the warmth of the stained, chipped mug the owners had left behind for us. It was better to be at work, because what else would I be doing? Not Christmas shopping. Not sitting in the kitchen with my mother, watching as she pressed circles of pastry into molds and filled them with mincemeat. Not gossiping with Laura. Not giggling at one of Troy's surreal remarks. I worked until my hands were raw and then I drove home and sat in the living room under the beam. *That beam.* I wished the ceiling would be dragged down in an explosion of plaster under the weight of it, all on top of me.

I sat there for about an hour, just sitting and listening to the rain dripping outside from the branches of bare trees. Then I picked up the phone because I needed to talk to someone. I pressed the first few digits of Laura's number but stopped. I couldn't speak to her. What would I say? *Help? Please help me because I think I'm going to go completely insane?* I had always turned to Laura but now she was a closed door to me. I thought about what had happened and felt sick. I thought about the future and felt a sense of vertigo — like looking into a dark pit at my feet, not being able to see the bottom.

So at eight o'clock I went to bed, because I didn't know what else to do with myself. I lay there holding an old shirt of Troy's against my face and waited for it to be morning. I must have slept at last because I woke to a gray dawn, sleet slicing through the circles of light from the streetlamps.

At exactly seven the next day I was knocking at the door of my parents' house. Kerry answered. She was wearing a gauzy pink shirt with beads around the neck that made her face look peaky. I kissed her on her cold cheek and stepped inside.

Work had stopped on the house. The gaping hole in the kitchen wall had been crudely boarded up and there was thick polyethylene billowing over the side window. Pots and pans that had been emptied out of the old units were piled on the linoleum. The microwave was on the kitchen table. In the living room, the carpet had been taken up, and a trestle table cluttered with tools stood where the bookshelf used to be. Everything had stopped at the moment when Troy had been discovered strung up on my beam.

Bill and Judy were already there, sitting in a cluster with my parents around the fire Dad had made. But Brendan wasn't there yet.

"He's seeing somebody about an idea," said Kerry vaguely.

Looking at my depleted family together, I realized they had all become thinner. But not Brendan. When he arrived, a few minutes later, I saw he had put on weight. His cheeks were pudgier, his paunch strained at his lilac-colored shirt. His hair seemed blacker and his lips redder than ever. He met my eyes and inclined his head, with a half-smile that looked like. . . . what? Victory, perhaps, graciously acknowledged.

He was less ingratiating now. His manner was slightly aloof. There was the touch of the bully in his tone when he told Kerry he needed a stiff drink. When he mocked my father about the rather feeble fire, there was an edge of contempt in his voice. Bill glanced up at him and wrinkled his brow. He didn't say anything, though.

In other circumstances we would have been drinking champagne, but Dad brought out red wine instead, and whisky for Brendan.

"What are you going to wear tomorrow, Kerry?" I asked after a moment.

"Oh." She flushed and looked up at Brendan. "I'd planned to wear this red dress I bought."

"Sounds lovely," I said.

"I'm not sure it suits me, though." Again, that anxious glance at Brendan, who'd refilled his tumbler. "I don't know if I can carry it off."

"You can carry anything off you want to," I said. "It's your wedding day. Show me."

I put my wineglass down. The two of us filed up the stairs together, into their room. The last time I'd been there was when I'd been caught rifling through Brendan's case. I pushed the thought away and turned to Kerry. She reached into a large shopping bag, unwrapped tissue paper. My face ached. I wanted to cry. It all felt so wrong.

"It looks gorgeous. Try it on for me," I said. All my anger at Kerry had gone. I only felt helpless love for her now.

She wriggled out of her trousers, pulled her pink top over her head, unclasped her bra. She was so thin and white. Her ribs and her collarbone jutted out sharply.

"Here." I took the dress off its hanger and passed it across to her and as she reached out for it we both became aware of Brendan standing in the doorway. No one said anything. Kerry started struggling into the dress, and for a moment her head was obscured by the red folds, only her skinny naked body was visible, shining in its whiteness like a sacrifice. It felt perverse that Brendan and I should be watching her together. I turned sharply and stared out of the window, into the night.

"There," she said. "Of course, it needs high heels, and I'd pin my hair up and put makeup on."

"You look lovely," I said, although she didn't; she looked washed out; obliterated by the bold red color.

"You really think so?"

"Yes."

"Hmmm," said Brendan. He stared at her appraisingly, then a funny little smile flitted over his face. "Oh well. They're all waiting to toast us downstairs."

"I'm coming."

"Back to being friends, are you?"

It was as if his words had lit a fuse and now anger was burning up toward my center. I turned to him.

"We're sisters," I said.

We stared at each other. I wasn't going to be the first to look away. For the few moments that we gazed into each other's unblinking eyes, I felt that there was nothing left inside me except for hatred.

★ ★ ★

On Friday morning, I got up early, had a bath and washed my hair, then I went into my bedroom and stared at the clothes in my wardrobe. What do you wear to the wedding of your sister to a man you hate, that is taking place only days after your brother has died? Nothing flamboyant, nothing sexy, nothing glamorous, nothing jaunty. But you can't wear black to a wedding. I thought of Kerry's white face staring out from the red velvet. I thought of a face in a lined coffin. Eventually I pulled a lavender-colored dress out of the cupboard and held it up to the light. It had a thin knitted top and a loose chiffon skirt and was really for the summer, but if I put my nice raw silk shirt over the top it would do. I applied makeup, blow-dried my hair, put earrings into my lobes, pulled on tights and clambered carefully into the dress. I looked at myself in the mirror, grimaced at the whey-faced, hollow-eyed creature I saw there.

I pulled on my long black coat, picked up the present I'd bought them and left. We were all going to walk to the register office together from my parents' house, so I drove there through the traffic and parked a few doors down.

I half-ran through the drizzle, lifting my

dress to keep it clear of the puddles. As I lifted a fist to hammer at the door, it opened.

"Miranda," said my father.

I was startled. He was in his tatty tartan dressing gown, and unshaven. Had I got the time wrong?

"We've got to leave," I said.

"No," he said. "No. Come in."

My mother was sitting on the stairs, in a pair of baggy leggings and an old turtleneck jumper I hadn't seen her wear for years. She lifted her head when she saw me. Her face was all folds and creases.

"Have you told her?"

"What?" I said. "Told me what? What's going on?"

"He's called it off."

"What do you mean?"

"He wasn't there when Kerry woke and he phoned her at eight o'clock. He said . . ." For a moment the dull monotone of her voice cracked. She shook her head as if to clear it, then continued. "He said he'd done his best to help us all but it was no good. He said he was tired of carrying all of us and he could do no more."

I sank onto the step beneath my mother.

"Oh poor Kerry."

"He said," she went on, "that he'd found

the opportunity of happiness with someone else and he knew we'd understand that he had to take it. He had to think of himself for once."

"Someone else?" I spoke dully as if this new information had been a physical blow to my head. It felt like that. My mother looked at me suspiciously.

"Didn't you know?"

I didn't reply. I just looked at her, baffled.

"She's your friend, after all," she continued.

"No," I said. "Oh no."

"So," said my mother. "There we are."

"Laura," I said.

I went up to Kerry's bedroom. The lights were off so that the room was dim. She was sitting on the bed, very upright, still in her pajamas. I sat beside her and stroked her thin, soft hair and she turned her glassy gaze on me.

"Stupid of me," she said in a brittle voice. "I thought he loved me."

"Kerry."

"Stupid, stupid, stupid."

"Listen . . ."

"He just loved *you*."

"No."

"And then your friend."

278

"Kerry," I said. "He's not a good man. He's not. There's something wrong with him. You're better off without him and I know you'll find —"

"Don't you dare say I'll find someone better," she whispered, her eyes burning.

"All right."

"Everything's ruined," she said softly. "It was ruined already, when Troy killed himself. Brendan's just knocked over the last few stones. There's nothing left."

I thought of Brendan trampling over my family, grinding his boots over all our hopes. I put my arm around my elder sister, her bony body that smelled of sweat and powder and flowers. Her red velvet dress hung in the corner of the room. I hugged her to me and kissed the top of her head. I felt her eyelashes prickling against my skin and I felt tears on my cheek but couldn't work out if they were mine or hers.

Some things, when you look back on them, seem like a dream. But this wasn't a dream, although later I remembered it like a moment snatched out of time and haunting my memory forever.

I woke and although it was still dawn, a soft light filled the room. Climbing out of bed, I opened the curtains to a world of snow. Large flakes were still falling, floating and spinning down on the other side of the glass. I hastily pulled on warm clothes and opened the front door onto the unmarked street. Snow lay thickly on the cars, dustbin lids, low garden walls, its pristine thickness occasionally blemished by cats' paw prints, the claw marks of small birds. It weighed down the trees, and as I walked, small flurries fell at my feet with a muted thump; flakes caught in my lashes and melted on my cheek. The world was monochrome, like an old photograph, and foreshortened. There was no horizon, just the steady flicker of falling flakes. There was no sound, save for the slight creak of my shoes against the snow. Everything was muffled, mysterious, beautiful. I felt entirely alone.

It was still not fully light, and there was nobody on the heath. No footprints, and as I walked, my own were swiftly covered, too. The ponds were frozen and covered in snow;

the paths were discernible because they were a smoother white than their surroundings.

I walked up the hill and stood there for a while. What was I thinking? I don't know. I just wrapped myself in my coat, turned up the collar and watched the snow fall all about me. Soon enough, there would be crowds here — walking, throwing snowballs, building snowmen, tobogganing down the hill with squeals of pleasure. But for now it was just me. I put out my tongue and let a flake catch on it. I tipped back my head and was blinded by the falling snow.

As I made my way back down the hill, I saw there were people now, like vertical smudges on a white canvas. And then I saw a figure, walking slowly along the path that crossed mine. As I drew closer I could make out that it was a woman. She had on a thick coat, a large hat pulled down over her eyes, a scarf wrapped around the lower half of her face. Nevertheless something about her remained familiar to me. I stopped where I was, with a tightness about my heart. Perhaps she felt my eyes on her, for she stopped, too, and looked up. She turned her head toward me and then she took off her hat and put a hand to her eyes, to see better. Flakes fell onto her dark hair. For a few moments, she didn't move, and neither did I.

I wanted to call out her name: Laura! Laura! *I wanted to cover the distance between us so I could see her face properly. And she, too, seemed to be drawn toward me. She took an uncertain half step, her hat still dangling from her mittened hand. But she halted and still I didn't move.*

Then Laura put on her hat and once more she started walking along the path, away from me. I watched her as she became a shadowy figure. I watched until, like a lonely ghost, she faded into white.

★ ★ ★

Somehow, days passed. Weeks passed. Whatever you do, time always goes by. Then something happened.

I was dreaming that I was falling, falling through the air, and then I woke with a start that made my heart pound. The phone was ringing. I stretched out my hand instinctively, though I was still stupid with sleep. I half noticed, as I fumbled with the receiver, that it was dark outside.

I mumbled into the receiver and someone started singing into my ear. For a moment, I thought this was part of my dream, a dream within a dream. Then the words resolved. "Happy birthday to you, happy birthday to you . . ."

I sat up in bed and clutched the phone. Behind the relentlessly cheery tune there was another noise: a rabble of voices, music and loud laughter.

"Happy birthday, dearest Miranda . . ."

"Don't," I mumbled.

"Happy birthday to you!"

I twisted my head around to see the green glow of the numbers on the clock. 12:01 clicked into 12:02.

"I wanted to be the first to say it. You didn't think I'd forget, did you? I could never forget."

"I don't want —"

"March the eighth. Did you know that was International Women's Day?"

"I'm going to put the phone down now, Brendan."

"You're always in my thoughts. Not an hour goes by. And I'm always in your thoughts, aren't I?"

"You're drunk."

"Just merry. And on my own now."

"But Laura . . . ?"

"On my own and thinking of you. Just thinking of you."

"Fuck off," I said.

I put the phone down, but not in time to miss him saying, "Sleep well, Miranda. Sweet dreams."

Chapter 27

Unbelievably, unforgivably, I arrived late at the church. I had a fistful of excuses. I'd been thinking what on earth I should wear, and whether it mattered, and suddenly I realized I'd been sitting on the edge of my bed staring at the wall for forty-five minutes and I didn't know what I'd been thinking about. The church was down in New Malden, where Laura's parents lived, and it turned out to be much farther than I thought, involving changes of train. And then I was in such a panic that I ran out of the station and took a wrong turn and found myself running along the edge of a golf course, unbelievably, with men in bright sweaters pulling their long leather bags on this bright spring morning.

There were two different doors to the church, both closed. I could hear people singing a familiar hymn inside, one I'd sung in school assemblies. I didn't know which door to take. I took the smaller entrance, down the side. I was worried I'd come out in some prominent place where I'd be stared at. I pushed at the door but there was some resistance. As it opened, I realized that the small church was full and people were standing in front of the door. A bearded man in a dark trench coat moved along to allow me inside. I thought of the crowded underground train I'd come on. Move along inside, please.

I was halfway down the nave, stuck by the wall behind a pillar with a severely restricted view of proceedings. The hymn finished and someone I couldn't see started to speak. I looked around for familiar faces. It was a collection of strangers and I wondered for a horrible second if I had blundered into the wrong church but then I saw someone who used to be at college with Laura and me. She caught my eye and I realized I couldn't remember her name. Someone to avoid afterward. At the back I saw Tony, gaunt, harrowed, but weirdly embarrassed as well, as if he had sneaked in without paying. I hadn't been concentrating on the speech and now I made myself listen. It was like a radio slowly coming on. I found it hard to follow the sense at first. I just picked out phrases: "happy young woman," "first flush of youth," "spring morning." They seemed nonsensical to me. From the artificial tone, I assumed this must be a vicar who didn't really know Laura, who had only heard about her. "Sometimes we want to ask God questions," said the voice. "We want to ask why bad things happen to good people. Why innocent children suffer. And now, why this beautiful, sunny young woman should die, so cruelly, so unfortunately, so unnecessarily. An accident of this kind would be horrible at any time, but for a woman like Laura, newly married, it is almost too much to bear."

Through the fog of confusion and misery, I felt a steely jab. "Newly married." I hadn't known that. So they had got married. Laura had got married.

"And so," the vicar continued, "our thoughts and our prayers must be with, not just Laura's parents, Jim and Betty, but with Brendan, her new husband."

I could see them now. I leaned across and saw the front row of pews. I could only see them from the back. A gray-haired woman leaning forward, a gray-haired man with his arm around her, and on her other side, sitting upright, facing forward, Brendan. I couldn't see his face but I could picture his expression. He would be the best mourner in the church. The world champion mourner. He would look sad but thoughtful. When the vicar mentioned his name, Brendan would have given him a glance, pursed his lips and given a modest nod of acknowledgment. I saw him turn slightly to Laura's mother. Exactly. In the midst of his suffering he would be helping others. What a star.

There was another hymn and then an uncle read a poem and the vicar said that the family would go out with the coffin and the other mourners should gather at the family's house. It was a short walk. There was a map on the order of service. I didn't have one. I would have to follow the crowd. It was all rather like a school assembly, what with the hymns and the announcements and having to leave in a particular order. When the coffin was carried past me, I hardly connected it with Laura at all. I just thought about how heavy it must be and how they chose the men to carry it. I wondered if they were all relatives and friends or employees of the undertakers. Laura had been my best friend but I had never met her parents. She had fallen out with them very badly about something to do with a boyfriend when she was in her last year at school. So when they followed the coffin out, it was the first time I had ever seen their faces. The funny thing was that Laura's mother, round-faced and fleshy, didn't look like her daughter. Laura had been the image of her father. She had been a beautiful woman and he was handsome. His face was gaunt, with prominent cheekbones. He looked ill at ease in his dark suit. Maybe he had borrowed it from someone.

Behind them was Brendan. He almost made me gasp, he looked so handsome. Everything about him was right. He was holding his hands together in front of him, slightly clenched, as if he were in pain but trying not to show it. His black suit was beautifully brushed, without even a hair or a speck of dust on it. He had a white shirt and a rather gorgeous crimson tie with a large knot. His hair was tousled, which clashed slightly with the care and precision of his dress, but that was appropriate, too, as a signal of his grief and his passion, a note of elegant disarray. His face was very pale, his dark eyes were fixed in front of him, so he didn't see me.

The parade passed by and out through the door. There was some awkward shuffling and murmuring while we waited to be sure that the family members were gone and safely away. Last in, I was one of the first out, blinking in the sunshine. My eyes were dazzled and I realized that I was crying. In the church it had all been too intense but outside I saw the acres of graves. For some reason the obvious thought that they had all been people once and that they were gone and that my friend Laura had now gone with them — it just made me cry. Crying again. My eyes were getting used to this. I felt a touch on my shoulder.

"Miranda?"

I turned to discover that it was the woman whose name I'd forgotten. Laura had shared a house with her in her first year at college. Lucy. Sally. Paula.

"Hello," I said.

She came forward and gave me the warmest of hugs. Kate. Susan. It was something quite common. Tina. Jackie. Jane.

"It's so good to see a friendly face," she said. "It's so long since I've seen Laura. I thought I wouldn't know anybody."

Lizzie. Frances. Cathy. Jean. Alice. No. I couldn't manage much more than a shrug.

"Isn't it unbelievably sad?" she said. "I just can't believe it."

"I know," I said. I should have asked her name straight away and apologized. It was too late now. Julia. Sarah. Jan. Maybe someone else would come up and address her by name. As long as I didn't have to introduce her to anyone.

"Are you coming along to the house?" she said.

"I don't know," I said.

"You must come," she said. "Just for a bit, at least. I want to talk to you."

"All right," I said, and we set off. She had a card with the instructions written on it. I had a moment of inspiration. I asked her if I could have a look at the instructions and she handed me the card. I turned it over. Written in pen in the corner was the name "Sian." Of course. How could I possibly have forgotten that? What a relief. Finally something in my life had gone right.

"It's funny," she said. "This is the first time I've ever been to the funeral of anyone my own age."

"Yes, Sian," I said, just to show her that I knew her name. "It's strange."

I didn't say anything about Troy. His death seemed something too precious to be brought out and bandied around in conversation as something interesting to talk about with someone I hardly knew and would probably never meet again. Sian talked about Laura and how they hadn't met for over a year and how she had heard about her marriage from mutual friends. They had just got married at the register office without telling anyone.

"She married someone I've never heard of," Sian said. "It must have been so sudden."

I didn't want to say anything but I knew that if I didn't, it was an absolute certainty that someone would come up to us and start talking about Brendan and me and it would make me look ridiculous again.

"I knew him," I said. "It was pretty sudden."

"He must have been the one walking behind the coffin."

"That's right."

"He was very good-looking," said Sian. "I can see why she might have fallen for him."

"I'll introduce you," I said.

Sian looked embarrassed.

"I didn't mean . . ." she started and then stopped. She seemed unable to say what it was she didn't mean.

The house was crowded. It was a big gathering, though I couldn't see Tony anywhere, the one person I wanted to see and to hug. There was a table with sandwiches, boiled eggs, dips, chopped vegetables, crisps. There was tea, coffee, juice. I thought of Laura's mother superintending the preparations. She wasn't invited to the wedding, but here she was, just a few weeks later, organizing the funeral. I looked around for someone I knew. I saw no sign of Tony. I assumed he must have slipped away after the ceremony. Laura's parents were leading a very old woman across the living room into a corner and helping her into an armchair. I thought of offering my condolences and then thought how could I possibly without getting myself lost in horrendous explanations and then told myself I ought to talk to them anyway. This argument with myself was still going on when I became aware of someone's presence beside me. I looked around. The face I saw was so unexpected that for a moment I had trouble placing him. It was the detective, Rob Pryor.

"What on earth are you doing here?" I asked.

He didn't answer, just handed me a cup of tea.

"I'd sort of hoped for something stronger," I said.

"There isn't anything stronger."

"All right."

"I know what you're going to say," he said.

I took a gulp of tea. It was scaldingly hot and it burned my mouth as I swallowed it.

"What am I going to say?"

"I thought you'd be here," he said. "I thought it was important that I head you off."

"I don't know what you're talking about."

"I've looked into this," Rob said. "Laura's death is terribly sad. But that's all."

"Oh, for fuck's sake, Rob," I said. "Do you mind if I call you Rob?"

"Go ahead," he said.

"Come off it," I said. "Don't insult my intelligence."

"I know what you mean," he said. "I thought of you as soon as I heard. I made calls. I talked to the investigating officer."

"Forget all that," I said. "Just think about it. I come to you with my suspicions about Troy. You pooh-pooh them. Fine. Then Brendan dumps my sister for my best friend and runs off with her. A few months later she's dead. Do you see a pattern here?"

Rob sighed. "I'm sorry," he said. "I'm not very interested in patterns. Facts are stubborn things. Laura died by accident."

"How many twenty-five-year-olds drown in the bath?" I asked.

"She'd been at a party," Rob said. "She was clearly intoxicated. She had some sort of altercation with Mr. Block. She left early. She returned to their flat alone. She ran herself a bath. She slipped and struck her head while the bath was running. She drowned. The bath overflowed and at just before twenty past midnight, Thomas Croft, who lived in the flat beneath, became aware of

294

water coming through the ceiling, ran up, found the front door of the flat unlocked and discovered Mrs. Block dead in the bath."

I hated to hear him call Laura Mrs. Block. It was another way that Brendan had got his clammy hands into somebody's life. I looked around to make sure nobody could overhear us. "That's exactly what he did when he and Kerry were living in my flat."

"What?"

"He deliberately let the bath overflow. It's a message."

"A message?"

"To me."

Rob Pryor looked at me almost with an expression of pity. "Mrs. Block's death was a message to *you?*" he said. "Are you insane?"

"It's easy to bang someone over the head," I said. "Hold them under the water."

"That's true," said Rob.

"And it wasn't a dinner party, was it?" I said. "There must have been lots of people around. In the house. In the garden. Were people keeping track of Brendan every minute?"

Rob gave an impatient frown.

"It's a twenty-minute walk from the party at Seldon Avenue back to their flat. Maybe twenty-five. Anybody who left the party to kill her would have been away for about an hour."

"They could have caught a cab," I said, a bit feebly.

"I thought your theory depended on nobody noticing," said Rob. "Your murderer calls a cab, it arrives at the party with nobody noticing. And what? Did he ask the cabbie to wait while he went inside and committed the murder?"

"He could have followed her back. Nobody noticed she was away."

"Oh, I forgot," said Rob, and at that very moment I felt hands on my shoulders. I looked around and a face leaned into mine, kissing me on both cheeks, hugging me too close. It was Brendan.

"Oh, Miranda, Miranda, Miranda," he murmured in my ear. "What a terrible thing. It's so good of you to come. It means a lot to me. It would have meant a lot to Laura." He looked over at Rob Pryor. "Rob has been a good friend to me, ever since the business with Troy." He looked back at me. "I'm sorry, Mirrie. I'm so sorry. I seem to bring bad luck wherever I go."

I didn't reply. I couldn't.

"I needed to talk to you, Mirrie." He smiled at me, looking me in the eyes. I always felt he was just a bit too close, his breath warm on my cheeks. "You're the one who understands me. Better than anyone else. There's something strange. Has Rob told you?" He looked over at Rob, who shook his head. "Almost at the moment when it — you know, the thing with Laura, I can't bear to say it — do you know what I was doing?"

"Of course I don't," I said.

"You do," he said. "I was talking to you."

Dearest Troy,

There's this memory that keeps coming back to me. When you were about nine you insisted on waking me up at four in the morning to listen to the dawn chorus. I staggered blearily out into the garden in my dressing gown even though it was freezing cold and the grass was soaking wet. I thought I'd just stay out there for a few minutes to humor you and then race back to my warm bed. But you were all dressed up in jeans and Wellington boots and a big jacket and you had Dad's binoculars hanging around your neck. We stood at the end of the garden in the dawn and all of a sudden — as if a switch had been thrown — the birds started to sing. A great wall of sound all round us. I looked at your face and it was so incredibly joyful that I forgot to feel cold. You showed me the birds in the branches and then I could match the sounds with the open beaks and pulsing throats. We stayed out there for ages and then we went into the kitchen and I made us hot chocolate and scrambled eggs. You said, with your mouth full: "I wish it could be like this all the time."

Of course you can't read this but I'm writing to you anyway because you're the only person I really want to talk to. I talk to you all the time. I'm terrified that one day I'll find that I've stopped talking to you, because that will mean you're dead.

Chapter 28

"I don't really know why I'm here," I said.

The woman opposite me didn't answer, just looked at me until I glanced away, down at my hands screwed together in my lap, at the low table between us where a box of tissues stood ready. Out the window I could see daffodils in the sunshine. The yellow color looked garish and excessive. I felt blank and dull and stiffly self-conscious. At least I wasn't lying on a couch.

"Where should I begin?"

At least she didn't say "Begin at the beginning." Katherine Dowling must have been in her late forties or early fifties; her lined, handsome face was without makeup, she had steady brown eyes, strong cheekbones, a firm jaw. Her hair was flecked with gray and she wore quiet clothes — a skirt down past her knees, old and wrinkled suede boots, a baggy, soft gray cardigan. She was focused on me, or trying to see into me, and I didn't know if I liked it. I shifted in my chair, unfolded my hands, scratched my cheek, gave a polite, irrelevant cough. I glanced at my watch — Troy's watch — on my wrist. I had forty-three minutes left.

"Tell me what brought you here."

"I've got no one else to talk to," I said and noticed the unsteadiness in my voice. I welcomed it — I wanted grief to overwhelm me, to pour uncontrollably out of me, the way it did sometimes at night when I would wake in the small hours and feel my pillow was wet with weeping. "The people I want to talk to are gone."

"Gone?"

"Dead." I felt my throat begin to ache and my sinuses thicken. "My little brother and my best friend." I made myself say their names aloud. "Troy and Laura. He killed himself, or that's what everyone says, though I think, I think — well, never mind that . . . I found him, in my flat. He hanged himself. He was just a boy really. He still hadn't stopped growing. If I close my eyes I can see his face. Except sometimes when I try to remember him, I can't. Laura died just a few weeks ago. She died in her bath. She was drunk and she knocked her head and drowned. Isn't that a stupid way to die? She was only my age. The last time I saw her we didn't speak. I keep thinking if I'd said something to her, if I'd done things differently, this wouldn't have happened. I know that probably sounds stupid to you but it's what keeps coming back to me."

Katherine Dowling leaned toward me very slightly in her chair. A lock of hair fell forward and she pushed it behind her ear without taking her eyes off me.

"I can't believe that I'll never be with them again," I said. I took the first tissue out of the box. "Of course, I know I won't, but I can't believe it. I can't," I repeated hopelessly. "It seems impossible."

I took another tissue and wiped my eyes.

"Bereavement," began Katherine Dowling, "is something that everyone experiences in —"

"This is his watch," I said, holding up my wrist. "He left it by my bed and now I wear it and every time I look at it I think, this is the time he doesn't have anymore. All those seconds and minutes and hours, ticking away. I always thought we'd grow old together. I thought I could help him. I should have helped him, my lovely little brother."

I was weeping in earnest now and my voice was coming out in hiccups.

"Sorry," I said. "Sorry, but it seems so unfair."

"Unfair on you?"

"No. *No!* I'm not dead, am I? I'm one of the lucky ones. Unfair on them, I mean."

I talked and my words came out in a jumble of memories and feelings, everything mixed up together. Troy, Brendan, Laura, Kerry, my parents, Nick. A body dangling from a beam, phone calls in the night, words whispered into my ear like poison trickling into me, weddings called off, funerals, first his and then hers. . . . Every so often I stopped and cried into the damp wad of tissues I clutched in my hand. My cheeks stung, my nose was snotty and my eyes were sore.

"I'm like Typhoid Mary," I said at one point. "I'm like one of those Spanish soldiers bringing plagues to the American Indians, poisoning their world. I'm like —"

"What do you mean, Miranda?" Katherine Dowling's calm voice broke into my tirade.

"I'm the carrier," I cried out, blotting my face. "Don't you see? They were all right, more or less. I brought him into my world, and that's my problem and I had to deal with that. But it was their world as well and he's infected them, destroyed them, wrecked their lives. I'm all right. Look. Here I am, sitting with a therapist working out ways to feel better about everything. You see, that's the problem."

"Listen," she said. "Listen to me now, Miranda."

"No," I said. "Wait. I've got to get this straight, for myself as much as anybody. It's like this: there are awful things in the world, right? I feel terrible about them. Your job as a therapist is to stop me feeling bad about it. But maybe what I should really do is deal with the awful things in the world."

"No," she said.

"There's something narcissistic about this, if that's the right word. I mean, if people came to you and were suffering from depression because of the poverty and suffering and injustice in the world and you had a pill to make them stop worrying about it, would you give it to them? Would you, as a professional, dole out this pill that would make people indifferent to what is wrong in the world rather than go out and make it better?"

There was quite a long pause. Katherine Dowling was probably starting to regret what she'd let herself in for. I blew my nose and sat up straighter in my chair. Outside the window, the sky was a lovely pale blue.

"This." She pointed at me. "This is called grief. Do you hear me?"

"He even made me into his fucking alibi," I muttered. "God, he must have laughed!"

304

"Listen!" she said, and I subsided again. "People come to me and often what I do is help them find patterns, make shapes out of chaos, make stories of their lives so that they can understand them. But here I am going to say something quite the opposite to you. You are making a pattern that isn't there. You are trying to find a meaning, an explanation, tie everything up neatly, take responsibility, place blame. In the past few months, you have lost two people whom you loved a great deal. And you have been through a painful and disturbing episode with a man. This Brendan. Because these things have happened together, you connect them, like cause and effect. Do you understand?"

"I *do* connect them," I said.

"Now, we can talk about what happened with Brendan; in fact, I think that might be helpful. We can talk about your bereavement, and why you feel such guilt. But we will be looking at *you* — at what is going on inside you after these traumas. We will not be looking at why these two young people had to die one after the other. They died. Now you must mourn." Her voice grew gentler. "You must let yourself mourn. Not cast around for explanations."

"But if . . ."

"It takes time," she said. "There's no easy way."

I made myself consider what she had said.

"Sometimes I have felt that I was going mad," I said at last. I felt like a rag doll lolling on the chair. "I used to have this life that I understood. Things made sense. I could work out what was going to happen next and make plans. I feel I've lost control. Anything could happen. Everything seems hostile and out of kilter. It's like a nightmare but I can't wake up out of it. It just goes on and on."

"Well, we can talk about that, too," she said. "We should. Would you like to come again, Miranda?"

I nodded. "Yes," I said. "I think I would."

"Good. This time next week would suit me if that's all right with you. Now, as your brother's watch will show you, it's time for you to go."

Before I had time to find excuses, I changed into my running clothes and stepped out into the spring afternoon once more. I ran to the heath. I ran up the hill where I had last glimpsed Laura but I didn't stop. I ran until my legs ached and my lungs hurt and I had a stitch in my side.

When I got home I had a shower and

made myself a bowl of pasta with olive oil, chopped spring onions and Parmesan cheese over the top. I ate it and stared around me. Everything was drab and neglected. I'd been stumbling through my life, coming back here just to sit staring out of the window, then crawl into bed at nine o'clock and sleep for hours and hours. I'd been sleeping for ten or eleven hours every night, sometimes even more, and still I woke in a fog of dreary, heavy-eyed, leaden-limbed fatigue.

I thought of Katherine Dowling pointing her finger at me. "This is grief." I'd let myself become clogged up by grief, sodden and hopeless with it.

I stood up and put my bowl in the sink. Then I filled a bucket with hot sudsy water and started to wash the windows, to let in the light.

Chapter 29

The next morning I woke early, and knew before I even opened my eyes that it was a warm and lovely day outside. The strip of sky between the curtains was blue. There was a warmth in the room. And, for the first time in a long while, I didn't feel clogged with tiredness but alert, as if there was something that I had to do. Although it was a Saturday and I didn't have to go to work, I got up at once.

I stripped my bed and put the sheets in the washing machine, then put on my running clothes. I went to the heath again, but this time ran to the wilder part, where the trees are thick and you can even fool yourself that you're not in the city with millions of people around you in every direction. The sun, still low and pale, shone steadily. There were primroses and tulips among the tangle of bushes, fresh, unfurling leaves on the branches above me. I ran as hard as I could, until my legs ached and, as soon as I stopped, sweat trickled down my forehead. I felt as though I was cleaning out the inside of my body, making the blood run faster, the heart pump stronger, opening out my pores.

Nearing home, I stopped at the baker's and bought a loaf of whole meal bread that was still warm. I had a quick, hot shower, washed my hair vigorously and pulled on a denim skirt and a shirt. I put on Troy's watch, but for once the sight of it didn't make my eyes well up with tears. I made a cup of peppermint tea and tore a hunk of bread from the loaf, eating it just as it was, chewing slowly and letting the doughy texture comfort me. I vacuumed the carpets, plumped up the pillows on the sofa, piled old newspapers and magazines into a box and opened the windows to let in the bright day.

Before I could change my mind, I pulled on a jacket and walked to the underground.

Kerry was already behind her desk when I walked in. Someone was sitting across from her, leafing through brochures and pointing things out, so she didn't see me immediately, and when she did her face flickered through various emotions: surprise, discomfort, pain, welcome. It smoothed out again into politeness as she turned back to the woman.

I watched her as she leaned across the desk, pointing at pictures with a finger whose nail was a delicate pink. She looked much better than I'd been expecting. I'd grown used to seeing her pinched and blotchy. Now she looked rosy and plumper. She was growing her hair again, and it fell in blond waves around her smooth, pale face.

"Fancy a cup of coffee?" I said, when the woman left, clutching a pile of brochures, and I eased myself into her seat. I smelled Kerry's perfume, something subtle and sweet. Her skin was satiny, her lips glossy, and she had tiny gold studs in her ears. Everything about her seemed considered, delicate, well cared for. I looked down at my hands on the desk, with their dirty, bitten nails. I saw the cuffs of my shirt were slightly frayed.

Kerry hesitated, looked at her watch. "I don't know if I can."

"Go on," called a woman at the next desk. "We'll be busy soon and then you won't have the time."

She looked at me and gave a nod.

"I'll get my coat."

We didn't talk until we got to the café down the road. We took our coffee downstairs, where they had a sofa and armchairs, and looked uncertainly at each other over the rims of our steaming mugs. I said something about the new flat she was renting, and she said something about being frantic at work. We lapsed into an awkward silence.

"Sorry I haven't been in touch," I said eventually.

"You've been busy."

I waved away the polite words. "That's not the reason."

"No, I suppose not."

"I didn't know where to begin."

"Miranda . . ."

"You said something to me — just after he, you know . . . just after Brendan walked out. You said everything was ruined and he'd just kicked over the last standing stones. Something like that."

"I don't remember." She put her mug down on the table. There was the faint red semicircle from her lips on its edge.

"Of course not. Why would you? I don't know why it stuck in my mind, but it did, maybe because of my job — that image of him razing everything to the ground until we were all just standing in the rubble of our lives. That's what he did to us."

"You shouldn't think about him so much, Miranda," she said. "You should let him go."

"What?" I stared at her.

311

"I have," she said. "He's out of my life. I never want to think about him again."

I was startled by what she had said.

"But everything that happened . . ." I said, stammering. "With you and me. The whole family. With Troy."

"That's got nothing to do with it."

"And Laura."

"Do you think I didn't care about Laura?"

"Of course not."

"Do you think I felt a little stab of pleasure when I heard? That some sort of revenge had been taken?"

"No," I said. "Of course not."

"Well I did. Just for a moment. I hated Laura so much and I'd wanted something bad to happen to her and then the worst possible thing did happen and I felt some kind of triumph for a second and then I felt terrible, as if I were responsible for it in some way." She had looked fierce for a moment but then her expression turned sad again. "In the end I just felt, well, what has any of it got to do with me? I decided we've just got to put it behind us."

"Don't you want to talk about it at all?" I asked.

"I want to get on with my life."

"Don't you want to think about it? To understand what happened?"

"To understand?" She blinked at me. "Our brother killed himself. My fiancé left me."

"But . . ."

"I'm not saying it wasn't terrible. I'm saying that it was quite simple. I don't know what there is to talk about."

I sat for a few moments. All the turbulence, the waves of emotions and hatred and despair that had battered our family, was now a calm dark pool.

"What about us?" I asked at last.

"Us?"

"Us, you and me, the two sisters."

"What about us?"

"You hated me."

"I didn't," she said.

"You blamed me."

"A bit, maybe." She picked up her mug and drained the last of the coffee. "That's in the past. Are you all right? You look a bit . . ." She left the sentence dangling.

"I've been a bit down."

"Of course."

I couldn't just leave our conversation there.

"Oh Kerry — I wanted to make it all right between us," I said. Then, realizing I sounded like a two-year-old asking to be kissed better, I added, "I thought there were some things that ought to be said. Made clear."

"I'm quite clear about everything."

"I hope you know now that I was never in love with Brendan. Never. I left him and . . ."

"Please Miranda," she said in a disgusted tone. "Let's leave that."

"No, listen, I just want you to understand that I was never trying to wreck things between you two, never. I wanted you to be happy, really I did. He was the one who was . . ." I trailed away, realizing what I sounded like. "Like you said, it doesn't matter anymore. That's all finished with. He's out of both of our lives. I wanted to know if you're all right, that's all really. And that we were all right. It would be terrible if we allowed him to alienate us from each other."

"I know," she said in a small voice. Then she leaned forward and for the first time her face lost its smoothness. "I should tell you something."

"What?"

"It feels almost wrong. After Troy and — you know, I thought I'd never be happy again. And it's all happened so suddenly." She blushed. "I've met someone."

"You mean . . ."

"A nice man," she said. "He's quite a bit older than I am, and he really seems to care for me."

I put my hand over hers. "I'm very, very glad," I said warmly. Then, "No one I used to know, I hope?"

The stupid attempt at a joke fell flat. "No. He's a hospital manager. His name's Laurence. You must meet him sometime."

"Great."

"He knows about everything . . ."

"Of course."

"And he's very different, from, you know . . ."

"Yes. Good. Great."

"Mum and Dad say they like him."

"Good," I said again hopelessly. "Really good. I'm so happy for you."

"Thank you."

I bought a big bunch of tulips and daffodils and irises and got on a bus that stopped a few hundred yards from my parents'. The scaffolding had finally gone from the outside of the house, and the front door had been painted a glossy dark blue. I knocked and listened; I knew they'd be there. They never seemed to go anywhere these days. They worked, and then my mother sat in the house watching television and my father

315

spent hours in the garden, plucking weeds from borders and nailing bird boxes to the fruit trees at the end.

There was no reply. I walked around to the back and pressed my nose against the kitchen window. Inside everything gleamed new and unfamiliar: stainless steel surfaces, white walls, spotlights on the ceiling. Dad's favorite mug stood on the table, beside it a plate with orange rind on it and a folded newspaper. I could imagine him methodically peeling the orange and dividing it into segments and eating them slowly, one by one between sips of coffee, frowning over the paper. Everything the same, and everything changed utterly.

I still had the key to the house so I fished it out and opened the back door. In the kitchen I found a vase and filled it up with water and crammed the flowers in. There were a couple of segments of orange left on the plate on the table, and I ate them absent-mindedly, gazing out at the garden that just a few months ago had been a mess of potholes and discarded kitchen units, and now was neatly tended and planted out. I heard footsteps on the stairs.

"Hello?" It was my mother's voice. "Who's there?" she said from the hallway. "Who is it?"

"Mum? It's me."

"Miranda?"

My mother was in her dressing gown. Her hair was greasy and her face was puffy with sleep.

"Are you ill?" I asked.

"Ill?" She rubbed at her face. "No. Just a bit tired. Derek went out to get some garden twine and I thought I'd have a nap before lunch."

"I didn't mean to wake you."

"It doesn't matter."

"I brought you some flowers."

"Thank you." She glanced at them without taking proper notice.

"Shall I make us some tea or coffee?"

"That'd be nice." She sat down on the edge of one of the chairs.

"Which?"

"What?"

"Tea or coffee?"

"Whichever you'd prefer. I don't mind."

"Coffee," I said. "And then we could go for a walk."

"I can't, Miranda. I've got, well, things to do."

"Mum . . ."

"It hurts," she said. "The only time it doesn't hurt is when I'm asleep."

I picked up one of her hands and held it

against my face. "I'd do anything . . ." I said. "Anything to make it better."

She shrugged. The kettle shrieked behind us.

"It's too late for anything," she said.

"I loved her," said Tony. He was on his third beer and his words were slurring together. Everything about him seemed to have slipped a bit — his cheeks were slack and stubbly, his hair was slightly greasy and fell over his collar, his shirt had a coffee stain down the front, his nails needed cutting. "I loved her," he repeated.

"I know."

"What did I do wrong?"

"That's not the way to look at it," I said weakly.

"I wasn't good at saying it but she knew I did."

"I think . . ." I began.

"And then" — he lifted up his beer and drained it — "then when she ran off like that, just a note on the table, I wanted her dead and she died."

"That's not connected, except in your mind."

"Your fucking Brendan. Charming her. Promising her things."

"Promising her what?"

318

"You know — whirlwind romance, marriage, babies. All the things we used to argue about in the last few months."

"Ah," I said.

"I would have agreed in the end though. She should have known that."

I sipped my wine and said nothing. I thought of Laura, laughing, her head tipped back and her mouth open and her white teeth gleaming and her dark eyes shining with life.

"Now she's dead."

"Yes."

On Sunday, I ran again. Seven miles through drizzling mist. I had coffee with Carla, who'd also known Laura and wanted us to spend the hour exclaiming with a kind of scarifying relish over how awful it all was.

I worked on the company accounts. I was restless and agitated. I didn't know what to do with my spare time. I didn't want to see anyone, but I didn't want to be on my own. I sorted through old correspondence. I threw out clothes that I hadn't worn for over a year. I went through all my e-mails and deleted the ones I didn't want to keep.

At last I rang up Bill on his mobile and said I'd like to talk to him. He didn't ask me if it could wait till tomorrow, simply said he was in Twickenham but would be back by six. We arranged to meet in a bar near Kings Cross that used to be a real dive but was now minimalist and chic, and sold cocktails, iced teas and lattes.

I had another bath and changed out of my sloppy drawstring trousers into jeans and a white, button-down shirt. I was there fifteen minutes early. When he arrived, he kissed me on the top of my head and slid into the seat opposite. He ordered a spicy tomato juice and I had a Bloody Mary, to give me courage. We clinked glasses, and I started asking him how his weekend had been. He held up a finger.

"What's this about, Miranda?"

"I want to stop working for you," I said.

Reflectively, he took a sip of his drink and put it back on the table. "That sounds like a good idea," he said.

"What!" He just smiled at me in such a kind and tender way that I had to blink back tears. "Here I was plucking up the courage to tell you and all you can say is 'That sounds like a good idea.' "

"It does."

"Aren't you going to beg me to stay?"

"You need to start over."

"That's what I've been thinking."

"Away from the whole family thing."

"You're not like family."

"Thanks."

"I meant that in a good way."

"I know."

"I feel like my life's one great big enormous ghastly mess and I need to scramble free of it."

"What are you going to do?"

"I guess I'll try and get a job with an interior decorating company, something like that. I've got enough contacts by now. Shall I give you three months' notice, or what? And will you be my reference?"

" 'I've known Miranda Cotton since she was one day old . . .' Stuff like that?"

"Something like." I swallowed and fiddled with my drink.

"Don't go all sentimental on me, Miranda. We're still going to see each other. It's not as if you were leaving town."

"I thought I might."

"What? Move out of London?"

"Maybe."

"Oh." He raised his glass. "Good luck to you. I've always been a believer in burning one's bridges."

"I know. Bill?"

"Yes."

"I never was in love with Brendan. It wasn't the way people thought."

Bill gave a shrug. "I never thought much of him. The way he would always squeeze my arm when he was talking to me and use my name three times in a sentence."

"Do you believe me then?"

"On the whole," he said with a half smile. "More or less."

"Thanks." My eyes burned with tears again. I felt floppy with gratitude. "I think I'll have another Bloody Mary."

"Well, I'm going home. Drink all you like but we start on the new house at eight."

"I'll be there, eight sharp."

He stood up and kissed the top of my head once more.

"Take care."

Chapter 30

I did it. I made myself do it and I did it. I put my flat on the market. I was sleepwalking through it, not thinking. I just didn't care, and so it went more smoothly than anything I've ever done in my life. A young man with a clipboard came and looked around and raved about how sellable it was. He said their commission rate was 3 percent. I said two and there was just a beat of hesitation and he said all right. The very next morning, a woman came to see it. She reminded me of me, except a bit richer, a bit more grown-up. She had a real job; she was a doctor. I saw the flat through her eyes. So much had been moved out that it had a minimalist look to it that made the space seem brightly lit, larger than it really was.

She said that the flat had a good feel to it. She smiled and said it must have good feng shui. I took a deep breath and said yes and thought about Troy hanging from the beam. Half an hour later the estate agent phoned saying that Rebecca Hanes had offered ten thousand less than the asking price. I said no. He said the market was looking a bit soft at the moment. I said it didn't matter. He rang back ten minutes later and said she had offered the full amount, but she wanted to move in straight away. I said I didn't want to be hurried. I would move in a month. He said he thought that might be a problem but he rang back after a few minutes and said that would be fine. As I put the phone down, I caught sight of my reflection in the mirror and I wondered: Is that the secret of doing deals? Is that the secret of life? If you care less than the other person, then you win. Was that me?

I was pretty far along in the process of jettisoning my own life, but I had done nothing about getting myself a new one. I took my old school atlas off the shelf and opened it at "England and Wales, South." Suddenly I realized that I had an existential freedom about my life. I had no particular family connection with anywhere outside London. I wasn't constrained. I was equally indifferent to everywhere. Should I draw a line an inch around London? Two inches? Three inches? Would I like to live beside the sea? And, if so, which sea? Village or town? Or open countryside? Or island? Thatched cottage? Houseboat? Martello tower? Decommissioned lighthouse? My freedom was like an abyss in front of my feet. It was almost awesome. It was also the wrong way around. I needed to think about work. What I needed to do was to find a job or jobs. I needed to make some calls, but there wasn't immediate pressure now. I'd bought myself a month by being horrible to a nice woman.

I made a resolution. I would contact two people every day who might be of some help in finding me work. I sat down with a piece of paper and after five minutes' thought I had a shortlist with one name on it, a guy called Eamonn Olshin, who had just finished training as an architect. So I phoned him up and asked if we could meet up so I could pick his brains about work. Eamonn was surprisingly — almost ridiculously — friendly. I had been seeing the world as a hostile, treacherous place for so long that it was startling when someone just sounded pleased to talk to me. He said it was funny I should call because he'd been meaning to get in touch for ages and how were things. I was enigmatic in my reply to that one. He said that, come to think of it, he was having people around for supper that very evening and why couldn't I come along? My immediate impulse was to say no, because I wanted to spend the rest of my life living in a hole in the ground and because it would make me seem pathetically needy. But I *was* needy. Maybe not pathetically so but definitely in need. A brutally simple thought struck me: Who would I normally turn to at a time like this? Laura. I said yep, all right, trying not to sound too desperate.

Eamonn's flat was down in Brixton. I wanted to arrive fashionably late, again in order not to show that I was too keen, and then lost my way so I was ludicrously late. Also, the plan had been to breeze in looking rather cool, but because I'd had to ask the way from about five different people, I ended up sprinting along back streets and then the flat was on the top floor, so I was puffing like a walrus, and clammy and disheveled, when I finally walked through the door, just before nine o'clock. There were eight people sitting around the table, two or three of whom were vaguely familiar. Eamonn introduced me to them in turn. The first was his girlfriend, Philippa, which was a relief. He really had invited me because he wanted to see me. After I had regained my concentration, it was too late. I'd missed almost all the names.

They were halfway through the meal and I said I'd quickly catch up, but I helped myself to just a token portion of lasagna. I sat next to Eamonn and talked briefly about my plans. He was very encouraging but he had assumed I was looking in London. I told him I was going to move away, probably to the countryside. He looked baffled.

"Where?" he said. "Why?"

"I need to get away," I said.

"That's fine," he said. "Take a weekend break. There are some great deals. But don't go and live there. London is where you live. Everywhere else in England is for . . ." He paused, as if it was difficult to remember what it was for. "I don't know, going for walks in, flying over on your way somewhere."

"I'm serious," I said.

"So am I," said Eamonn. "We can't afford to lose you. Look, there are people from all over the world stowing away on ships and in containers and under lorries, just because they want to get to London. And you're leaving. You mustn't."

Philippa raised an eyebrow at her boyfriend. "She said she was serious."

Maybe Philippa thought that Eamonn was being too nice to me. He sulked a bit and said he would talk to his boss to see if he knew any people who "weren't good enough to make it in London." We chatted for a bit and then the conversation lapsed and I felt a nudge. It was the man sitting on the other side of me. He was one of the ones who had looked familiar. Of course I hadn't caught his name. Unfortunately, he remembered mine.

"Miranda," he said. "It's great to see you."

"David! Blimey!" I said. He'd cut his hair short and had a small mustache over his upper lip.

He waggled his finger at me roguishly. "Do you remember where we last met?"

"It's on the tip of my . . ."

"I saw you sitting on your arse on the ice at Alexandra Palace."

A wave of nausea swept through me. Oh yes. He had been one of the group on the day I met Brendan. What was it? Was God punishing me? Couldn't he have given me a single evening free of this?

"That's right," I said.

David laughed. "A good day," he said. "It's the sort of thing you ought to do more often and you never really get around to it. Didn't we do a sort of conga on the ice?"

"I wasn't really secure enough, I . . ."

He narrowed his eyes in concentration. I could see he was trying to remember something. I thought to myself, Please, God, no.

"Didn't you . . . ?" he said. "Someone said

that you had a thing with that guy who was there."

I looked around quickly, and I was relieved that an animated conversation about life in the country was proceeding without me.

"Yes," I said. "Briefly."

"What was he called?"

Couldn't he shut up?

"Brendan," I said. "Brendan Block."

"That's right. Strange guy. I only met him a few times. He was an old friend of one of the guys but . . ." David laughed. "He's out there. He's just one of these people, the stories you hear about him. Amazing."

There was a pause. I knew, I just knew, that I should start talking about anything else at all. I could ask him about where he lived in London, what his job was, if he was single, where he was going on holiday, just anything except what I knew I was going to say.

"Like what?"

"I don't know," said David. "Just odd things. He'd do things, things the rest of us wouldn't do."

"You mean, *brave* things?"

"I mean things you'd think of as a joke, he'd actually go ahead and do."

"I'm not following you."

David looked uncomfortable. "You're not still together, are you?"

"As I said, it was just a brief thing."

"I just heard about this from someone who was at college with him."

"He went to Cambridge, didn't he?"

"Maybe later; this was somewhere in the Midlands, I think. From what I heard, Brendan was really winging it. He did no work at all. Apparently his idea of hard work was to photocopy other people's essays. He was doing one course where the tutor got so pissed off that he failed him altogether. Brendan knew where he lived and he went round there and saw his car parked outside the house. He'd left one of the windows wound down about an inch. What Brendan did was to put some rubber gloves on — you know, the kind you use for washing up — and what he did was he spent an entire night going round the area picking up dog shit and pushing it through that crack in the window."

"That's disgusting," I said.

"But amazing, don't you think? It's like a stunt in a TV show. Can you imagine coming down in the morning and opening your car door and about a million dog turds fall out? And then trying to clean the car. I mean, try getting *that* smell out of the car."

"It's not even funny," I said. "It's just horrible."

"Don't blame me," David said. "He wasn't *my* friend. And then there was another story about a dog. I'm not exactly sure of the details. I think they were renting a house somewhere and a neighbor was getting on their nerves. He was some old guy with one of those scraggly, mangy dogs. It used to run around the garden barking, driving everyone mad. Brendan was very good with animals. My friend said that the most ferocious Rottweiler could run at you and in about five seconds Brendan would be scratching it under his chin and it would be rolling on the ground. So Brendan got hold of the dog and he put it in the back of some builder's lorry that was just about to drive off. There were these other people around who thought he was just joking and that he'd get the dog out but he didn't. Someone came along and got in the lorry and drove off and it headed off down the road with this barking coming out of the back. Insane."

"So this man lost his dog?"

"Brendan said he was testing those stories you hear about in the local papers about dogs finding their way home from miles away. He said he definitively disproved it."

331

I looked around once more and the table had fallen silent. Everyone had been listening.

"How cruel," said a woman from across the table.

"I must admit," said David, "that the story came out sounding less funny than I thought it was going to. This guy was always talked of as a practical joker but you don't want to be on the receiving end of his humor. Better to hear about it." He looked around warily. "Maybe better not even to hear about it." The rest of the people started talking among themselves again. David leaned closer to me and spoke in a murmur. "Not someone you want to get on the wrong side of. And if you do, roll your windows up, if you get my meaning."

"I don't understand," I said. "How could you be friends with someone like that?"

"I told you," David said, shamefaced now. "I didn't know him that well."

"That behavior sounds psychotic."

"Some of the stories were a bit extreme, but he seemed all right when I met him. I didn't know the people he played jokes on. Anyway, you know more than I do. You . . . well, you went out with him."

Fucked him. That's what David meant. I breathed deeply. I couldn't stop myself now.

I was furious, but I wasn't exactly sure who to be angry with. I tried to speak calmly. "I wish I'd heard these supposedly amusing stories about Brendan before I went out with him."

"It might have put you off."

"Of course it would have fucking put me off."

"You're a grown-up," said David. "You have to decide for yourself who you go out with."

"I didn't have the information," I said. "For fuck's sake, I thought I was with friends. I feel like someone who's been given a car with dodgy brakes."

"It's not like that. I remember you talking to him. I only heard about you as a couple later."

"Did you think of us as a nice couple?"

"I wouldn't have chosen him for you, Miranda. Maybe someone could have said something. Does it really matter? You said you weren't seeing him anymore."

"I think it does matter," I said. "You know what I'm thinking? I'm thinking of a group of people I thought of as friends watching me get into conversation with someone who had filled a car with dog shit because he got an 'F.' "

"I'm sorry," said David. "I didn't think of it at the time."

"Whose friend was he?"

"What?"

"You said he was an old friend of one of the guys. Which one?"

"Why do you want to know?"

"I just do."

David thought for a moment.

"Jeff," he said. "Jeff Locke."

"Do you have his phone number?"

David gave a half smile. "You want to get in touch?"

I looked at him. The half smile vanished. He started to rummage in his pockets.

Chapter 31

When I woke, I was drenched in sweat and my heart was thudding. I had been dreaming, but the dream was breaking up and sliding away. I tried to hold on to a corner of it. Something about drowning. Drowning, not in water but in a substance that was slimier. Thrashing around and looking up at the bank and there were people sitting there, talking to each other and smiling. Lots of faces: my mother's face; an old friend from school whose name I no longer remembered; and my own face, too, suddenly there on the bank. I lay in bed, my skin prickling, and tried to draw more of the dream back up into my conscious mind. Something about Troy. I saw his face in my mind now, chalky white, his mouth calling something except no sound came out.

I sat up in bed, drawing the duvet around my shoulders. It was just past four, but there was still orange light from the streetlamps and blue light from the moon shining through the half-open curtains into my room. I waited for the panic to subside. It had just been a dream, I told myself. It didn't mean anything, just random images flickering in the night. I was scared to go back to sleep again because then I'd see Troy shouting for help in my head.

I hauled myself out of bed, pulled on my dressing gown and padded into the bathroom. In the mirror, my forehead looked shiny with sweat and my hair was damp, though I was now shivery with clammy cold. I rubbed a towel over my face, then went into the kitchen and made myself a mug of hot chocolate, which I took back to bed with me, along with an *A to Z* of London. I opened it at the right page and squinted down at the tiny letters, the network of roads. When I'd found what I had been half dreading I would see, I put it on my pillow and lay down. I closed my eyes. Soon it would be light and the birds would be singing and the sounds of the morning would start.

I had to be in Bloomsbury by eight-thirty, so I got up at half-past six, pulled on my shorts and singlet and put a sweatshirt over the top. I had two glasses of water and then went out to my van. The traffic wasn't thick yet, so it only took me fifteen minutes to drive to Seldon Avenue in E8. It was a broad

336

road, with apartment blocks and terraced houses on either side, not really like an avenue at all. I parked directly opposite number 19. I looked at the *A to Z* one more time, to make absolutely sure I had the route in my head, then took off my sweatshirt and got out. It was still quite cool and there was a slight mist softening the horizon. I jogged on the spot for a few minutes to warm up and loosen my limbs, then ran up and down the road twice, getting ready to start properly.

I looked at my watch. 7:04. A deep breath and I set off, quite fast: halfway down the road, right onto a parallel road, right again and then up through a small alleyway with scrub land on one side and houses the other. It led to a housing estate, and I dodged around the fire gates, into the parking space, and out the other side. Along the small road with lockups and a railway bridge, left onto a cul de sac, through a narrow cutting that led onto a pedestrian bridge over the railway line. I knew exactly where I was now; I'd been here dozens of times. Hundreds of times. I sprinted along the street, turned right and stopped, panting for breath. Kirkcaldy Road. Laura's road. Laura's house. I gazed up at her window. The curtains were not drawn but no lights were on. I looked at my watch. 7:11. Seven minutes.

I waited for a minute or so and then ran back, retracing my footsteps. This time it took just over six minutes. It would take around twenty minutes, maybe, if you followed the streets, which went the long way, along a railway embankment, across a bridge and around a series of builders' yards. But the direct pedestrian route, the alley, cutting through the flats, the one you couldn't see if you were driving around in a squad car, that was a quarter of the distance at the most. Not twenty-five minutes at all.

I arrived at eight in the morning at the flat in Bloomsbury, letting myself in with the key I'd been given. I was going to sand the floorboards. It wasn't my favorite job; it's noisy and stirs up a storm of dust. I covered the shelves with sheets and put on my ear protectors and mask, and for three hours I moved steadily up and down the spacious living room, planing the dark grot of decades off the wood and seeing it turn honey-colored and grainy again.

At last I was finished. Squatting on the floor, I ran a finger over the wood, which was full of new patterns and knots. Once it was varnished, it would look beautiful. I stood up, pulled off the headphones and mask and shook myself, like a dog coming out of water. I opened the large windows to let in the spring air and the buzz of traffic. I swept up the sawdust, and then vacuumed it, making sure the nozzle got into all the corners. I pulled all the sheets off the bookshelves and started to vacuum them, too, running the nozzle up the cracks between each volume, sucking up the fine layer of dust that lay over their tops.

This man had strange books. The first shelf was full of general things — two thick atlases, several dictionaries and encyclopedias, a tall book about birds of prey, another one about remarkable trees. But as I lifted the nozzle up to the second shelf I saw titles like *The Addictive Personality*, *Maternal Ambivalence*, *Psychotic States in Children*, *Forensic Perspectives on Erotic Obsession* and a thick green tome called *The Handbook of Clinical Psychopharmacology*. I turned off the vacuum cleaner and pulled down a book with the title *Erotomania and the Sexualization of Torture* and opened it at random. "In the structure of unmaking," I read, "there is a fundamental differentiation to be established between the intricacies of this conflation . . ." I rubbed my grimy face. What on earth did that mean? My brain felt thick with effort. I sat down on the floor and flicked forward a few pages. Karl Marx was being quoted: "There is only one antidote to mental suffering and that is physical pain." Was that true?

I heard a movement behind me. I was surprised in different ways at the same time. I had assumed the owner was at work. Not only was he not at work, he was wearing striped flannel pajamas of the sort that I hadn't seen since visiting my grandfather when I was a small child. How could anybody have slept through what I'd been doing in that flat? He looked as if he had just woken up after several months of hibernation. He had long dark curly hair, and "tousled" was an inadequate word to describe its state. He rubbed his hand through it and made it worse.

"I was looking for a cigarette," he said.

I handed him a packet from a bookshelf.

"And matches."

I found a box on a loudspeaker. He lit the cigarette, took a couple of deep drags on it and looked around him.

"I hope you're not going to say that I've got the wrong flat," I said.

"You're not Bill," he said.

"No," I said. "He subcontracted the job."

I looked at my watch. "Did I wake you? I didn't know you were here."

He looked puzzled. He didn't seem entirely to know that he was here either.

"I had a late night," he said. "I've got to get to work at twelve."

I looked at my watch again. "I hope it's nearby," I said. "You've got thirty-five minutes."

"It's very nearby," he said.

"Still, you'll probably be late."

"I can't be," he said. "There're people waiting for me in a room. I've got to talk to them."

"You're giving a lecture?"

He took a drag of his cigarette and winced and nodded his head. "Interesting book?" he said.

"I was just . . ." I gazed down at the book in my hand, then pushed it back into its space on the shelves.

"Coffee?" he said.

"No, thanks."

"I meant, could you make some for me? While I'm getting dressed?"

I was tempted to say that I wasn't his butler but this was obviously an emergency.

He flinched as he took his sip of the coffee.

"You've got twenty-five minutes," I said.

"It's only across the square." His eyes were more widely open now. "You've done a good job," he said, looking at the boards. "Not that I'd know the difference between a good job and a bad job."

"It's the machine that does it," I said. "I'm sorry I was messing with your books."

"That's what they're there for."

"Are you a doctor?"

"In a way."

"Interesting," I muttered inanely. I was thinking about Brendan pushing dog shit through the car window. And then about my dream; fragments of it rose in my mind, like the mouths of small fish nibbling at the surface of the water.

"My name's Don."

"I know. I'm Miranda." I sipped at my coffee. It tasted chocolatey. "Do you deal with mental illnesses?"

"That's right."

"I know you must get really pissed off with people asking you stupid questions, but can I ask you a stupid question?"

"What?"

"It's about someone I heard about. A friend of a friend." I put some shortbread into my mouth. "Of a friend," I added thickly.

"Yeah, right," he said with a faint smile.

342

"I just know little bits about him really."
That was true anyway.

I started to tell Don about Brendan. I
began with the dog turds and then I went
on, and when I got to the bit about the bath
flooding and was saying: "And then she
went back and found that her bath was overflowing when she *knew* that she hadn't —"
Don held up a hand.

"Hold on," he said. He lit a second cigarette.

"What?"

"This is you, right?" he said. "The
woman?"

"Well, yes, in fact."

"Good."

"Good?"

"I was worried you might be the one who
put the dog shit in the car."

"That was a man."

"You could have changed the sex. For
purposes of concealment."

"This is pathetic, I know," I said.

"Go on with the story."

So I did. Even though time was getting
short before his lecture, I told him everything. I even backtracked and told him how
Brendan had whispered to me about
coming in my mouth. And then, at the end, I
told him about Troy and Laura but very

quickly, so I wouldn't start weeping again. When I finished I picked up my mug and took a last gulp of stone-cold coffee.

"So what do you think?" I asked. For some reason, my heart was hammering.

"Fuck," he said.

"Is that your considered verdict?"

"You're well rid of him."

I gave a snort.

"*I* could say that. What I want to know is, is he a psychopath? Could he be a murderer?"

He held up his hands in protest. "It's a bit early in the morning," he said.

"It's actually very late in the morning."

"I don't want to be pompous and say that I would have to conduct my own investigation before making any comment like that. And I don't want to start throwing technical, clinical terms around. The point is, it doesn't really work that way round. I can't say that this pattern of behavior means that he is a murderer —"

"*Could* be a murderer," I interrupted.

"The way it would work is if someone was found to have committed certain types of violent acts then I wouldn't be surprised to find the kind of behavior you've described."

"So there we are," I said.

"No, we aren't," he said. "The majority of

344

murderers show earlier signs of dysfunctional behavior. But a very large number of people display dysfunctional behavior and the vast majority of them don't cross the line."

"But if he has crossed the line, which is what I think, even if nobody else agrees with me, is that it? Is he finished? Is he still dangerous?"

Don sipped at his coffee. "You're piling assumptions on assumptions here," he said.

"I'm not in court," I said. "I can pile anything I want onto whatever else I want. I want to know if he could have burned himself out." I heard the wobble in my voice and coughed to cover it up.

Don shook his head. "I'm sorry," he said. "This is all about hindsight. When people have acted, when they have committed a crime and been caught and imprisoned, then the psychologists and the psychiatrists come out of the woodwork and do their tests and pronounce their verdicts with great authority. And you'll be able to find experts to argue for or against any issue you want."

"Thank you," I said dully. I turned to face him. I noticed he had a thin face and auburn hair and he was looking at me kindly.

"Keep away from him," he said.

"Yes."

"Are you all right?"

"I don't know." I pulled the window shut sharply and the room became quieter. I looked at my watch. "You've got four minutes."

"I'd better go," he said. "You don't look happy."

"It doesn't make it all right that it might be just a stranger, does it?" I started to gather up the sheets. "You can't just sit on the bank and let people drown."

Don looked as if he were going to say something but had changed his mind.

"What are you going to talk about?"

He frowned for a moment. "A very rare psychological syndrome. Very very rare. Only about four people have ever had it."

"So what's the point of lecturing about it?"

He paused.

"If I started asking myself questions like that," he said, "then where would I be?"

I went to see the therapist, Katherine Dowling, again. I sat for a long time in silence, trying to come to a decision. Was I going to deal with the world or with my own head? I looked at my watch. It had been over ten minutes. I told her my dream.

"What does that mean to you?"

"I'd like to continue with you," I said. "But in a few weeks. Or a few months."

"Why?"

"I've got things to sort out."

"I thought that was why you were coming here."

"I can't sort them out here."

I left after half an hour. They still charge you the full amount, though.

You didn't kill yourself, did you? Of course you didn't. I should never have let myself doubt that, not even for a second. You didn't kill yourself and Laura didn't bump her head and drown. I always knew it. The question is, what should I do now, Troy? I can't just not do anything, can I?

No. Of course I can't.

The weird thing is, I should be scared myself, but I'm not. Not a tiny bit. The truth is, I don't care anymore. Not about my safety. I feel like I'm standing on the edge of a cliff in the howling wind and I don't mind if I fall off or not. Sometimes I think I almost want to.

I hope it didn't take too long. I hope you never knew. I can't bear it if you knew.

Chapter 32

I couldn't let it go. I was like a bee buzzing around a honey pot. No, that's not right. Honey pots are good for bees. I was like a honey pot knowing that there was a bee buzzing around somewhere. I was like a moth drawn to . . . No, I'm not going to say it because in fact it's all wrong. I had a boyfriend once and he was studying insects, which was part of the problem. The very first time we met he told me that moths weren't actually drawn to flames. It was a myth. "A moth myth." He actually said that. We were in the student union and he was pissed. Our relationship was doomed from the start, of course. It was just impossible to imagine myself for long with a boy who would introduce himself to a girl by telling her an interesting fact about moths. The funny thing is that now, about five years later, virtually all I can remember about him is that he was called Marc and the interesting fact he told me about moths, which made me fall out of love with him instantly. Because it was pretty interesting.

I had insisted to Marc that he was wrong. I had once been camping with my family and there had been a blur of moths and mosquitoes around the lamp that my father tethered to the tent pole. Marc shook his head. "It's an illusion," he said. "They're trying to align themselves with the moon, which means that they keep the rays of the moon at the same angle. The only way they can do this with a nearby lamp is to circle it. In practice, what they'll do is to spiral into it, closer and closer. There's no attraction. It's just a navigation error." I remember pondering it for a moment. I was probably a bit pissed myself. "It doesn't do the moths much good," I said. "They still end up in the flame." "Who cares about a fucking moth?" said Marc. That was a further bad sign. He was cruel to animals.

So there we are. Moths aren't really drawn to flames. All those songs and poems are wrong. But the fact remains that the moth's progress is not helped by the flame. God knows I had plenty else to do with work and looking at estate agents and making huge decisions about my life, the sort you can't possibly make rationally, which you really ought to make just by tossing a coin. Even so, I rummaged in the pockets of jackets hanging in my cupboard and found the number that David had scrawled on a ripped-off corner of a newspaper, the number of the person at the skating rink who had known Brendan. Jeff Locke.

"Brendan Block? The guy who used to order weirdly flavored pizzas?"

"Did you think there was something odd about him?"

"Sure."

"You should have warned me about him."

"You can't go about like a policeman. Anyway, didn't he get married?"

"She died."

"What? You mean his wife?"

"She was a friend of mine," I said.

"I'm sorry."

"That's all right. How did you meet him?"

He had to think for a moment. "I think a guy called Leon was an old friend of Brendan's. I don't have his number but I know where he works."

"Is this Leon Hardy?"

"Right."

"I'm trying to track down Brendan Block."

"Oh, *him*. I hardly know him. But I think Craig does."

"Craig?"

"Craig McGreevy. He works for the Idiosyncratic Film Distribution Company in Islington."

"Hi, sorry to trouble you. My name's Miranda Cotton and I'm a friend of Brendan Block. I need to reach him urgently. Can you help me?"

"I'm not sure," he said. "I haven't seen him for ages. I've got a number."

I couldn't resist a smile when he read out my own phone number to me. "I've tried that one," I said. "He's not there anymore. Maybe someone else could help me. How did you get to know Brendan?"

There was a pause that I had got used to. Is it like that with all friends or was there something particular about Brendan? When I thought of my own friends, I just knew where I had met them. It was at school or college or because they had been at school with someone else or they were someone's cousin. But everybody seemed a bit vague about Brendan. Suddenly he had been there in their lives and they weren't quite sure how he had got there. Craig McGreevy gave me a couple of names and numbers. One of them didn't answer but the other did and put me onto someone else who put me onto someone else who put me onto a man called

Tom Lanham who, as soon as I mentioned Brendan, said: "Are you ringing about his stuff?"

"His stuff?"

"When he moved out, he left some boxes. He said he was going to collect them but that was about a year ago."

"You shared a flat with him?"

"He stayed here for a bit, then took off and I haven't seen him since. Are you a friend?"

"That's right. I'm trying to track him down. I might be able to help you with his stuff. I could take it to him."

"Are you sure?" Tom said. "That would be great. It's still in a corner of my room. I don't know what to do with it."

"Could I come round and talk to you?"

"Any time. What about tonight?"

I was disconcerted by his eagerness. How much stuff was there?

"Where do you live?"

"Islington. Just off Essex Road. I'll give you directions."

He wasn't going to take no for an answer, so I took down the details and three hours later I was knocking on his door. Tom had obviously just got back from work. He was still in his suit, his tie loosened. His hair was carefully brushed. I guessed that he worked in the City. I was in overalls. He grinned at the contrast between us.

"Sorry," he said. "I didn't have time to change."

He escorted me in and offered me a drink. I asked for coffee. He embarked on a ridiculously pretentious process involving a single paper filter placed over a mug. But it was very good, very strong, so that it made me wince as I sipped at it. He poured himself a glass of wine in a large glass.

"So you don't know where to find Brendan?" I said.

"Why do you want to find him?"

"I'm worried about him," I said.

Tom smiled. "I thought he might owe you money," he said.

"Why?"

"Because he owes *me* money."

"What for?"

"It's not such a big deal," Tom said. "He was meant to be contributing towards the mortgage, the heating, the phone, but he never quite got around to it. He went off to work on a film somewhere and I haven't seen him since."

"A film?" I said.

"He said he was helping with some location scouting."

"When was that?"

Tom sipped at his wine. I didn't feel too sorry for him. He didn't look as if the money mattered very much.

"About a year ago," he said. "Did you say you were going to take his stuff away?"

"I could pass it on to him," I said.

"That would be great," Tom said. "I was thinking of putting it on a skip. Someone came to stay in the room he'd been using, so I put his things in a couple of empty wine boxes. It's just a few odds and ends."

"I'll take it off your hands."

"Why are you doing this?" he said.

"It's a bit like you and the money he owes you," I said. "Except it's not money."

Tom looked at me with a puzzled expression. "I suppose what it is is none of my business?"

I tried to make myself smile as if none of this was very important.

"It's like with you," I said. "Not a big deal."

He was still looking at me in a way I found disconcerting.

"Can I take you out to dinner?" he said.

"I'm sorry, I . . ." For a moment I tried to invent an excuse and then thought, Why bother? "I just can't."

I hadn't been tempted. I didn't like his suit. Anyway, I wanted to look at the things

355

Brendan had left behind when he met me. The things he didn't need. Tom carried one of the boxes out to the car. Then he asked for my number. I gave it to him. What did it matter? It wouldn't be mine for much longer.

As soon as I got home I tipped the boxes onto the floor of my living room and sifted through the pile. At first it looked enticing but as I sorted through each item, it quickly began to seem impersonal and disappointing. Much of it was just the sort of scraps that might be lying by anybody's bed, and I couldn't see why Tom hadn't just thrown them away. There were a couple of yellowed newspapers, a brochure for holidays in Greece, a couple of paperbacks. There was a brown shoelace, a London street map, a watch with a plastic strap, some blank audiocassettes. There were quite a lot of letters, of the anonymous kind, offering credit cards or loans. Almost all of them were unopened. There were some dried-out pens without tops, a pair of plastic scissors for cutting paper, a cardboard beer mat, a cheap calculator, a small plastic torch with no batteries, lots of paper clips, a plastic bottle containing eyedrops. It was just a collection of objects. There didn't seem anything that connected, no touch of the personal.

Except right at the end, there was a hand-written note written on lined paper that looked as if it had been torn from a note-book. The writing was a childish scrawl. It said: "Nan's in St. Cecilia's." This was fol-lowed by an address in Chelmsford and a room number.

I looked at the piece of paper and I wished I'd never seen it. If I'd had a friend — a friend like Laura — sitting with me now she would have asked me what I was doing, and I would have said to her, *I don't know.* She would have said, *He's gone. Let him go. What's it to do with you?* I might have said, *I'm in a zoo and by mistake I open a cage and let a dangerous animal escape. He scratches and bites me and then he is gone. Should I just be glad and get on with my life or is it still my responsibility?* My friend might say, *You didn't let him into the world. You stumbled into him. It was bad luck. He did ter-rible things to you and he's gone. What are you going to do? Are you going all the way to Chelmsford to see someone you don't know for some reason you don't understand?*

At that point I would have thought for a long time and I would have said, *I wish that that man Tom had just thrown all this in the bin and that would be the end of it. But I keep thinking of those people back at the skating rink last year. They knew there was something weird about Brendan. And if they didn't know, they fucking should have. They saw him flirting with me and they saw us getting on. One or two of them were my friends and they should have told me about him.*

My friend would say to me, *You're worrying about people you don't know, people you'll never see.*

And I would say, *Yes. Stupid, isn't it?*

It was as if God himself was trying to discourage me. It rained all the way up the A12 and I missed the turnoff because I was looking at the map on my lap. It was difficult to find St. Cecilia's, a grimy pebble-dashed square building at the end of a row of houses, and I had to park in the next street, so that I was soaked. St. Cecilia's was a residential home. As soon as I opened the swing door I was hit by a smell of cleaning fluid and all the smells that the cleaning fluid was trying and failing to cover up. Nobody was at the front desk. I looked around. There was another door that led to a corridor. An obese woman in a light blue nylon housecoat was mopping something up. When she dipped the mop into her metal bucket it clattered, as if she couldn't see it properly. I cleared my throat and she looked around at me.

"Hello," I said. "Have you got a Mrs. Block here?" That was a guess. I wondered if Nan was a relation.

"No," said the woman.

"Her first name's Nan," I said.

"There's no Nan here," she said and returned to her mopping.

I took the letter from my pocket. "She's in room three, Leppard Wing."

The woman gave a shrug. "That's Mrs. Rees. Along the corridor, up the stairs, first floor, along the corridor past the TV room. She might be watching TV."

I went upstairs. There were three old women and one old man watching a cooking show on the TV. Another woman was sitting with them but looking to one side.

"Is Mrs. Rees here?" I asked.

They looked up, irritated at the disturbance.

"She's in her room," said one of the women. "She doesn't go out much." As if this counted as going out.

In room three there was a bed and a chair and a table in the corner. There was a sink, a wastepaper basket, a window with a crack in the top corner and a nice view over a playing field. Mrs. Rees was sitting in the chair with her back to the door. I walked around. She was in her dressing gown. Her face was directed toward the gray light outside, but she didn't seem to be looking at it.

"Mrs. Rees?"

I moved into her line of sight but she didn't respond. I knelt by her chair and put my hand on her arm. She looked at the hand but not at me.

"I'm here about Brendan," I said. "Brendan Block. Do you know him?"

"Tea," she said. "It's tea."

"No," I said, more loudly. "Brendan. You know Brendan."

"It's tea," she said.

"Can I get you some tea?" I said.

"It's tea."

"Your nightie?" I said.

She just gave a whimper. This was a disaster. I didn't even know if this was Mrs. Rees. I didn't know if Mrs. Rees was the woman referred to in the letter. Maybe she was a new occupant of the room. I didn't know if the woman referred to in the letter was really connected to Brendan. If she was connected to him, I wasn't at all clear what I wanted to know. And if this was the right woman, it was immediately obvious that she

360

wouldn't be able to tell me anything about anything. In desperation I stood up and walked around the room. There were plastic dishes and cups, nothing sharp, nothing that could be dropped and broken. Above the table, stuck on the wall with tape, were two photographs. The first was an old picture of a man in uniform. He had a mustache and a roguish look. He wore his cap at a jaunty angle. Husband probably. In the other a woman stood holding the hands of two children. I looked closely. It was the woman in the chair, years ago when her hair was gray rather than white. The boy, about ten years old, smart in his school blazer, grinning at the camera, was unmistakably Brendan. I took the picture from the wall and showed it to the woman.

"Mrs. Rees," I said, pointing at the photograph. "That's Brendan —"

She frowned and stared. "That's Simon," she said.

"Simon?"

"Simon and Susan."

I tried to ask more questions but she started talking about tea again. I tried to stick the picture back on the wall but the tape was too old and dry. I just leaned it against the wall. I tiptoed out of the room and then ran down the stairs. The woman was gone from the corridor. I found her in a room behind the front desk. She was pouring water from a kettle into a mug.

"I talked to Mrs. Rees," I said.

"Yeah?"

"I need to talk to her daughter, Susan."

"Granddaughter."

"Yes, of course. I've got something important for her. Could you give me her address?"

The woman looked at me, her mouth half open. I wondered if she had heard me. But she started to rummage through a box of filing cards with her chapped fingers.

Chapter 33

Susan Lyle lived at 33 Primrose Crescent, which was on the eastern outskirts of the town, near a cemetery. It was a row of beige and gray houses. Number thirty-three had closed curtains, a peeling red door; and its bell, when I pressed it, rang out a tune: a few notes from "(How Much Is) That Doggie in the Window?"

Because I hadn't let myself think about what I was doing, and because I had imagined that Susan Lyle would not be at home, I was taken aback when the door opened almost immediately and a woman stood in front of me, filling the entrance. For a moment, all I could think of was her size. She had a vast stomach that looked misshapen; her white T-shirt, on which was written in bold pink "Do Not Touch!" was stretched across her bulky chest; her neck was thick; her chin fell in folds; her hands were dimpled. I felt myself blushing with a kind of shame as I tried not to look anywhere but into her eyes, small in her wide white face, at the person beneath the mountain of flesh. In her grandmother's photograph she had been skinny and knock-kneed; what had happened in life to make her like this?

"Yes?"

"Susan Lyle?"

"That's right."

I heard a child's wailing come from behind her.

"I'm sorry to disturb you like this. I was wondering if I could have a quick word with you?"

"What's this about? Are you from the council? They already checked the premises you know."

"No, not at all. Not the council, nothing like that. You don't know me — I'm — my name's Miranda and I know your brother."

"Simon?" She frowned. "You know Simon?"

"Yes. If I could just . . ."

I took a small step forward but she didn't budge from the entrance. The wailing inside grew louder, joined by more high-pitched shrieking.

"You'd better come in before they kill each other," she said at last and I followed her into the hall, where the radiator was hot even though the day outside was mild.

It was dim in the living room, because the

curtain was drawn, so it took me a few minutes to make out exactly how many children there were in the stuffy, cluttered room. There was a baby sitting placidly in the playpen among a giant heap of soft toys, pacifier in its mouth. There was a wailing toddler strapped into a high chair, with a streak down its bib and an upturned bowl on the floor. There was another toddler on the sofa, staring at the television screen where there was some kind of game show going on, though the sound was turned down. She was gripping a lollipop in her fist. I peered into the carry-cot on the floor and there was a baby in there, fast asleep in spite of the noise. It held its hands straight out in front of it, as if holding on to some invisible object, and its eyes flickered rapidly. What do babies dream about?

"What a lot of children," I said brightly. There was a glowing bar fire behind a guard, giving out scorching local heat, and a smell of nappies and air freshener clogged my nostrils. I felt a sense of acute oppression, a thickness in my chest. "Are they all yours?" As soon as I asked this, I realized it was a stupid question, mathematically impossible.

"No," she said, staring at me with mild contempt. "Just the one." Then she added with pride: "I have three more who come after school three days a week, too. I make a good living. I'm registered."

Tenderly, she lifted the screaming boy out of the high chair and wiped his mouth with a corner of the bib. "Quiet now," she said. "Shush!" And he immediately quieted, his smeared mouth breaking out into a grin, and he put a hand into her thick dark hair.

Perching the child on the great swell of her hip where he clung like a tiny koala, she said, "So — Simon?"

I hadn't rehearsed an opening, so it came out abruptly. "When did you last see him?"

"Are you police?"

"No."

"Social?"

"No, I just —"

"So what gives you the right to barge into my house and stand there looking as if there's a bad smell under your nose and ask me questions?"

"Sorry. I didn't mean to . . . I'm just worried and I'd be really grateful if you could help me."

"Has he dumped you or something?"

"What?" For a ghastly moment I thought that perhaps Brendan had even got to his sister before me and told her his version of our relationship.

"Why else would you come running to me for help?" She lowered herself onto the sofa with her son, and the other child immediately clambered onto her lap, too, and pushed her sticky face into the folds of her neck. Susan seemed not to notice. She picked up the remote control and flicked through channels randomly before saying, "Not for ages. We've gone our separate ways. He's got his life and I've got mine. Why? What's it to you?"

"Like I said, I know Simon. I've known him for nearly a year now. And I'm a bit worried about him." I sat down on the edge of the sofa. "I think he might not be very well."

"Are you a doctor?" She flicked away the lollipop that was being waved in front of her face as if she was swatting a fly.

"No."

"He should go to a doctor. What am I supposed to do about it? He's a grown-up."

"I don't mean ill like that — I mean . . . well, his behavior has been rather disturbing and . . ."

"Oh. I *see*. You mean ill in the head, do you? Mmm?" She suddenly sounded like Brendan.

"I'm not sure. That's why I wanted to talk to you."

367

"There's nothing wrong with Si." She stood up with surprising agility and the children fell back into the depths of the sofa, letting out yelps of surprise. "Who do you think you are?"

"I didn't —"

"Get out!"

"I just want to help," I lied.

The anger suddenly went out of her. "I could do with a fag," she said. She picked a video up from the side table and slid it into the player under the TV. Cartoon characters ran across the screen. She turned the sound up high, and then reaching up to a shelf, she brought down a tin of biscuits and fished out three chocolate bourbons, which she pushed into three eager hands.

I followed her into the kitchen where she sat down heavily on a chair. She poured herself a large glass of fizzy lemonade and lit a cigarette.

"Is he in trouble?"

"I don't know," I said cautiously, aiming for a vague and misleading truthfulness. "It's more that I want to prevent trouble, if you see what I mean. So I thought I'd come here and just talk to someone who knew him before he got taken into care."

"What?"

"I thought . . . ?"

"Care?" Her laugh was a high, thick wheeze. "Where did you get that idea from?"

"You mean, he didn't get sent away?"

"Why would he, with our mum and then our nan there to look after us? We were never in care. You should be careful what you say."

"I must have got the wrong end of the stick," I said in a placating tone.

She pulled on her cigarette and then released a trail of blue smoke. "Si wasn't a bad boy," she said.

"What about school?"

"Overton. What about it? He was good at lessons but he hated people telling him what to do or criticizing him. He could have done all right if they hadn't . . ." She stopped.

"If what?"

"Never mind."

"Did they punish him?"

"They don't like boys like him being clever."

"He was expelled?"

She ground out her cigarette, swilled back the remains of her lemonade and stood up. "I'd better see what they're up to in there," she said.

I stared at her. "What happened then, Susan?"

369

"You can see yourself out."

"Susan, please. What did he do after he was expelled?"

"Who are you anyway?"

"I told you, I know Brendan."

"Brendan? *Brendan?* What is all this?"

"Simon, I meant."

"I've had enough of people poking their noses into our business. Live and let live, I say. I don't believe you want to help Si, anyway. You're just *snooping*."

Again, with that word, uttered with such hostility, I heard a weird echo of Brendan. He might have left his past, changed his name, reinvented himself utterly, and yet still at some deep level he remained connected to it all.

"Get out of my house," she said. "Go on. Fuck off before I call the police."

So I left, out into the fresh air and a sky that was clearing after heavy rain, with blue on the horizon and the deep gray separating out into clouds. I drank some water and popped a Polo into my mouth, then started the van. I headed back the way I'd come, through the gleaming wet streets, but after a few minutes stopped again. Brendan didn't let things go, I thought grimly. Never.

I wound down the window and when a

woman walked past I leaned out and said, "Excuse me, could you tell me where Overton High School is?"

Children were coming out of school, weighed down by backpacks, carrying musical instruments and PE bags. I sat and watched them for a few minutes, unsure what I was doing here. Then I got out of the van and wandered over to a couple of women standing by their cars chatting.

"Sorry to bother you," I said.

They looked at me expectantly.

"I'm moving to the area," I said. "And my children — well, I was wondering whether you'd recommend this school?"

One of them shrugged. "It's all right," she said.

"Does it do well academically?"

"All right. Nothing to write home about. Your Ellie does well though, doesn't she?" she said to the other woman.

"Is there much bullying?"

"There's bullying in every school."

"Oh," I said, stumped. Then, "I had a friend who came here about, let's see, twelve or thirteen years ago. He mentioned something about an episode."

"What d'you mean?"

"I can't remember now what it was, exactly. Just, he said something . . ." I allowed myself to trail away.

"I don't know. Things are always happening."

"That'd be the fire," said the other woman. "It was before our time, of course, but people still talk about it."

I turned to her, my skin prickling. "Fire?"

"There was a fire here," she said. "You can see. A whole year eleven classroom was burnt to the ground, and half the IT area."

She pointed across the yard to a low red-brick building that was newer than the rest of the school.

"How awful," I said. I felt hot, and then cold all over. "How did it happen?"

"Never caught no one. Probably kids fooling around. Awful what they get up to nowadays, isn't it? There's Ellie now." She raised an arm to a lanky girl in plaits walking our way.

"So no one was caught?"

"Good luck with the move," said one of them over her shoulder. "Maybe see you again, if you decide to come here."

I got back into the van and put another Polo into my mouth. I sucked on it, feeling its circle become thinner and thinner until it broke and dissolved. I turned on the ignition but still sat with the engine idling, staring at the new classroom, imagining a blaze of leaping orange flames. Simon Rees's revenge. I shivered in the warmth. Like a sign I knew how to read, like graffiti scrawled on the wall: BRENDAN WOZ HERE.

Chapter 34

Don was his own worst enemy, in all sorts of ways. He smoked too much. He kept irregular hours. He existed in a general state of vagueness, which I began to think was largely deceptive but not entirely. When I was sealing the floor, he wandered in with two mugs and I had to wave him back before he caused disaster. I joined him out in the corridor and he handed me a coffee and started thinking aloud about other things that needed doing in his flat. Did I think the window frames looked a bit worn? (Yes, I did.) Could anything be done about the cracks in the living room door? (Yes, if money wasn't an object.) I sniffed at the strong black coffee to try and rid myself of the resinous reek of the floor lacquer.

"It's dangerous to think of things as you go along," I said. "That's how costs get out of control."

"I've heard that," Don said, sipping his coffee. "The problem is that it's easier to think up ideas once the work has started.

Don't you find that?"

I shook my head. "There's always more you can do," I said. "Always something else that can be fixed. What I like is getting a job finished."

"You don't want more work?"

"That's a funny thing," I said. "I have this feeling that not only should I be working at the moment. Shouldn't you be as well?"

Don looked a bit shifty.

"I have this problem," he said. "I suffer from attention deficit disorder."

"Is that a real illness?"

"It's more like an excuse with a long name. This is my day when I work from home."

"Does this count as work?"

"It's fallow time. I think and write and make plans."

"What do you do the rest of the time?"

"Bits of teaching, I see some patients, other stuff."

"You look too young for that," I said.

"You mean 'immature'?"

"You should learn to take a compliment," I said. "I was saying I was impressed."

"I think it's cleverer to be able to do what you do," he said.

"You don't know the half of it. Remember Brendan, that man I told you about?"

"Yes."

"I found his sister. She lives in a council house in Chelmsford."

"You went to see her?"

"Yes."

"Why?"

I couldn't think of a short answer, so I told what I'd done. I told him how Brendan wasn't his real name, about what he did to his school. "Isn't that scary?"

"Are you scared yourself?"

"Me?" I shook my head. "This isn't about me. This is about other people, don't you see?"

"It's hard to tell."

"You said yourself he sounded dangerous. And look at all the signs."

"Maybe."

"He set fire to his school. Would you admit that that's a symptom of mental disturbance?"

"You didn't say what happened. Was he charged with arson? Did he get any kind of treatment?"

I took a deep breath. "He was never caught."

"Did the sister tell you he did it?"

"Reading between the lines, it's obvious.

Can't you see the pattern? Everything fits. Is it true or is it not true that setting fires as a child is one of the earlier signs of being a psychopath?"

I'd finished my coffee and Don gently took the mug from my hand.

"This conversation isn't going the way I planned," he said.

"What do you mean?"

"I was going to work my way around to saying that it's fun having you working here and how I wondered if we could have a drink sometime. I was also going to say at the same time that you probably get hassled all the time like this. I was probably also going to apologize as well because it's probably difficult for a woman like you because you can't do your job without being harassed by people like me."

I couldn't help smiling at this. "Instead I started going on about this psychopath I used to know."

"That's the thing," said Don. "I don't want to offend you."

"I'm not easily offended."

Don paused and looked at me as if he was trying to decide if I was telling the truth. "I worry that you misunderstood what I told you before."

"Why do you worry?"

"I don't think you should have gone to see those women."

"You think it's dangerous?"

He took a sip of his coffee and then gave an expression of disgust. "Cold," he said. "You should be careful about interfering in other people's lives."

"I've told you," I said, with a harder tone in my voice. "Brendan is dangerous. Do you disagree?"

"There are colleagues of mine who carry out assessments for social workers about children who are at risk. Every so often a child will be murdered and the social workers and the psychiatrists and the police will be blamed in the press for having known the child was in danger and not having acted before. What the press won't mention is the hundreds and thousands of other children who are also in that gray area of being poor, vulnerable, threatened, hopeless. But most of them will turn out more or less all right. There's no magic checklist, Miranda. You wouldn't believe how many people I see who are on the edge. You can tick all the boxes. They have been bullied and beaten and sexually abused. Yes, they may have set fires. Whatever the profilers say, that doesn't make you Jack the Ripper. Above all, he's out of your life and it's not your business anymore."

"Don, if you had sold a car and then you got a report that there was something dangerous about it, that the brakes didn't work, would you just forget about it? Would it not be your business?"

Don looked genuinely troubled by this. "I don't know, Miranda. I want to say that I admire you for doing this. You're being a Good Samaritan. Better than that, you're being a Good Samaritan for someone you don't know. I just want to say two things. The first is that people aren't like cars. And the second is, what are you actually going to do?"

"It's very simple," I said. "I want to find out if he's going out with anybody else. If he is, then she will be at risk and I'll warn her."

"She may not be grateful," said Don. "A gesture like that could be misconstrued."

"That doesn't matter," I said. "I'm not easily embarrassed."

"And you may be putting yourself in danger."

When he said this, I felt a shiver go through me. It wasn't apprehension though, more like a surge of exhilaration. I had a strange sense of stepping out of my life and all the things that trapped me.

"That's not important," I said to Don.

"Will you be careful?"

"Yes," I said, meaning no. I would not be careful; I would be unstoppable.

I wanted to find Brendan without his knowing I'd found him. It was more difficult than I expected. I phoned an old friend of Laura's called Sally, who I'd seen at the funeral. I guessed that she'd been in touch recently. Her tone became awkward and constrained when I identified myself. Obviously she must have heard some version or other of the tangled relationships between Brendan, Laura and me. Did they feel sorry for me? Did they think I was to blame in some way? I hardly gave it a thought. I told her I wanted to get in touch with Brendan. Was he living in Laura's flat? She said that she didn't think so, but that I should check with Laura's parents.

I phoned Laura's parents. I talked to Laura's mother. She sounded tired and spoke slowly as if she had been woken from sleep in the middle of the day. She was probably on something, the poor woman. Like my mother. I told her my name and that I was an old friend of Laura's.

"Yes," she said. "I think Laura mentioned your name."

"I was at the funeral," I said. "I'm so sorry. It's a terrible thing."

"Thank you," she said, as if I had paid her a compliment.

"I wanted to get in touch with Brendan," I said. "I wondered if you might know where I could reach him."

"I don't know," she said.

"Is he staying in Laura's flat?"

"No," she said. "It's being sold."

"I'm sorry for bothering you, but do you have an address for him?"

"We haven't seen him. He said he needed to go away."

I couldn't believe that Brendan had left his parents-in-law without even a forwarding address. What would happen with Laura's estate? Would he get half of it? All? But these weren't questions I could pursue with Laura's numb, mourning mother. I could think of only one thing to do, but I felt a lurch of apprehension as I did it. I phoned Detective Inspector Rob Pryor and indeed he sounded a long way from pleased to hear from me.

"Don't worry," I said. "I've just got a simple question. I know you've become friendly with Brendan. I need to get in touch with him and I wondered if you could tell me where he is?"

"Why?"

"What do you mean, 'why'? Is it such a big deal?"

"You told me I should be investigating him for — what? — murder? Why do you want to see him?"

"Are you his receptionist? I just need an address." There was a pause. "All right," I said. "I've got some stuff he left behind in a flat he lived in."

"*Your* flat?"

"*A* flat."

"How did you get it?"

"What is all this?" I said. "What business is this of yours?"

"I don't know what's going on with you, Miranda, but I think you should give it up and move on."

"I just want his address."

"Well, I'm not going to give it to you." Another pause. "I'll tell him to call you. If I speak to him."

"Thank you."

"And don't call me again."

I put the phone down. That hadn't gone very well.

Chapter 35

Why do phones always ring when you're in
the bath? I left it for ages, but it went on, insistent, until at last I wrapped myself in an
unsatisfactorily skimpy towel and headed for
the living room, at which point it stopped. I
swore, and returned to the bathroom where I
stepped gratefully back into the warm, soapy
water and submerged myself. At which point
it rang once more. I got there quicker this
time, trailing water.

"Hello?"

There was a short pause, during which I
knew for a certainty who was on the other
end. I flinched and pulled my damp towel
more tightly around me.

"Mirrie?"

At his voice, just the utterance of that
single word, I felt the familiar, choking disgust. It was as if the air were suddenly thick
and dirty, and I could barely breathe. Sweat
prickled on my forehead, and I wiped it
away with a corner of my towel.

"Yes."

"It's me."

"What do you want?"

"What do *I* want?"

"Look . . ."

"It's what *you* want, I think."

"I don't —"

"Or what you have for me."

I clutched the receiver and didn't reply.

"Rob just called me," he went on. "I hear that you're looking for me."

A kind of groan escaped me.

"You want to see me."

"No."

"You want to give me something. Something I left behind. I wonder what that can be."

"It's nothing."

"It must be important, if you're going to all this bother. Mmm, Mirrie?"

"A book," I stuttered feebly.

"A book? What book would that be?" He waited and when I didn't answer said, "Would the book be an excuse, perhaps? You just can't let go, can you?"

For a moment, everything went misty.

"Cut the crap," I said. "This is me. Nobody else is around. You know what I know about you. You know and I know you know and every hour of every day I think about what you did to Troy and Laura and

Kerry and if you think —"

"Hush," he said in a soothing voice. "You need help. Rob thinks so, too. He's very concerned about you. He says that in his opinion there's a word for what you've got. For your syndrome."

"Syndrome? *Syndrome?* I just want to send you this fucking book."

"The book," he said. "Of course. The one whose name you can't remember."

"Give me your address and then piss off."

"I don't think so." I could hear him smile.

"Jesus," I said, with a sob of rage. "Listen . . ."

But I was talking on a dead line. Brendan had put the phone down. I gazed at the receiver in my hand, then rammed it down on its holder.

I climbed back into the tepid bath. I ran hot water and then, holding my nose, slid under the water. I listened to the booming of the pipes and the beating of my heart. I was so violently angry that I felt I would fly apart.

I came up for air with a thought that made me leap from the bath and run naked and slippery back to the phone, crouching low as I passed the window so no one would see me. I dialed 1471 and waited until the automated voice told me the caller's number. I'd forgotten to have a pen ready so I held the digits in my head, chanting them as I scrambled in the drawers looking for pen and paper. I jotted it down on a stray playing card I found, then dialed 1471 again, just to check it.

It was a 7852 number. Where was that? Somewhere in South London, maybe. It wasn't a code I rang often, that was for sure. I shuffled on all fours under the window, then went to my bedroom, yanking out the bath plug on my way. I got dressed in baggy cotton trousers and a loose top and then started flicking through my address book, looking for those four digits, trying to find out which bit of London Brendan was in now. There had to be a better way of doing this. I found a telephone directory and ran my finger down the lines and lines of names looking for the area code. My eyes were starting to swim with the effort until I found the area: Brackley. That was reasonably accessible.

What now? I couldn't wander around Brackley looking for him. Maybe I should call the number and — well, and what? Talk to Brendan again? I couldn't do that; just the thought of it made me tremble. I poured myself a large glass of red wine and then turned on my laptop computer. Two minutes, a couple of search engines, and I was looking at the name Crabtree's, a café in Brackley. I toasted my perseverance with a gulp of red wine that tasted rather vinegary. I looked at my watch: 7:35.

Now that I knew it was a café, I did risk calling the number. It rang and rang and just when I was about to put the phone down, someone answered.

"Yes?"

"Is this Crabtree's?"

"Yes. It's the payphone. You want someone?"

"Oh — well, can you tell me the opening hours?"

"What?"

"The opening hours of the café."

"I dunno exactly; I've never been in here before. It's new and I thought I'd give it a go — eight till late, that's what it says on the board outside."

"Okay, thanks."

"It's not a pub though."

"No."

"You can't get drinks — it's all cappuccino and latte and those herbal teas that taste like straw."

"Thanks."

"And vegetarian meals. Organic this, that and the other."

"You've been very helpful . . ."

"Alfalfa. I always thought it was cows that ate alfalfa."

I didn't stop to think. I poured the wine down the sink, picked up my denim jacket and left. No underground goes to Brackley, so I drove there, through the balmy evening. The sky was golden and even the dingy streets were softened in its glow.

Crabtree's was in the upmarket bit, between a shop that sold candles and wind chimes and a shop that sold bread "made just as the Romans used to make it." I drove past it and then found a place to park a few minutes' walk away just in case Brendan was around.

I walked slowly past the café, with the collar of my jacket turned up, feeling excruciatingly visible — an absurd and ham-fisted parody of a private eye. I imagined Brendan sitting by the window and seeing me shuffle by. I cast a few rapid glances through the glass, but didn't see him. Then I turned around and walked past once more. The café was practically empty and he didn't seem to be in there.

I went inside. It was brightly lit and smelled of coffee, vanilla, pastry, herbs. I ordered a pear juice (with a hint of ginger) and a flapjack and took them into a corner. What would I do if he walked in now? I should have brought a large newspaper to hide behind. I could cut a hole in it and stare out or something. Even a book to bend over would be better than sitting here exposed. But it was warm and clean and aromatic and for a moment I allowed myself to relax. I was tired to my bones, tired in the kind of way that sleep can't cure. I put my head in my hands and gazed through the lattice of my fingers at the street outside. People walked past, men and women with purposeful strides. No sign of Brendan.

After half an hour of nibbling at the flapjack and sipping at the juice, I paid up and asked the young woman behind the counter what time they closed.

"Nine," she said. She had silky blond hair twisted onto the top of her head, a scattering of clear freckles over the bridge of her nose and a lovely candid smile. She glanced at the watch on her delicate wrist. "Just seven more minutes, I'm glad to say."

"And what time do you open in the morning?"

"Eight o'clock."

"Thanks."

I knew it was ridiculous, but I was back at

eight, with a newspaper. I ordered a milky coffee and a brioche and took up my seat again, wedged behind the coat stand so that if Brendan did come in he wouldn't see me. There were two middle-aged women behind the counter this time, and a man in the kitchen, behind the swing doors.

I stayed an hour and a half, and had two more coffees, and then, shaky with caffeine and fatigue, went outside and sat in my van for a bit. I called Bill and said I wouldn't be at work for a couple of days, and then I left a message on Don's machine apologizing for not turning up to finish the job, but promising I'd be back soon. I didn't say when, because I didn't know when and I didn't want to think about the hopelessness of my task. London was a huge, swarming place in which you could hide and never be found. Brendan may have been passing by and would never return to the café again, and I was hiding in a corner, camped out behind a newspaper, waiting with a dry mouth and a pounding heart for something that wouldn't happen. Or he could be just across the road, at an upstairs window, looking down. Maybe he was coming along the street now and if I didn't hurry I'd miss him. Maybe this was what going mad was like, crouching in a café, hiding in my van, pacing the streets in an area of London miles from home.

I went to the candle and wind chime shop and took my time choosing and buying a glass bowl and some floating candles in the shape of water lilies, all the while peering out at the street. I went to the baker's and bought a wheel of brown sourdough bread that cost so much that at first I thought the decimal point was in the wrong place. I walked very slowly up the street and down again. I went into a bookshop and bought a book of walks in and around London. I poked around in a hardware shop until the glares of the man behind the counter drove me out. I bought a pad of ruled notepaper and a pen at a stationers, and some toffees to suck during my vigil. I returned to Crabtree's once more, which was filling up now.

The young woman from last night was back, as well as a couple of waiters, who looked like students. She was flustered with the lunchtime rush, but she nodded at me in recognition when I ordered white bean soup and a glass of sparkling water. I sat in my obscure corner and leafed through the book of walks. I ate very slowly and when I'd finished got myself a cup of tea. When the door opened I would bend down, as if tying my shoelace, and then peer around the bottom of the table to see who was coming in. At just after two, I started trudging up and down the streets again, aimless and footsore and wretched with the impossibility of my task. I told myself I'd give it until closing time and then call it a day.

At half-past four, the young woman looked mildly surprised to see me again. I had a pot of tea and a slice of lemon drizzle cake.

At seven, I came back for vegetable lasagna and a green salad, but I just pushed it around my plate and left. I got the van and parked it near the café and huddled in the dying light, waiting for it to be closing time. I sat for a while, doing nothing, just staring out at the shapes of the buildings against the sky. I felt very far from home. Forlorn.

On the spur of the moment, I rang Don again and when he answered, before I could change my mind, said, "That drink you mentioned, did you mean it?"

"Yes," he said without hesitation. "When? Now?"

"Not now. Tomorrow?"

"Great."

He sounded genuinely pleased and the glow of that stayed with me after I'd said good-bye, a little bit of sunlight in the gloom.

★ ★ ★

I must have dozed off because I woke with a start and found the light had faded and the crowds on the street had thinned, although there was still a pool of people outside the pub up the road. It was just before nine, and I was stiff and sore and thirsty. I turned the key in the ignition, switched on the headlights, put the gear into reverse, released the handbrake, glanced in the rear mirror, and froze.

If I could see him in the mirror, could he see me? No, surely not. I was only a strip of face, two eyes. I turned off the ignition and the headlights and slid down low in the seat. In a few seconds, he was walking past the van. He was just a couple of feet away from me. I held my breath in the dark. He stopped at the door of Crabtree's, where the young woman was turning the OPEN sign to CLOSED. When she saw Brendan, her face lit up and she lifted a hand in greeting before opening the door to him. I sat up a bit straighter in the seat and watched as he took her in his arms and she leaned into him and he kissed her on her eyes and then her lips.

She was very beautiful, Brendan's new girlfriend. And very young — not more than twenty-one or -two. She was besotted. I watched her as she pushed her hands into his thick hair and pulled his face toward her again. I closed my eyes and groaned out loud. Whatever Don had said, whatever my common sense told me, I couldn't leave it — not now I'd seen the freckles on her nose and her shining eyes.

The woman collected her coat and shut the door. She waved good-bye at someone still inside and then she and Brendan walked arm in arm down the road, back the way he'd come. I waited until they were nearly out of sight, then got out of the van and followed them, praying he wouldn't turn around and see me skulking in the distance. They stopped outside a door between a bicycle shop and an all-night grocery and broke apart while the girl fumbled in her pocket for the key. Her flat then, I thought. That made sense. Brendan was the cuckoo in other people's nests. She pushed the door open and they disappeared inside.

The door swung shut and a few moments later a light in an upstairs window came on. For a second, I saw Brendan standing, illuminated. He closed the curtains.

Chapter 36

It wasn't exactly an orthodox first date: poking around in an abandoned church in Hackney that a few years ago had been turned into a reclamation center. But maybe it was better this way — there's something awkwardly self-conscious about sitting face-to-face over a pub table, sipping cheap wine, asking polite questions, testing the waters. Instead, Don was at one end of the church, where the altar used to be, bending over an iron bath with sturdy legs, and I was down the aisle looking at stone gargoyles. There was no one else around, except the man who'd let us in, and he was in his office in the side chapel. Everything was bathed in colored, dusty light, and when we spoke to each other our voices echoed.

"Why have I never been in this place before?" he called out to me, gesturing around him at the stone slabs, the vast wooden cabinets, the porcelain sinks leaning against the walls, the boxes full of brass handles and brass padlocks.

"Because you're not a builder."

"I want everything here. Look at these garden benches. Or this birdbath."

I grinned across at him, feeling suddenly dizzy with unfamiliar happiness, tremulous with relief.

"You don't have a garden," I said.

"True. Do you have a garden?"

"No."

"Oh well. Tell me what I should get then."

"What about a pew?"

"A pew?"

"It would go perfectly in your room. Look here."

He walked down the aisle and stood beside me. But he didn't look at the old wooden pew with carved arms. He looked at me. I felt myself blushing. He put his hands on my shoulders.

"Has anyone ever told you you're gorgeous?"

"Never in a church," I said. My voice caught in my throat.

And then he kissed me. We leaned against a wood-burning stove that cost £690 and I put my hands under his jacket and his shirt and felt his warm skin beneath my palms, the curve of his ribs. Then we sat down on the pew, and when I looked at him he was smiling at me.

We had our drink after that, sitting in a pub garden in the warm evening, holding hands under the table, and then we went and had an Indian meal together. I didn't speak about Brendan all evening, not once. I was sick and weary of him worming his way into every thought, present even when he was far away, whispering softly and obscenely in my skull. So I pushed him away. I pushed Troy and Laura away, too. I only let them back in my head after I dropped Don off at his flat and drove home. Though it wasn't really home anymore — it was the place where I lived, with the SOLD board outside and an air of neglect settling over its rooms.

The ghosts came back, but tonight I didn't feel quite so wretched because I was doing something, at last. I had a task, a purpose, a goal. I had a man who thought I was gorgeous: that always helps to blunt the edge of loneliness.

I was at Crabtree's at eight the next morning, but she wasn't there. Instead, one of the men I'd seen two days previously was behind the counter, serving up double espressos, hot chocolates, chamomile teas. I perched on a tall stool, ordered a coffee and a cinnamon bun, and then asked if the young woman who'd served me before was coming in soon because I might have left a scarf behind, and maybe she'd picked it up.

"Naomi? No."

"When will she be in next?"

"I dunno. She only comes in a couple of days a week as a general rule. She's a medical student in real life. She didn't say anything about a scarf, though. Do you want me to have a look out back?"

"Don't worry. I'll come back later," I said.

I joined the rush hour queue at the bus stop a few yards down the road from the door I'd seen Naomi and Brendan enter. The curtains in the upstairs room were still drawn. I stood there for fifteen minutes, shifting from foot to foot and watching the buses arrive and go. Eventually the curtains in the flat were opened, though I didn't see by whom. If I waited long enough, one of them had to come out. If it was Brendan, I'd knock at the door and hope she was there. If it was Naomi, I'd catch up with her and talk. If it was both of them together — well, I'd think about that when it happened.

In the event, it was Brendan who emerged. He was wearing baggy black trousers and a gray woolen jacket and carried a silver rucksack over one shoulder. I pressed myself against the bus stop, among the crowd, worried that he might be coming my way. He passed by on the other side of the road, walking with a jaunty step and whistling to himself.

I waited until he was out of sight and then crossed the road and went up to the door. I ran an anxious hand through my hair, took a deep breath, and rang the bell. She took a bit of time answering and I was beginning to think that she had left earlier than Brendan, but then I heard feet coming down the stairs. When she opened the door, she was wearing a white towel robe and her hair was bundled up in a towel. She looked even younger than before.

"Hello?" she said, peering through the gap. "Can I . . . ?" Then recognition and puzzlement came into her face. "But aren't you the woman in Crabtree's?" she asked.

"Yes. Sorry to intrude like this. I'd really like to have a word with you."

"I don't understand. What are you doing here? How did you know where I lived, anyway?"

"Can I come in? Then I could explain. Just a few minutes."

"Who are you?"

"If I could just —"

"Tell me your name."

"Miranda," I said. I saw her eyes widen and inwardly cursed. "You may have heard of me."

"Oh yes, I've heard of you all right," she said in a hostile tone. "Now I think you'd better go."

She started to push the door shut but I put my hand against it. "Please. Just a few words," I said. "It's important. I wouldn't be here if it wasn't important."

She hesitated, biting her top lip as she stared at me.

"I won't be long," I said. "But there's something I have to tell you. Please."

At last she shrugged and stood back to let me pass.

"Though I can't for the life of me think of anything you could tell me that I'd want to know."

I followed her up the stairs and into the tiny living room. There was a splaying bunch of bluebells in a jam jar on the table, and medical textbooks. A man's leather jacket was slung over the chair. She turned to face me, hands on her hips, and didn't ask me to sit down.

"I don't know what you've heard about me," I began.

"I know that you used to go out with

Ben," she said, and I blinked at her. He was Ben now, was he? "And I know you couldn't let go when he ended it; that you made his life a misery for a while."

"What about Laura?" I demanded. "Did he tell you about her?"

"Of course. Laura was his wife and she died and his heart was broken." I saw tears start up in her candid gray eyes. "He's told me everything. Poor Ben."

"And Troy? He's told you about Troy, has he?" I asked harshly.

"He still has nightmares about it."

"Naomi, listen. You don't know what you're getting into here. Brendan — Ben — he's . . . There's something wrong with him. Really wrong, I mean."

"How dare you say that. *You*, of all people. He's suffered more in his life than anyone has a right to suffer, but it hasn't made him bitter or closed-off. He's even nice about *you*; he understands why you've behaved like you do."

"He makes things up," I said.

"No."

"He lies, Naomi. But there's more to it than that." I felt quite sick with frustration and wretchedness.

"I don't want to hear any more."

She actually put her hands to her ears as

she said this. I raised my voice. "I think you're in danger."

"You're talking about the man I love."

"Listen. Just hear me out. Please. Then I'll go. But please listen, Naomi. *Please*."

I put my hand on her arm and when she tried to pull away, I gripped her harder.

"I don't think she wants to listen. No one wants to listen to you anymore, do they? Mmmm? Now take your hands off her."

I turned.

"Brendan," I said.

"Ben," said Naomi. "Oh Ben!" She crossed the room and put her arms around him.

"I wonder how you found me? You must have gone to a lot of effort."

I glanced quickly at Naomi. All I could think of was that I might have put her in greater danger by trying to save her.

"I'm very sorry that you've been dragged into this," Brendan said to Naomi. "I wanted to protect you. I blame myself. Are you all right?"

"Oh, you don't need to protect me!" she said. She gazed at him tenderly and put a hand up to touch his cheek. "Anyway, it was my fault. I let her in."

"I'll go," I said.

"Do that," said Brendan. He took a few

steps toward me, until he was gazing down at me. He had a very faint smile on his lips. "My poor Mirrie."

Chapter 37

Three days later I got a call from Rob Pryor.

"I thought we weren't meant to talk anymore," I said brightly.

"We need to talk now," he said.

I felt a ripple of alarm. "Has something happened with Naomi?"

"No," he said. "Nothing has happened with Naomi. I couldn't believe that you'd been to see her. That you were watching her."

"I had to," I said. "It felt like a moral duty."

"I want you to come and see me."

"What about?"

"This whole business with you and Brendan. It can't go on like this."

"I know what you mean," I said. "I feel like someone with a disease."

"We're going to sort it out," he said.

"When do you want me to come?"

"One other thing first. Miranda, do you have a solicitor?"

"What do you mean?"

"I think it would be useful if you had some sort of legal representation."

"The only time I've had a solicitor is when I bought my flat."

The whole idea seemed laughable but Pryor didn't give up. He asked me if I knew anybody at all who was a lawyer. I thought for a moment and then remembered Polly Benson. The main thing about Polly is that when we were at college she was the biggest party animal of us all, which was saying something. Pryor said it would be a good idea if I brought her along. I wasn't sure if this was a good idea. I hadn't been in touch with Polly for ages. But Pryor was insistent. I began to get suspicious.

"Is there some problem?" I said.

Pryor's tone was soothing. "We're going to sort this out," he said. "But you may benefit from some advice. Talk to your friend, then phone me. We'll make a date."

I phoned Polly and she gave a cheerful scream when I identified myself. She was so excited. It was so great. We must get together. We must have a drink. What were my plans? I could hear a clatter as she searched around on her desk for her diary. I said that would be great but first I had something I needed to talk to her about. I asked her if she could come with me to see someone. In fact, a detective, but it wasn't what she thought. She said sure, no problem, straight away, just as a friend should. I said I would pay her, just like a normal client, and she laughed and said forget it and, anyway, I wouldn't be able to afford it. She asked me what was up, so I gave her the two-minute version of the Brendan story while she murmured sympathetically.

"What a creep," she said when I'd finished. "But you don't know what's up?"

"Brendan's become friendly with this detective. He may have made some complaint." I laughed. "Or maybe he's going to confess to murder."

"Maybe Brendan objects to what you've been saying about him," said Polly. "You have to be careful about things like that."

"I'm a bit worried about needing a solicitor," I said.

"Then it'll be good that I'm there," she said.

I wasn't sure if that really answered my question but I found a time she was free the next day and also a time we could meet for a drink later in the week. I phoned Rob Pryor and that was fine and so — weirdly — the next afternoon found me standing outside the police station talking with one of my old college friends. I had made an effort to smarten up with a dark jacket and black trousers but Polly had popped out of her office and she was on an entirely different level of looking businesslike. She was wearing a gray pin-striped suit and with her jet-black, very straight hair and brown skin she looked stunning. We hugged each other.

"I'm sorry to waste your time like this," I said. "We should be in and out in a moment."

A uniformed officer showed us through to Pryor's office, which seemed full of people. Brendan was there and a middle-aged woman, also formally dressed, who Pryor introduced as Deirdre Walsh, Brendan's solicitor. She looked at me with a puzzled expression, as if I wasn't the person she was expecting or as if I'd said something she didn't understand. I introduced Polly to them and tried very hard not to look in Brendan's direction. Pryor asked if she knew about the situation.

"I filled her in," I said. "But I'm not quite sure what this is all about."

Pryor, Brendan and Walsh exchanged glances. Something was up. Pryor was fidgeting with a file on his desk. He flipped it open.

"At Mr. Block's request," he said. "This is an informal meeting."

"What does that mean?" I said.

"You'll see," said Pryor, picking up a sheet of paper from the file. "We all know what's been going on, more or less. But it might be worth going through some of the salient episodes." He pursed his lips and hesitated for a moment before continuing. "Last year the two of you had a brief, intimate relationship which Mr. Block ended."

"That's not true," I said.

"Please, Miss Cotton, let me just —"

"No. I'm not going to sit here and nod to a lie like that. It was simple. I caught Brendan reading my diary —"

"Please, Miss Cotton — Miranda — let me go on and then you can have your say."

I clenched my teeth hard and said nothing.

"According to Mr. Block, he ended the relationship. Maybe unfortunately he then began a relationship with your sister and then with a mutual friend —"

"She was *my* friend," I said.

"A relationship," said Pryor, as if I hadn't spoken, "which ended tragically."

"For *Laura*," I said. "Not for Brendan."

There was a sort of angry sigh from Deirdre Walsh and I saw that she was actually glaring at me.

"Please, Miranda," said Pryor.

Polly leaned over and put a hand on my arm. I nodded at her. Pryor continued.

"I won't go through all the episodes of tension during the time when Brendan was engaged to your sister. I'll only mention the occasion when you were caught searching through Brendan's possessions in his bedroom."

I looked around at Polly. I hadn't mentioned that to her. She was looking entirely impassive.

"Mr. Block admits that his severing of ties with your sister was a painful process, but he was, at least, no longer connected with your family. However, your erratic behavior only intensified. There were, for example, the wild accusations you made against him to people . . . well, to people such as myself. Even when I went to the trouble of showing that the accusations for example, concerning the death of Laura . . . were demonstrably false."

"That's just not true," I said. "It all depended on time and the route. I checked it, and if you took the direct route through the council estate, Brendan could easily have got there in the time."

There was a silence. Deirdre Walsh leaned forward and spoke for the first time. "I'm sorry, Miss Cotton. I'm not sure I've got this right. Do I take it that you have walked the route yourself and timed it?"

"Someone had to," I said.

"Excuse me," said Polly to the others. She leaned close to my ear and whispered to me, "I think it would be better if you didn't respond to these claims point by point until the detective has finished."

"Why?" I said.

"Please," said Polly.

"All right," I said. "Go on, then."

Pryor took another piece of paper from his file. "Do you know the name Geoffrey Locke?"

I thought for a moment. It sounded familiar. "Oh, you mean Jeff? I've met him."

"You phoned him about Mr. Block."

"I wanted to reach him."

"Have you tried the phone book?"

"He wasn't in it," I said.

"Leon Hardy?" asked Pryor.

"I've only talked to him on the phone."

"About?"

"I wanted to get in touch with Brendan."

"Craig McGreevy?"

"I don't see the point in just reading these names out."

"You actually visited Tom Lanham."

"I'm sorry, I don't see the problem."

I looked over at Brendan. He had the very

faintest of smiles on his face. It reminded me of the way he looked at me when we first met, when I first suspected that he really liked me. I looked at Pryor. He had no kind of smile on his face.

"You didn't just talk to Lanham. You took property of Mr. Block's away with you."

I looked at Polly again. She didn't catch my eye. "If I saw him," I said, "I could give it to him. That was the idea. He just wanted to get it out of his flat. And if you talked to him, you also know that Brendan skipped without paying rent."

Pryor looked at his file again.

"Mr. Block's grandmother, Victoria Rees, is severely demented. You visited her at her nursing home."

"Yes."

"Did you think she would be able to give you Mr. Block's address?"

"I wanted to find out about his childhood. For various reasons."

"And you called on his sister," said Pryor. "And you asked offensive and invasive questions."

"I wouldn't say that."

"After all the tragedies he has suffered, Mr. Block is trying to put his life back together. He has a new relationship. You approached his new partner. You had been spying on her and you threatened her."

"I did not threaten her."

"It was agreed with Mr. Block and his legal representative that I would coordinate this meeting and speak on his behalf. But I just want to call on Mr. Block to say what this has meant to him."

Brendan gave a cough.

"I'm sorry, Mirrie," he said. "I feel sorry for you, I really do. But I've felt . . ." There was a pause as if it were all too painful to talk about. "Violated. Threatened. Invaded. Unsettled."

"Ha! My heart bleeds for you," I said angrily.

"Miranda," said Polly sharply.

"I have one more thing to say," said Pryor. "Ms. Walsh and Mr. Block came to see me with this information. Much of it I knew already. I have to say that there is an overwhelming case for dealing with this under the Protection from Harassment Act of 1997."

"What the hell do you mean?" I said. "Is Brendan pretending that I've been stalking him?"

"Listen, Miss Cotton," said Pryor. "It is my professional opinion that there is no doubt whatever that harassment has occurred. I want to say this very clearly in front of you and your legal representative. When I first read through this file, I was minded to arrest you. Your solicitor will be able to tell you that harassment under section two of the act is a summary offense with a penalty of up to six months' imprisonment, a fine of up to five thousand pounds, or both. I would be quite within my powers to arrest you here and now and conduct a search of your property. I should also say that the Harassment Act also allows for a civil remedy."

I was so dismayed and angry and shocked that I could barely speak. "That is just such a travesty," I said. "I just . . . well, for a start, in no way have I harassed Brendan. I talked to friends of his."

"The harassment isn't defined in the act," said Deirdre Walsh in a chilly tone. "If you believe you are being harassed and a reasonable person, such as a magistrate, agrees, then harassment is proved. I must say that I have never seen a clearer case."

"Ms. Walsh is right," said Pryor. "It was my view that the case should proceed. I consider you a possible threat to Mr. Block. But he was eager to settle the case informally. If this case reached a criminal court, you would be subject to a restraining order. If it was a civil court it would be a restraining injunction. It doesn't matter. They amount to the same thing. Mr. Block is willing to accept a personal commitment from you. If you won't make such a commitment, we'll think again."

"You mean, you'll arrest me?"

"That's right," said Pryor.

"This is completely insane," I said. "If anything, Brendan is the one who has been stalking me. I was the one who broke off with him and then he insinuated himself into my family, into my life. I should take an injunction out against him."

There was quite a long awkward silence.

"You're going about it in an unconventional way," said Pryor. "And now I think you might like a few moments with your legal adviser. We'll leave you alone together."

The three of them stood up and walked past me. I had to stand up to leave space for them. Pryor closed the door behind him but the inside wall of his office was entirely transparent. I saw them walk across toward the coffee machine, a group, speaking. Deirdre Walsh glanced back and I looked away too late. Polly was staring down at the carpet.

"That isn't exactly what I was expecting," I said.

She turned to me. Her face was drained of color.

"I'm not sure if I'm right for this," she said. "You may need someone more senior."

"I just want your advice, Polly."

She bit her lip. "Is this true?" she said. "Did these things happen?"

"They're not exactly false," I said. "In themselves. But . . . I mean, for example, the point about being caught looking through Brendan's bags. He was staying in my parents' house at the time, so it wasn't as if I was breaking and entering. And all those phone calls, it was a matter of A saying phone B and B saying phone C and so on. I was just trying to find him. The idea that I was stalking Brendan is grotesque. I think he's dangerous. What was I supposed to do?"

Polly stood up. She seemed reluctant to meet my gaze.

"I shouldn't have agreed to this," she said. "We know each other. It's not professional. I didn't realize . . . But look, Miranda, I think apart from everything else — you should see someone."

"If you mean a therapist, I have been talking to someone."

"You didn't tell me that," said Polly. "Among other things."

"I was talking to her about my feelings after losing my brother and my closest friend."

"You should have told me."

"So you could have discounted what I said as some psychological symptom?" Polly didn't reply but she didn't deny it either. "I'm not going to accept this."

Polly shook her head urgently. "No, Miranda, stop that. They are being generous with you."

"Let them prove it in court."

"Miranda!" Polly grabbed my arm with a grip that almost made me cry out. "If you go to court you will lose. Let me tell you, you do not want to be cross-examined on what that detective read out from his file. You will be convicted, I promise. If you have the wrong judge, you could spend four months in Holloway. Is that what you want, for the rest of your life, every time you fill out a form, every time you apply for a job or a visa?" Polly was looking at me with a pity that revolted me. "I don't know what's happened, but I'm so sorry. Miranda, let me be your lawyer for five minutes and we'll just accept whatever they're offering. Whatever it is, they're letting you off easy. Will you let me ask them back in?"

I could hardly speak. My skin felt hot and clammy, while my mouth was dry.

"All right," I said.

On the way out I caught sight of Brendan

in the corridor. He was in conversation with Rob Pryor. He caught my eye and then he smiled. He raised his right index finger and wagged it slightly at me, like a teacher reproving a pupil. Then he passed the finger across his neck. Around the neck. What did that mean? Was it like a knife across a throat? Was it Troy's noose around the neck? Was this a warning? *Don't mess with me.*

"Did you see that?" I said to Polly.

"What?" she said.

Nobody but me ever seemed to see.

Afterward, back on the steps outside in the sunshine that made my eyes hurt, Polly said I should be very relieved. I had signed an undertaking drafted by Deirdre Walsh according to which I promised not to approach or contact Brendan or his friends or members of his family. Polly also said on my behalf that I was sorry and that I'd been under a lot of pressure and that I was already receiving psychiatric help. Before we parted, Polly held out her hand.

"I don't mind any of this," I said. Polly looked puzzled. "It's all crap. Brendan was always going to outwit me at something like this. If you're as good a liar as Brendan is, you'll always make someone like me sound

417

like she's lying. I think you gave me good advice. I had to sign that document. So I should thank you for saving me from going down in flames. But I need to ask one thing: Do you believe me?"

Polly seemed unwilling to speak.

"Well, do you?"

She gave an unhappy gesture. "How can I be sure?" she said.

"Because you're my friend," I said. "If you were a real friend, you would know me and you would trust me."

"I'm sorry, Miranda," she said. "Even friends get ill."

I held out my hand and shook hers and said good-bye. That evening Polly rang me, canceling our drink.

Chapter 38

I went to a sweetshop along the road and bought a pad of notepaper. The only shade they had was some awful sort of violet. But, after all, what did the color matter? I opened it on my table. The first ballpoint I found didn't work. I licked it and shook it and held it under hot running water and then snapped it and threw it in the bin so that it couldn't cause me pain again. It took a lot of rummaging around in drawers to find another one. I made another resolution. When I found my new home, wherever it was, I would buy a hundred — no, *two* hundred — pens and I would scatter them around like little chocolate eggs at Easter. I would hide them in drawers and at the back of shelves and in cupboards and behind books and down the back of sofas and in the pockets of my coats and jackets, so that I would always be able to find one.

I didn't feel in the right mood now. I made myself a cup of coffee and I disproved the saying that a watched pot never boils. I filled it with cold water and stood looking at it, in a dream, until I heard the hissing and saw the lid rattling. I held my hands around the hot mug, feeding off its heat, and stood by the window, seeing nothing. I turned to face my room. Soon they would be packed in boxes and in storage somewhere and then later they would be unpacked and re-arranged somewhere else. For the moment they looked as if everything were normal, but I already felt like an emigrant leaving my old life behind. But there were one or two things I still had to do, and this was the most important. I sat at the table and began to write.

Dear Naomi,

If you're reading these words, that means at least that you didn't throw the envelope in the bin, so that's something.

As you probably know, if you give this to Brendan/Ben or to the police — it amounts to the same thing — then I'll be arrested and charged with harassment. That's what they told me. I hope you don't. I don't want to go to prison. But if you do hand the letter over, could you read it first? And I want you to read this promise as well: This is my last message to you. I'll never contact you again. It's up to you now.

I'm not going to attempt some defense of my behavior to you. It would all be too complicated and this letter would have to be as long as a book and I probably wouldn't have the words to explain it, anyway.

All I can do now is to be as clear as possible. I've been accused of being a threat to Brendan. I happen to believe that it's the other way round. I wake in the night and every creak I hear, I think he may have come to finish me off. Well, that's not your concern. I'm frightened for myself but I'm even more certain that you are in danger. Maybe not today; maybe not tomorrow, but if things go wrong, the way things go wrong in relationships. I don't think Brendan can take it when things don't go the way he has planned it.

What am I saying to you? I was going to send you a sort of checklist. Do you think he is telling the truth? Is he caring for you or controlling you? Is he being secretive? Are there hints of anger? Violence? Do you know what he's doing when he's not with you? How much do you really know about him? Do you believe what he tells you?

But this is all rubbish. Forget all I've said. You'll know.

You'll never hear from me again and I

wish you happiness and that you'll never want to contact me. I'm about to leave my flat. I don't know where I'm going, yet. But if you ever want to contact me, I'll put some numbers of various people at the bottom of this letter. One of them should be able to put you in touch with me.

I'm afraid that I think you've had bad luck. But I wish you good luck.

Miranda

Before I could change my mind I put the letter in an envelope, addressed it to her, care of Crabtree's and walked out and posted it in the box on the corner.

It's a rule of life that the way to find your missing sock is to throw away the sock that isn't missing. And if you want to know why you shouldn't post a letter, you'll realize it the moment you post, the very second your thumb and finger release it. As I heard the letter to Naomi clatter down onto the other letters inside the postbox, I realized there was another alternative I hadn't yet considered. With Brendan, there generally was. I had thought that Naomi might throw the letter away unread or keep it to herself. In either case I would hear nothing. She could give it to the police or to Brendan, who would give it to the police. In either case, I would receive a very unpleasant visit from a police officer in a day or two.

Now I thought of another possibility. Naomi would give it to Brendan and he wouldn't pass it on to the police. He would read the letter and he would realize that I was implacable and he would tell Naomi that it wasn't worth bothering about and he would decide that something would have to be done.

I stood by the postbox for forty-five minutes until a red van pulled up and the postman emerged with a large gray canvas sack. I told him that I'd posted a letter by mistake and that I'd like to get it back. He unfastened a catch on the side of the postbox and emptied dozens and dozens of letters into his sack. Then he looked at me, as so many people had looked at me, as if I were insane, and shook his head.

Chapter 39

"Hello! Miranda?"

His voice boomed up the stairwell, and then I heard his footsteps, taking the steps two at a time. I applied one last precise lick of gloss paint along the skirting board, then laid my brush down on the lid of the paint pot.

"The paint's still wet," I said as he came through the door, loosening his tie as he did so. "Don't touch anything." I stood up and crossed the beautiful bare room.

"Except you," he said. He put his hands on my aching shoulders and kissed me and bit by bit all my stiffness eased away. I thought: How is it possible to feel excited and safe all at the same time, to know someone so well and yet feel there's so much more to yet know?

"Good day?" I asked.

"This is the best bit. I've got exactly fifty minutes before I have to get back to work. I've bought us some sandwiches from the deli."

"Shall we have those in a bit?" I said and took him by the hand. I led him up the next narrow flight of stairs, along bare boards and fresh-painted walls, into the small attic room I was using as a bedroom, where a mattress lay under the window and my clothes were stacked in wooden boxes. I took off his jacket and tie and he unbuttoned my overalls and we grinned at each other like idiots because here we were on an ordinary Wednesday lunchtime, about to make love in an empty, echoey house. Light fell through the blinds in bars across the room. I hung his suit on a hanger for him. He tossed my paint-stained gear into the corner of the room.

"I'd like to stay here the rest of the day," I said a bit later, stretched out on the mattress while he lay propped up beside me and stroked my hair.

"Roasted vegetables with mozzarella or farmhouse Cheddar and pickle?"

"Half of each?"

"Okay."

"We can have them in the kitchen, then I can show you what I've done since you were last here."

I had tried to move out of London, to the country. I really had. I'd burned my bridges, leaving Bill, selling my flat in record time, putting my stuff into storage. At the same time, I'd written to all the people I knew in the trade and gone for informal talks and considered all my options, just like you're meant to. I'd thought about relocating to Wales and Lincolnshire and even, for a few days, Brittany, where apparently lots of English people were desperate for a builder-slash-interior designer to revamp their picturesque farmhouses. But, like Alice when she goes through the looking glass and finds she had to go backward in order to advance, the result of all my labors was somehow the exact opposite from the one I'd intended. By attempting to move out of the great churning wheel of the City, I'd somehow ended up at its very hub.

I was now living in a tall, narrow house just south of Kings Cross, completely renovating it while the owner was in America for nine months. When he'd offered me the job — an extravagant modernist conversion of the kind I'd dreamed of, with free accommodation thrown in — it had seemed like too good an opportunity to pass up. I'd started at the bottom and moved upward — gutting the kitchen and turning it into a laboratory for food preparation, building a minimalist conservatory into the garden, opening out the living room, turning the smallest bedroom into an en suite bathroom. Eight of the nine months had now elapsed. Now only the attic room where I slept was still to be plastered and decorated and opened to the skies.

"You've done a great job," he said, popping the last of his sandwich into his mouth and pulling on his jacket.

"It's all right, isn't it?"

"And now you're nearly finished."

"Yes."

"Miranda?"

"Yes."

"After that . . ."

But then my mobile phone started bleeping from the bedroom, so we said good-bye hastily, and I pounded up the stairs to get it, while downstairs I heard the door slam shut. I caught up the vibrating phone. If I stood on tiptoe and craned my neck, I could just see him from the dormer window, walking briskly along the street. He'd forgotten his tie.

We went for a bike ride in the early evening and had coffee, sitting on the pavement outside even though it was getting chilly. We'd been together nearly one year now, all the seasons. He'd seen me through the anniversaries — Troy's death, Christmas, Laura's death. He'd met my beaten-down, bewildered parents; met Kerry and her fiancé; met my friends. He'd let me wake him up at three in the morning to talk about the things I tried not to talk about in the day. He'd trailed around builders' yards with me, trying to take an interest in grains of wood, or held ladders while paint dripped onto his hair. I looked at him as he biked beside me, and he felt my gaze, glanced up, swerved. My heart contracted like a fist.

At his flat, he made supper for us — smoked mackerel and salad with a bottle of white wine — while I sat on the church pew he'd bought at the reclamation center and watched him. When he sat down he took a small bite but then pushed his plate away.

"Um — what I was saying this afternoon . . ."

"Yes?"

"About your plans, you know. Well, I was thinking you could move in with me."

I started to speak, but he held up a hand.

"Hang on. I'm saying this all wrong. I don't mean, 'You could move in with me.' Well, I do of course, but that's not what I'm really saying. And when I say, 'I was thinking you could move in' as if it had just

occurred to me — well, it's what I'm thinking about all the time."

"You're confusing me."

"I'm nervous, that's why." He took a breath
and then said, "I very much want you to come
and live with me." He twisted the wineglass
around by its stem. "I want you to marry me,
Miranda."

Happiness bubbled up in me like an
underground stream finding the surface.
Unlooked for, undeserved happiness that
had come into my parched life when I met
him.

"I want to have children with you . . ." he
continued.

"Don," I said.

"I want to grow old with you. Only you.
Nobody but you. There."

"Oh," I said.

"I've never said anything like this before."
He gave a grimace and rubbed his eyes.
"Now you're supposed to reply, I think."

"Listen, Don," I said.

"Just tell me."

I leaned toward him and put my hands on
either side of his lovely, clever, kind face,
kissed him on the eyelids and then on the
lips. "I love you, too," I said. "I love you
very, very, very much. Only you."

"That's good," he said. "Isn't it?"

"Can you wait a bit?"

"Wait?"

"Yes." I held his gaze.

"Well, of course I can wait — but does that mean you're not sure? About me, I mean?"

"No. It doesn't mean that at all."

"Why?"

"I am sure about what I feel," I said. "I used to wonder how you knew when it was the real thing. Not anymore."

"So why?"

"It's complicated," I said evasively.

"Are you scared?"

"Do you mean, of commitment or something?"

"Not exactly. But after everything you have been through, maybe you feel it's wrong to be happy."

"It's not that."

"Or maybe you feel you're not safe, and therefore anyone who's with you isn't safe either. We've talked about that — about how you felt you were the carrier. Is that it? Everyone you love dies."

"You're the psychologist," I said.

"Because I don't mind," he said. "Everything's a risk. You just have to choose the risk you want to take. I chose a long time ago. Now you have to as well."

I put my hands over his, turned his palms

upward, kissed them both. "I have chosen," I said.

"You're crying," he said. "Into your food."

"Sorry."

"Of course I'll bloody wait."

I've met a man. Don. I wish you could meet him as well. I think you'd like him. I know he'd like you. It feels — oh, I don't know, odd, unsettling, not right, to be in love with someone again. I never thought it would happen, not after everything. I thought all of that was over. And sometimes — well, a lot, really — I get this sudden rush of panic that it's wrong. Wrong to be happy, I mean, when you're not here and Laura's gone and Mum and Dad are wrecked and so many people have suffered and I feel that it was because of me. It was me who spread the terrible contagion. I can see that sardonic expression on your face when I say that, but nevertheless it's true. I'll always miss you, Troy. Every minute of every day of every week of every year that's left. So how is it possible that I can allow myself to be happy? Maybe it isn't. We'll see.

Chapter 40

My eyes were closed, hard, my breath coming in gasps. My heart was beating so fast that my body seemed to hum with it. I was sweating. I could hardly feel the pain. I knew it was there. On my face, around my jaw. I could taste blood, warm, metallic. Around my neck, the scraping. My ribs, sore, bruised. My eyes still closed, afraid of what was in store. I felt the sounds of someone approaching, the vibration of footsteps on the stairs. The touch, when it came, was gentle on my face and cheeks but it still made me flinch. I didn't open my eyes. I murmured something.

"Jesus, Miranda," said the voice. "I heard glass breaking . . . What the fuck? Miranda?"

I opened my eyes. The light hurt them. Don. Don's lovely face looking down at me, close, distressed. He ran over to the window. I spoke in a murmur but Don couldn't make it out. He leaned close to my face.

"Said he was going to kill me," I said in little more than a whisper.

"Who?"

"Hurt me," I said. "He hurt me."

His expression darkened. "Was it him? Brendan?"

"Said he'd come for me."

"What's he done to you?"

I felt him gently touching my face, stroking my hair, unfastening my shirt, assessing the damage.

"You're bleeding."

I just groaned. He was looking around.

"There's blood on the . . . What the fuck did that bastard do to you? I'm calling the police. And an ambulance."

"No," I said, half raising myself and flinching at the pain it caused me. "Don't . . . It's not . . ."

"What are you talking about?" Don said, almost angrily. "I'm sorry, Miranda. I'm not listening to you." I heard three little bleeps as he punched the numbers in his mobile phone. I sank back almost sobbing, partly with the pain, partly at the thought of what was to come.

I wasn't there when the police examined the room, when they dabbed at the blood on the wall and picked hairs off the carpet and put the knife in a plastic bag. I was grateful for that. It would be like the death of Troy all over again. I might have found it hard to retain control. Don told me about all that later. He had wanted to come with me in the ambulance but a policeman told me he ought to stay and help identify objects at the scene. What was mine, what was his and what was "foreign." Much, much later Don told me that he had been — in the midst of his distress — rather interested to see the scene-of-crime procedures with all their special gloves and tweezers and scalpels, plastic bags and labels, flash photography. He'd been rather excited to be on the inside of the tape that was shutting the crime scene off from the outside world.

Meanwhile I had been taken away in an ambulance with a female police officer for company. She was like a free pass that took me to the front of the queue. I was led through a waiting area full of people who, whatever their own injuries, were inordinately interested in me — a young woman being led by two nurses and a uniformed police officer. What could have happened to me? They would probably have to wait hours. Within two minutes I was being examined by a young doctor and a nurse. A minute later he stepped aside when a consultant in a suit and a spotted tie arrived. I felt nervous, as you do with doctors.

He examined my face and the inside of my mouth.

"What were you struck with?" he said.

"A wall," I said.

"Do you know who did this?" he asked.

I nodded. He turned to the police officer.

"You'll need to photograph this. The neck as well."

"He's on his way," said the WPC.

"We'll be taking an X ray but the cheekbone is probably fractured."

I gave a cry because as he said it he had given a dab on my cheek with his finger, as if to test his theory. He shone a light into my eyes and into my ears. He held up his finger and asked me to look at the point as he moved it around.

"Were you sexually assaulted?" he asked.

"No."

Even so, he asked me to take off my clothes so that he could examine me. The female police officer said that she was called Amy O'Brien and did I mind if she was present for the examination? I shook my head. As I took my clothes off, she said that she would need them for evidence. Was that all right?

"What am I going to wear?"

"We'll get you a nightie," the doctor said.

"You're, erm . . . you know . . ." said Amy.

"My boyfriend."

"Could he bring you some clothes?"

"I guess so."

I was X-rayed and I was photographed and taken to a private room with a vase without flowers and a window without a view. The doctor said they wanted to keep me under observation for a night. Amy said that they would like to take a statement. They said they could wait if I didn't feel well enough, but the sooner I could manage it the better. I said I could do it immediately. Things were happening so quickly. Within the hour a detective knocked on my door, took his jacket off and removed a sheaf of paper from his bag. He was called Seb Brett and he looked pale, as if he were kept in the dark. He pulled a small table alongside my bed and started to take dictation.

Now things got slow. It was like being back at school. He took my name, my address and my date of birth. He laced his fingers together and pulled them back sharply in that unpleasant way that makes the joints crackle like dry sticks of wood.

"Now," he said. "From the beginning."

There was no pressure of time, no shortage of paper. I gave him the story in every detail: Brendan ringing at the door, forcing his way inside, grabbing the back of my head and slamming my face into the

437

wall, pulling the knife from somewhere and pushing it against my throat, my pleading, his smile and telling me that this was the end, then the sound of the door, Brendan jumping up in alarm, running, I couldn't see where. It had only taken a few minutes but it took a couple of hours and fourteen pages to make the statement. At the end I was exhausted but Seb Brett asked me to read through it and sign at the end of each page. My words seemed different in Seb Brett's rounded, precise handwriting. They were all mine, but he had selected particular phrases and made alterations. It wasn't inaccurate but it sounded a bit like something translated by a computer into another language and then back into English by another computer. I found it difficult to concentrate, so this was a slow process as well. Halfway through there was a knock at the door. I felt a spasm of something not good. It was Rob Pryor.

"Miranda," he said. "I just heard. I came straight over. How are you?"

"Shaken," I said.

"I'm not surprised." He walked over to the bed and picked up the pages I'd finished with. "Do you mind?"

I looked across at Brett, who just gave a shrug. So I said I didn't mind. This was even worse. I read the pages with Rob reading the earlier pages beside me. I kept losing my place, so he quickly caught up with me. Each time I signed a page, he would take it from me and read it with a tut-tutting sound that I found infuriating. I signed the last page and passed it over to Pryor, but he gave it straight back.

"You need to sign it immediately where the text ends," he said. "Just here."

"Why?"

"So some wicked policeman can't add a hit at the end saying 'I woke up and it was all a dream,' and you would have signed it off."

I signed my name hard against the last word, which was "police."

"How did you get here so quickly?" I asked.

"Mr. Block is being questioned. He rang me."

"But what are *you* doing here?"

"As you very well know, I've been involved with him previously, so it seemed like a good idea to have continuity . . ."

"But you're making it sound like he's your client."

"Not at all," he replied brusquely.

I turned to Brett.

"Is this legal?" I said. "Pryor is a friend of Brendan's."

Brett looked quizzical. Pryor walked across and they had a whispered conversation that I couldn't quite hear. It went on for several minutes with puzzled looks from Brett. At the end of it he nodded and looked at me.

"DI Pryor has asked if he can have a quick word with you. Is that all right?"

"What about?"

"It'll only take a minute," Pryor said.

"I don't believe this," I said, looking at Brett. "Do you realize who this man is? This is like letting Brendan's lawyer come in and nobble me when everything has just happened. I just can't . . . I've just been attacked."

"I was telling Seb about your previous connection with Mr. Block."

"So?"

Pryor walked across and sat by my bed. It was like having Brendan himself there. His proximity made me want to gag. He looked at me closely. I held his gaze.

"It looks nasty, Miranda," he said. "It must hurt."

I didn't reply.

"What time did the attack happen?" he said.

"You've read the statement."

"Your boyfriend made the call at — what was it? — five past seven this evening."

I still didn't speak. I wasn't going to be drawn into a conversation.

"Your boyfriend," said Pryor. "Some sort of doctor, isn't he?" I only shrugged. He leaned in closer, his eyes narrow. "You know what?"

"No," I said. "What?"

"I don't believe you."

"What?"

"Did he help you? Your boyfriend? He could do it, couldn't he? A few bruises, things that would show but not do too much damage."

"What the . . . ?" I stuttered. "What are you saying?"

"There was a knife," Brett said. "He dropped it. We're checking the prints."

"They lived together," said Pryor. "She could have saved it."

"We never lived together," I said. "What the hell are you doing?"

He was so close to me now that I could almost smell him.

"He's got an alibi," he said.

I took a deep breath. I had to control myself.

"I don't care," I said finally. "Why are you telling me this? I was there. I know what I know."

"Don't you want to know?"

"All right," I said. "Who?"

"His girlfriend, Naomi Stone." He looked at me with an expression of mild triumph. I'd seen it before. "You don't seem very concerned."

"Maybe I'm used to being disbelieved," I said. "As I said, I was the one who was there. He had his knife against my throat. Look." I lifted my chin.

He clapped his hands gently. "Oh, very good," he said. "It's a brilliant performance. Dignified. Not overdone. Pretty convincing. But then you've had a bit of practice."

I tried to concentrate. *Don't let him rile you.*

"Have you ever thought that it's just possible that you could be wrong and that Brendan could be dangerous?"

"None of this matters," said Pryor. "He couldn't have attacked you. He was at home. He was at home when the police called and Ms. Stone places him there for the entire evening." He picked up the statement and glanced at it once more. "You mention a dark blue shirt. When I saw him a few minutes ago, his shirt looked brown to me."

"He might have changed it," I said. "Did that occur to you?"

He shook his head and smiled. "Mr. Block

442

is making a statement. We'll make some calls and then we can bring this charade to an end. If you really want to know . . ." And now Pryor was interrupted by the ringing of his own mobile phone. With a sigh of exasperation he took it from his pocket. "Yes?" Suddenly his expression changed. "What the hell are you talking about?" He looked at me with glassy eyes as he listened to the phone. "I'll be right there."

He mumbled something to Brett and then walked out of the room, banging the door behind him. Brett pulled a face at me. I think he was on my side, mostly. He ran out after Pryor. I was alone for several minutes and I lay back and stared at the ceiling, trying to empty my mind. I felt as if I were in another world now, unengaged by these events and disputes. When the door opened I barely looked around. It was another female police officer. She sat in the corner but made no attempt to start a conversation. I tried to sleep but it was hopeless. I closed my eyes so I wouldn't be bothered.

Much later, it must have been after an hour, the door opened and I was aware of someone by the bed.

"Are you awake?"

I opened my eyes. Brett.

"Sort of," I said. "You look cheerful."

"Sorry," he said. "Are you all right?"

"I don't know."

"It'll feel worse tomorrow."

"The doctor told me. I've got pills for that." There was a pause. "So what's happened? What happened with Pryor?"

The smile spread across Brett's face.

"He's not a happy man," he said. "My colleague was talking to Naomi Stone. Just to see if she was sure about that alibi. They told her about some of the hairs recovered at the scene. And the knife."

"So?"

"She's withdrawn her alibi. And better still, we've found the dark blue shirt."

"Where?"

"It wasn't in his drawer. It was in the bottom of a rubbish bag outside his house. It has some stains on it. They are as yet unidentified but we already know they are drops of blood. Human blood."

"Mine?"

"We'll see. I told Rob Pryor that he should come here and apologize to you."

"What did he say?"

"He had a previous engagement. Off the record, I think I can tell you that we shall be filing charges against Brendan Block in the morning." He took my hand. "We'll leave you now."

Brett and the policewoman left the room, switching off the light before they closed the door. I tried to go over things in my mind for a while, to get things straight, but I was tired now and slept and had no dreams.

Chapter 41

I spent a long time choosing the place. First I thought about somewhere with many people, Oxford Street or Trafalgar Square, because at least you lose yourself in a crowd, become anonymous and invisible. But I dismissed the idea immediately. I considered a motorway service station, heading north on the M1 say, standing in a car park or sitting at a table in the corner by a window eating doughnuts and drinking bitter, tepid coffee. But too many people pass through service stations, on their way somewhere else, and it would only take one. Perhaps outside an under-ground station in the suburbs: the last stop on the line, where London peters out and the countryside has not yet begun. Or in a muddy field somewhere. I could rehearse the route and draw up complicated instructions: *Take the M11 until Junction 10, head east on the A505. A landfill site, a laundrette in some charmless town, a lay-by off a dual carriageway, a wood at night . . .*

On a bright and freezing New Year's Day I

got up early, kissed Don's cheek very softly so he didn't wake. Before I left, I looked down at him. Yes. He'd do. I took the car and drove out of London. The roads were almost empty. I went over Blackfriars Bridge from where I could see the dome of Saint Paul's shining in the icy light, through New Cross, Blackheath, and onto the A2. Just past Gravesend, I pulled into a garage and filled the car up with petrol. I was handing over my credit card when I changed my mind and paid in cash. I bought a cup of coffee as well, and drank it in the car before setting off again. I felt calm, and in the brightness of that winter's day, things took on a clarity and precision.

I joined the M2 and a few miles later exited toward Sheerness. I could see the Medway estuary now, the mud flats and shabby clusters of houses with a few bare trees bending in the wind and the sky was vast and empty of clouds. Soon I was crossing onto the isle of Sheppey. I pulled over and consulted my map, then drove on, right at the roundabout, right a couple of miles farther, onto a bumpy minor road, left toward the church, which was visible for miles, the one vertical marker rising out of the marshy land. At the church, I parked and looked at my watch. It was ten o'clock. I had about two miles to walk and just less than an hour to do it in.

It was bitterly cold when I opened the door and I could hear the desolate call of sea birds on the wind. I pulled on my thick jacket, my scarf, woolen hat and thick biking gloves. Even then, my cheeks felt scoured. I started to walk. If Don had been with me, he could have told me the names of the birds that circled above me in the streams of air, or flew low over the water, calling. I clapped my hands together to keep the blood circulating. There was nobody around; just a few sheep grazing at the tufts of grass, birds picking their way delicately over the mud with long hinged legs. I turned my back on the sea and walked toward the inland marshes.

After about forty minutes, I saw a dot on the level horizon. The dot became larger, clearer. Became a figure that was walking toward me. Became a woman in a heavy coat with blond hair escaping her hat and whipping around her pale cheeks. Neither of us made a signal or lessened our pace. We just continued walking toward each other across the marshes until we were a few feet away from each other.

"Naomi," I said.

"Hello."

"Everything go all right?"

"I was careful, like you said."

I had not seen her since those days in court, when I'd tried so hard not to look at her, although I'd been acutely conscious of her, aware of her even when I was looking in the other direction. Once, our glances had touched for a second, less, and then we had both looked hastily away as if we had been scorched. She had lost weight and her pallor was striking. More than that, she seemed older, years older, than the candid, sweet-faced woman I'd met in Crabtree's. Perhaps it was that the innocence had gone, blasted away in just a few months. Brendan had done that.

"Shall we walk, just for a bit?" I said, and she nodded and turned back on her path. We went single file for a bit, until the path widened at a mobile home park that was deserted and eerie. From here the track led to the seawall; the wide estuary lay before us, and on the other side the low Kent coastline. There were pebbles and broken shells at the water's edge, and also old cans, broken bottles, shredded plastic bags.

"Was it easy to get away unnoticed?"

"There's no one really to notice anymore." Her voice was quiet and flat; I had to strain to hear it. "What about you?"

"I told Don I was inspecting an empty property."

"Oh."

For a few minutes there was just the crunch of our feet over frosted grass. I was sure we were remembering the same thing — that strange hour when we'd met and like two witches muttered plans and exchanged tokens. From her bag, she'd produced a little sandwich bag with some coarse dark hair inside that she'd pulled from Brendan's brush, and the jagged-edged carving knife wrapped in soft paper towels that she'd handed over by the bottom of its blade, careful not to touch its handle. And then she'd unfolded a dark blue shirt and laid it out before us. I'd held out the index finger on my left hand for her, and she'd taken a safety pin, opened it, and, biting her lower lip, jabbed the point into my finger. A dark ball of blood had welled up and after a few seconds I'd shaken it over the shirt, by its collar, and then wiped it there as well.

"Can I ask something?" she said at last.

"Sure."

"How did you do that to your cheek? You looked awful in court, even all those weeks after."

It all seemed a long, long time ago.

"When I saw Don pulling up outside, I

smashed my face against the kitchen door as hard as I could, as if someone was holding me by my hair and doing it to me. I did it over and over until I couldn't see for the blood."

"How could you do that?" she said in a whisper.

"I thought of Troy — Laura as well, but mostly Troy. Then it was easy — welcome, even. It was nothing."

Naomi nodded as if she understood.

"Now tell me something," I said. "Something I never had time to ask before."

"Yes?"

"How were you so certain about Brendan?"

She hesitated. "Are you sure you want to know? You might find that . . ."

"Tell me."

"He told me what he'd done to Troy. He said he'd do it to me, too, if I left him."

There was a pain in my stomach and a burning sensation behind my eyes when she said this. I squinted into the wind and kept on walking. Somehow it's easier to talk about devastating things when you're moving, your eyes on a fixed point ahead of you.

"He actually told you about Troy?"

"Yes."

"Why?"

She shrugged. "For the same reason he

kept that rope, perhaps? A kind of insane self-confidence. Some things we'll never know, will we?"

"I guess not. But why didn't you go to the police?"

"I thought of what had happened to you. I couldn't be sure."

"What did he say?"

"He said he'd filled him up with pills and strung him up on the beam and left him to die there."

"Go on."

"He said" — she looked around at me and then back at the path again — "he said he'd tried to call out."

"What?" My voice was a whisper.

"He'd tried to say your name."

I went on walking. One foot in front of the other. It's hard to understand how it's possible to keep on walking when you hurt so much and you just want to bend over with your arms around your stomach, curl up into a tight ball and wail like a baby. He called out for me because he thought I was coming home soon. I'd promised him I'd be there and he must have thought I could rescue him. But I was late. I didn't come.

"Are you all right?"

I managed a noise of assent.

"I think this might have been his." Naomi

pulled one hand out of her pocket; she was holding a bracelet made of leather, with three dull wooden beads on it. "Was it?"

I took the bracelet in my gloved hand. "Yes. Since he was small. He bought it in Italy, when we were all there together as a family. It's just a cheap old thing." But I held it against my cheek for a moment then slipped it over my wrist.

Naomi said, "My car's not so far from here."

We stopped and looked at each other.

"What are you going to do?" I asked.

Naomi looked around, as if there might be someone hiding in the reeds or in the long rippling grass.

"I caught his eye in court," she said. "When I gave evidence. He smiled at me. One of his nicest smiles. That's when I was certain about what to do. I'm leaving every-thing. Starting over from fresh."

"Can you do that?"

"Why not? I've got no family. Maybe that's why I fell in love with Brendan — I thought we were these two orphans who'd come together to protect each other in the wicked world." She gave a harsh laugh, more like a bark, and then shook her head as if to clear it. "One day he'll be free again and then he'll try to find me."

"Not yet though."

"No, but how long? How many years?"

"They gave him ten, so he'll be out in five or six — you can be sure he'll be a model prisoner; he'll charm everyone. But Pryor's said they're going to reinvestigate Laura and Troy's deaths, so . . . well, who knows. Maybe he'll be in for longer."

"Maybe, maybe not."

"Where will you go?" I asked.

There was a pause and she looked at me intently, as if she was committing my face to memory.

"Abroad. But it's probably better if I don't tell you."

"You're probably right."

"I know I'm right."

"Good luck," I said. "I'll be thinking of you."

"What will you do?"

"Nothing."

"Nothing?"

"I've got six years. I'll take that, a day at a time, and I'm going to try to love as well as I have hated. After that — well, I'll see."

"Oh," she said faintly. "So you're still waiting?"

I winced. But in a way of course she was right. I was still waiting for Brendan, and when he came I would be ready for him, like a soldier who can feel his enemy approaching even in his sleep.

"We'll never meet again, will we?"

"I guess not."

"This is good-bye," I said, and I smiled at her for the first time.

We both reached out at the same time; our hands met in a fierce grip. We stared into each other's eyes and didn't look away. It was like looking into the abyss.

"It was probably wrong, wasn't it?" she said. "I try to imagine myself justifying it to people and I'm not sure I could, except . . ."

"To save your life," I said.

"I hope so," she said. "So what about you? Are you telling your . . . your boyfriend?"

"Don?" I said. "I think I should. But I won't. I'd better keep it to myself."

There was nothing really left to say. We let our hands drop back to our sides.

"Good-bye," she said.

"Good-bye."

She turned and walked back the way she had come and I watched her figure getting smaller and smaller, until it was a dot on the horizon, until it was nothing at all. Then I turned, too, into the stiffening wind, and went back over the bleak marshland under the circling birds, back to the old gray church and my car. Back along the small road to the larger one, to the motorway; back to the teeming city where my life was. Back up the stairs to Don.

"I'm home," I said, listening to the word as I spoke it. I repeated it, to make sure. "Home."

"I missed you."

"Well," I said, kissing him. "I'm here now."

Dearest Troy,
I think I need to let you go now. I don't know how I'll manage without you but I'm going to try.
I'm sorry.

About the Author

Nicci French is the author of the bestsellers *Land of the Living*, *The Red Room*, *Beneath the Skin*, and *Killing Me Softly*, as well as two earlier books, *The Memory Game* and *The Safe House*, both published in England to great acclaim.